PRAISE FOR
HOLM

THE SPELLBREAKER SERIES

"Romantic and electrifying . . . the fast-paced plot and fully realized world will have readers eager for the next installment. Fans of Victorian-influenced fantasy won't want to put this down."

—Publishers Weekly

"Those who enjoy gentle romance, cozy mysteries, or Victorian fantasy will love this first half of a duology. The cliffhanger ending will keep readers breathless waiting for the second half."

—Library Journal (starred review)

"Powerful magic, indulgent Victoriana, and a slow-burn romance make this genre-bending romp utterly delightful."

—Kirkus Reviews

THE NUMINA SERIES

"[An] enthralling fantasy . . . The story is gripping from the start, with a surprising plot and a lush, beautifully realized setting. Holmberg knows just how to please fantasy fans."

—Publishers Weekly

"With scads of action, clear explanations of how supernatural elements function, and appealing characters with smart backstories, this first in a series will draw in fans of Cassandra Clare, Leigh Bardugo, or Brandon Sanderson."

—Library Journal

"Holmberg is a genius at world building; she provides just enough information to set the scene without overwhelming the reader. She also creates captivating characters worth rooting for, and puts them in unique situations. Readers will be eager for the second installment in the Numina series."

—*Booklist*

THE PAPER MAGICIAN SERIES

"Charlie is a vibrant writer with an excellent voice and great world building. I thoroughly enjoyed *The Paper Magician*."

—Brandon Sanderson, author of *Mistborn* and *The Way of Kings*

"Harry Potter fans will likely enjoy this story for its glimpses of another structured magical world, and fans of Erin Morgenstern's *The Night Circus* will enjoy the whimsical romance element . . . So if you're looking for a story with some unique magic, romantic gestures, and the inherent darkness that accompanies power all steeped in a yet to be fully explored magical world, then this could be your next read."

—Amanda Lowery, *Thinking Out Loud*

THE WILL AND THE WILDS

"An immersive, dangerous fantasy world. Holmberg draws readers in with a fast-moving plot, rich details, and a surprisingly sweet human-monster romance. This is a lovely, memorable fairy tale."

—*Publishers Weekly*

"Holmberg ably builds her latest fantasy world, and her brisk narrative and the romance at its heart will please fans of her previous magical tales."

—*Booklist*

THE FIFTH DOLL

STAR
MOTHER

ALSO BY CHARLIE N. HOLMBERG

The Spellbreaker Series

Spellbreaker
Spellmaker

The Numina Series

Smoke and Summons
Myths and Mortals
Siege and Sacrifice

The Paper Magician Series

The Paper Magician
The Glass Magician
The Master Magician
The Plastic Magician

Other Novels

The Fifth Doll
Magic Bitter, Magic Sweet
Followed by Frost
Veins of Gold
The Will and the Wilds

STAR MOTHER

A NOVEL

Charlie N. Holmberg

47NORTH

Text copyright © 2021 by Charlie N. Holmberg
All rights reserved.

No part of this book may be reproduced, or stored in a retrieval system, or transmitted in any form or by any means, electronic, mechanical, photocopying, recording, or otherwise, without express written permission of the publisher.

Published by 47North, Seattle

www.apub.com

Amazon, the Amazon logo, and 47North are trademarks of Amazon.com, Inc., or its affiliates.

ISBN-13: 9781542030465
ISBN-10: 1542030463

Cover design by Micaela Alcaino

Printed in the United States of America

To Taylor Swift,
one of my favorite storytellers,
ever since my roommate sang "Fearless"
in a dark bathroom
with the door closed.

CHAPTER 1

I thought making love to the Sun was the most unbearable pain I would ever experience.

Giving birth to His child was far worse.

But my story starts a little before that, and ends long, long after. And so we begin.

It wasn't quite time for the corn to be worthy of birds, or the cornfields to be in need of a scarecrow. But that did not mean the scarecrows could not be put to good use.

I slipped from a copse of trees, my feet bare, my skirt tied in a knot around my calves. My hair hung wildly over both shoulders, a few strands catching on my eyelashes, as I hurried in a half crouch toward Farmer May's home. She lived on the edge of Endwever, my small hometown that was nestled in the forests of Helchanar. Near the exact center, or so the maps of the time claimed.

My sister, two years my junior, hissed behind me, "Are you mad? They'll see you!"

"Then hurry!" I whispered back, keeping my eyes on the kitchen window. It was large and open, but so far I'd not seen any movement behind it. When I drew within six paces of the house, I dropped to my knees. Mud from yesterday's rain seeped into my skirt, but one could not stay clean if she wanted to pull off a successful prank. It was not possible. That was why Idlysi could never do this on her own. She cared far too much for cleanliness.

I motioned for her to follow. Her blue eyes looked huge in her pale face, and her gaze never broke from the window as she hurried to my side. As she did every time I coerced her into having fun with me, she said, "I can't believe I agreed to this. Mother will be furious."

I shushed her. "Follow me and she won't know."

Idlysi passed me a withering look. "Who else in town would do such a thing?"

I paused, considering. I *had* earned a bit of a reputation, and Endwever was a small place. There were only so many people one could point a finger at. "Todrick?"

Idlysi rolled her eyes.

Grinning, I crept around the back of the house, pausing over a sudden noise—but that was just Farmer May's old cow, whapping her tail against the weathered fence of her pen. My prize was in sight: a narrow shed connected to the back wall of the house, right beside the back door.

Idlysi froze as we neared. If anyone stepped out that back door, we would be caught. But I would just straighten and claim I was looking for a missing chicken. Idlysi . . . well, she would likely start crying and admit to everything before being asked, but it wasn't nearly as fun to do these things by myself, and Caen claimed he was getting too old to participate. He was busy working on our cottage today, anyway. The cottage we would move into in five months, after I turned twenty, which was marrying age in Helchanar. We'd been betrothed since I was twelve and he fourteen.

The thought brought butterflies to my stomach and a smile to my cheeks. I reached the shed and pulled up the latch holding it together.

Idlysi lingered behind, ready to run to the woods should someone approach.

When I moved a rake and shovel, my prize smiled at me.

Scarecrow.

He was old, his shirt tearing at the shoulders, the buttons long since pulled free for other mending, but he was large and awful and perfect.

"Help me," I whispered, and Idlysi slunk around the shed, shaking with nerves. She grabbed one of the scarecrow's straight arms, and I took the other. Together we heaved the thing free. No time to return the tools or close the shed; Farmer May would soon be out. Such was part of my plan.

Stifling a laugh, I pushed Idlysi back toward the house, both of us crouching as we dragged the scarecrow past the kitchen window and around to the front of the house. I hurried up the two wooden steps leading to the small porch, and Idlysi, who had refused to remove her shoes, clunked behind me. I shushed her again, pushing her and the scarecrow toward the gap in the floorboards of the porch. I'd noticed the gap when I came for butter yesterday, which was how I'd gotten this idea. The hole was just the right size for a scarecrow stump.

It took more effort than I would have liked to secure the thing; someone moved inside, and Idlysi squeaked and dropped her side of the scarecrow, leaving me to finish the task while she bolted for that copse of trees. But I got the stump planted, swallowed a fit of laughter, knocked on the door, and fled after her, sprinting on my toes to reach the copse before anyone could open the door.

I dived into the trees before I was seen, but not in time to turn around and see Farmer May's face. I only heard her scream.

Giggles burst from my throat, and I doubled over, forehead against the young spring grass, laughing.

"Oh, what a horrible thing we've done!" Idlysi cried.

Farmer May's voice tore through the morning air. "I know it was you, Wendens! Get back here!"

Idlysi looked ready to sick up. "I *told* you." Then, "Sun save us, she's coming this way!"

Still laughing, I grabbed my sister's hand and dragged her through the trees, into the greater forest, dancing across familiar trails and raised tree roots. She barked at me to slow down, but I didn't. The trick to the forest was this: so long as you could see the spire of the cathedral, you would never get lost, so I kept the copper point in my peripheral vision, angling closer if ever it dipped beneath the canopy, dragging my sister all the way.

Like most towns in Helchanar, our greatest attraction was the cathedral on the northeast side of town. It was circular in shape, as celestial things are, with a lily garden at its center and a bright copper spire above its southwest doors. It was built before my time and would surely last beyond it, structured by dedicated, faithful, and forgotten hands. My great-great-grandfather was said to be the one who crafted the stained glass. I paid little attention to it; when one grows up so close to beauty, it is easy to dismiss.

Fortunately, my soon-to-be cottage was close by, so we darted from the trees to its finished walls. Caen sat on a joist of the roof, working thatch into place. He looked up as we darted inside.

A small smile tugged up the side of his mouth. "Oh, Ceris. What have you done now?"

I beamed at him, his attention warmer than the Sun's own light. "Nothing terrible!"

Farmer May shouted again, far more distant.

Caen frowned. "Nothing terrible?"

I pulled the knot from my muddy dress and twirled, letting the skirt fan out. "Only propped up Farmer May's scarecrow by her front door. We hardly moved it!"

Caen chuckled, but Idlysi was biting off the tip of her thumbnail, as though terrified Farmer May might run us through with a shovel.

Hands behind my back, I peered up at Caen. "And how are you today?"

"Better than you're going to be." His focus returned to the thatch.

I shrugged. "Mother hardly cares what I do."

It was true, or at least it was true now. She'd been distant all of my adolescence, ever since my betrothal was secured. Simply put, she considered me someone else's problem. I often felt like a cow whose milk had dried up, simply taking up space in the backyard until someone could sell me for meat.

"I wasn't talking about you."

Idlysi began working on the nail of her index finger.

I sighed. On *my* part, my mother hardly cared, but Idlysi, at seventeen, had yet to make a match. There were so few bachelors around, and since my father was the cathedral steward, he preferred not to take long trips from home, even if it were to secure a future for Idlysi. He'd have to start looking soon enough, but there was still time. Idlysi couldn't marry for another three years.

It wasn't long before my mother's voice came barking through the town. There were only so many places we could hide; it didn't take a scholar to determine the cottage was one of them.

"Idlysi Wenden!" She trudged toward the gap where the front door would go. Caen passed us a sympathetic look. Idlysi, tears in her eyes, scowled at me before stepping out. I followed, right on her heels.

"Terrorizing Farmer May? Really?" Mother look tired, the lines around her eyes deep. "You are too old for such things!"

"It wasn't *terrorizing*," I said in a feeble attempt to defend our actions. "It was moving a scarecrow from one side of the house to the other. We can move it right back."

"You certainly will." But Mother only had eyes for Idlysi. She would have grabbed my sister by the ear, were Caen—and likely a few other villagers—not watching. "And you'll spend the rest of your day indoors, taking my share of the chores, since you have so much free time."

5

I couldn't bear to watch Idlysi crumble beneath the scolding. And it was *only* Idlysi being scolded. I had been the mastermind behind the joke. I had goaded her into it.

I stepped in front of my sister, forcing my mother to pay attention to me. "*I* will move the scarecrow, and *I* will take the chores, if that's what you insist on."

Mother frowned at me, like my presence exhausted her. "Can you not just leave her be?" Then, to Caen, "I'm sorry to drag you into this."

Caen offered her a warm smile. "I don't mind, Mrs. Wenden."

Mother sighed and grabbed Idlysi by the wrist, forcing me to step aside. Head down, Idlysi followed her back to our home, leaving me behind.

Once they'd gone, Caen set down his tools. "She let you off easy."

I folded my arms. "She always does." I had always been different from my sisters. To me, rules were things to be bent and tried, if they detracted from happiness—mine or others', it didn't matter. Joy was my primary motivator. I believed that was why my parents betrothed me at so young an age. To inflict me with responsibility, yes, but also to assure themselves someone else would take the burden of *ruling* over me. Once the agreements were made, I didn't matter anymore. Regardless of what I did, I was still the milkless cow in the backyard, watching through the window as my sister took my fall, again.

I wouldn't be able to bring her along next time. The consequences hurt too much. But little did I know then how true that statement would be, or how wide our separation would become.

I helped Idlysi with her chores anyway, when my mother wasn't there to supervise, though my sister refused to speak to me. When the chores were done and I was bored, I sat on my bed to work on my latest embroidery, though I should have been finishing my wedding dress.

The embroidery was a gift for Caen, a small token to show I thought about him, a trinket to perhaps endear him to me, for while Caen was kind and long-suffering, I knew he didn't love me. Not in the way I had grown to love him. Not in the way I so dearly wanted him to love me. He looked at me as a little sister rather than a woman to be desired.

I worked on the tapestry until the Sun had passed, and though it was but half-finished, I was so eager to show him I snuck from my home after my parents turned out their light. It was an image of Caen fighting a dragon, only the dragon wielded a sword and Caen breathed fire. I'd yet to add Caen's legs, and the dragon's tail was only an outline—but I thought myself so clever I wanted to share it. I wanted to impress him. I also grasped at any excuse I could to see Caen, even improper ones.

So I trotted across town to his home, climbed up his woodpile, and rapped on his window, quietly, for he shared his room with two others. His bed was closest to the pane, so I felt confident in my sneakiness.

But Caen's head didn't appear behind the glass, and no candles lit within. I knocked again, louder. Then a third time.

Color appeared behind the dark glass, and the pane opened, but it was Todrick, Caen's baby brother, only twelve years old. He blinked sleepily at me. "Oh, Ceris"—he thickened my name with his lisp—"he's not here. He's out in the wood somewhere."

I blinked. "Out in the wood?"

Todrick shrugged and closed the pane, for there was a slight chill in the air, and he clearly wished to return to the warmth of his bed.

Concerned, I clutched my embroidery to my chest and wrapped around the house, peering into the south wood. It was summer, the leaves still bright and green. I knew it wasn't wise to venture into the wood at night—there were wolves and godlings, though the latter were rare—but Caen also knew not to wander deeply, which meant he couldn't be far off. I followed the worn dirt path left by many members of his family, passing a little shrine to the Earth Mother, and pushed myself between the trees beside it, walking among them until the brush around my hips grew thick. I didn't go far before I saw a lamplight ahead and heard murmuring voices. Creeping as close as I could without detection, I stuffed my embroidery into my mouth and climbed a tree for a better look.

I couldn't make out what they were saying, only a word here and there, but it was Caen and Anya, the weaver's daughter. I wasn't surprised to see them together; they had been good friends since childhood, and I'd often suspected Anya of harboring feelings for Caen.

I'd just never thought he'd reciprocate.

She held the lamp. He bent low, talking close to her ear. I heard my name a couple of times, saw Caen caress the side of Anya's face. That was all he did, for I stayed up in that tree until long after the two parted. Their voices were laced with regret and sadness and love, but I knew them both, and they were too good in their hearts for a tryst. They would neither shame their parents nor break my heart.

But after that night, it started splintering.

He will learn to love me, I told myself again and again. I had learned to love him. He just needed more time.

After that, I doubled my efforts. Brought Caen larger lunches, showed him the embroidery, and made him laugh. I put more time into my wedding dress, perhaps thinking that if the gods saw my dedication, they might be willing to help turn my betrothed's heart away from the weaver's daughter.

But once I knew, I saw his sorrow whenever Anya passed by, and her ache during noon worship. Their pain mirrored inside me. I'm not sure they noticed. I hope they didn't. For even if I could be selfless enough to give up Caen, the choice wasn't mine to make. Our parents had bound us together when we were little more than children, under the eyes of the Sun. They would never tolerate a parting. All of the arrangements had been made, and our cottage was nearly finished.

I looked forward to the future, to having Caen as my husband and babes scattered around our little cottage. Babes I would love with all the love within me. Babes I would never forsake no matter how old they grew, or who they were promised to. I wanted to give them everything my parents had failed to give me. I wanted a place to call home, and people who would be mine as I was theirs.

I avoided wondering if Caen would still look at the weaver's daughter with such anguish, even with our children sitting in his lap. At her, or at the memory of her, should she leave. I avoided it, and yet in the minutes before falling asleep, when my mind was its weakest, the worries surfaced, churning and bitter, and I was afraid.

It was only a few months before my twentieth birthday when the Sun reached down and lit the torch upon the roof of the cathedral. A torch wide as a man lying down and deep as a child standing up, kept filled with wood and oil.

It had never once been lit, in all the centuries the cathedral watched over Endwever.

The torch burst alight just an hour after dawn one morning, and stayed alight long after the fuel ran out. The flames burned higher and brighter than any man-made fire, for the Sun Himself had reached down and touched the fuel, though none had seen His finger.

The faithful knew what this meant, once we were done reeling from the spectacle, reeling from being chosen. A star had died, and the Sun had turned His eyes toward Endwever for its replacement. Stars are perhaps the most powerful of godlings, which makes them incredibly long-lived. But unlike demigods like the moon, or full gods like the Sun, they are not immortal.

They are children of the Sun, and can only be born through a mortal mother.

I sat in a tree not far from my home, staring at the flames crowning the cathedral. They heated the cathedral beyond a bearable temperature,

9

so no one could enter, and yet none of the stone or glass had scorched. The whole town was bathed in warmth. A meeting among the men had already been called, but there would be another for the women. There would have to be, for only a woman of childbearing years could appease the will of the Sun.

It was a great honor to be a star mother. Though Endwever had never been chosen before, tales were whispered of star mothers from other places, sometimes in other towns or cities in Helchanar, sometimes in the lands beyond our borders. There were poems about them, songs, tapestries. The star mother's home would be greatly blessed, and her name would be woven with praise and admiration. Her face would be numbered among the stars, and her rest would be heavenly and eternal, in a paradise beyond what any mortal mind could conjure.

For no mortal woman could survive the birthing of a star. Once a woman left to be a star mother, she always returned nine months later, her body cold but strewn with heavenly treasures, a smile on her face. Or so it was said. It happened infrequently, only once every hundred or so years, so tales were all we had to go on.

The call had gone out, and we could not be long in answering it. No one wanted to test the patience of the Sun, who could burn all of Helchanar with a touch, if He so wished.

The women gathered on the second day. There were twenty-seven women in Endwever of childbearing age. Some of them were already married, but the honor of being a star mother was so great even married women could volunteer. Our meeting had not yet officially begun, and already the women whispered to one another about who was worthy, quoting scripture and gossiping. I listened with only half an ear. Having worshiped the Sun all my life, I knew of the honors, the promises. But my path was already set before me. I would marry Caen, have a mortal family, lead a mortal life, and die as any mortal would.

"Gretcha would be well for it," the midwife whispered to Gretcha's mother, though Gretcha, a year my junior, stood right beside her and could hear every word. "She is fair and unspoken for."

Gretcha's mother startled at the notion, but Gretcha did not. She took the suggestion reverently. There were not a lot of eligible bachelors in these parts; towns were small, with wide spaces between them. What better future could a young girl hope for than to be chosen by a god?

Jani, the herbalist, wished it could be her and said so over and over again. Her husband had passed away the year before, and she hungered for the salvation guaranteed to a star mother and, so it was said, her family. But Jani's youngest child was already older than I was. The torch had been lit too late for her.

While the talk went on, I surveyed the familiar faces and found one missing. Idlysi was not here, though both Pasha, my baby sister, and my mother were present. Curious, I slipped away from the delegation and returned to our home, where I found her in our shared bedroom, cocooned in blankets, staring wistfully out the window.

"Lys?" I approached her.

She must have been lost in thought, for she tensed when I spoke. "Leave me alone."

"But the torch—"

"I know about the torch!" she shrieked, then cowered into her blankets, apology written in her eyes. "How could I not know? I can feel it, even here!" She shook her head. "Pasha is young yet, and you are spoken for. I'm a prime candidate, aren't I?"

Her fear struck me like a dull knife running the length of my breastbone. "Idlysi, they will only take a volunteer—"

"And what if no one volunteers?" she whispered, pulling her blanket-covered fist to her mouth, pressing it against her teeth.

I gingerly sat on the edge of the bed and touched her foot. She shrunk from me. "Why would no one volunteer? It's a glorious path to have."

But my sister bowed her head. "Is it so glorious, to die?"

"The spirit never dies." It was a verbatim quote from scripture.

She shook her head like we spoke different languages and shifted her gaze back to the window. In an attempt to comfort her, I said, "I think it will be Gretcha."

Idlysi drew in a shuddering breath. "I hope so."

Pressing my lips together—I was unsure what else to say—I let her be. I did not return to the meeting, but to the beading on my wedding dress, which hung from a dress form in my parents' bedchamber.

My heart twisted inside me as I worked on the gown. Was I naïve, to believe scripture? To believe the promises passed down from the generations before us? Or was it merely easy to believe because I knew someone else would volunteer and it was not a decision I would be forced to make?

I wondered what would happen if no one volunteered. Would the Sun punish us? Would He turn away?

Or was Idlysi right? Would one of our women be *forced* to go?

Eager for distraction, I focused on the task at hand. My wedding dress was simple but lovely, cut from linen I'd woven with the aid of the village midwife and edged with lace I'd braided myself. I thought to try it on, but found I could not pull it from the dress form.

Instead, I went to visit Caen.

It was just past noon. The village was eerily quiet, the women's meeting having adjourned, families sheltering in their homes instead of completing their daily labors. Even the birds withheld their song, and the hounds their play. My footsteps felt unnaturally loud, and I slowed to quiet them.

I spotted Caen's profile on his back step, his head in his hands, the shadow of the forest across his lap. I paused, breath catching against a great rising ache within me. He looked so sorrowful, so stooped, so small. I approached with care.

"Caen?" I asked.

I startled him. His head shot up, eyes like a child's, wild until they found me and softened. "Ceris." His voice was rough.

"Are you all right?"

He nodded, but the way he sat said otherwise. I lowered myself beside him on the step and ran my palm down the length of his back. Felt his spine move as he breathed.

"I am afraid," he admitted.

"We all are. One never believes lore and legend will come alive before their eyes."

He leaned into me, and I relished his weight. I brushed my fingers through the ends of his hair, cut across the nape of his neck. Caen was such a strong man, and although he was always quick to laugh, I had never seen him cry. Now, he seemed on the verge of tears.

"Caen, what's wrong?"

He swallowed, hesitant, but my silent persuasion eased out the words. "Gretcha or Anya. No decisions came of the women's meeting, and now the council will debate between the two."

His words drove an iron spike through the center of my chest. My fingers stopped. His sorrow flooded me, choked me, weighed me down as an anvil hanging from either shoulder.

Anya. I had not even considered her.

If Anya was chosen, she and her family would be honored for all time. But Caen's heart would break, for despite my best efforts, I knew he still didn't love me. Not the way I loved him. Not the way he loved Anya.

And if I knew Anya, she would accept the call. She could not have the man she loved on Earth, so why not end her torment in the most glorious manner possible?

I resumed tracing the planes of his back, but my fingers grew numb. We stayed like that awhile, sitting in complete silence, for even the creatures of the forest were reverent of the burning torch. Not a single cricket chirped nor dog barked.

It was in that silence that a small spark lit within me, little more than an ember, glowing within the pit of despair sucking beneath my skin. I ignored it at first, or tried to, but it seared so painfully I could not bear it. Leaving a kiss in Caen's hair, I left him to mourn alone and walked aimlessly, unsure of where to go. The cathedral was out of the question, as it was uninhabitable. The forest felt eerie. My home seemed too crowded, too unwelcoming, and Idlysi still brooded there, terrified for her own fate. So I merely walked around, without a clear path, without a destination, trying to squash that spark, for I feared it more than I had ever feared anything in my life.

I knew how to make Caen love me more than any other, without breaking his spirit, without dishonoring my family.

The problem was, I would have to die for it.

CHAPTER 2

With a few words, a single promise, I could give Caen what his heart truly wanted. I could spare Anya's life and break the ties of our betrothal. I could honor my family and have my name in song, passed down from generation to generation, to be remembered always.

I could be a star mother.

The thought possessed me so strongly I could think of nothing else. I found my way home after several hours, only to climb onto the roof and stare at the torch atop our cathedral. Even from there, I could feel its heat. Heat that thrummed with my own heartbeat.

I had the power to earn my betrothed's heart, to take away my sister's fear, to give Anya a chance at happiness. To show my worth to my parents, and to all of Endwever. Perhaps if Caen could not love me, the Sun would.

I tried fruitlessly to push the thoughts away, but they stuck to me like burrs. The men met that evening. I did not sleep that night. It didn't help that my window faced the cathedral, and the Sun's fire burned His face into my eyelids whenever I tried.

I thought of Caen in the forest, touching Anya's cheek. I thought of him curled up on his back step, bowed over by the fear he might lose her once and for all. The way he'd said her name echoed inside my skull.

Come morning I was miserable and overtired, and angry that it went beneath the notice of my mother and my youngest sister, though I could not fault Idlysi, who couldn't even stomach breakfast, nor my father, who had not yet come home. After breakfast, I took up refuge in our small kitchen, the room farthest from the cathedral, and drew its thin curtains over the window, trying to block out the eyes of the Sun. Trying to quiet my own pestering ideas. I managed to doze in one of the chairs, only to dream of the torch and start awake with a crick in my neck. I went to my parents' bedchamber, where I attempted to work on my wedding dress, but my fingers could not thread the needle, and it all seemed so very pointless.

It was that evening, my father still not home, my mother in the kitchen, pushing her food around her plate, and me staring at my nearly completed gown, that I finally freed that spark, that pestering ember, and let it ignite.

I will be the star mother.

My fatigue, my anger, and even my fear abated the moment I thought those words, as though the Sun Himself had soothed me.

My dress blurred in my vision. My hands shook. I swallowed. Straightened. "I will be the star mother," I whispered.

And Caen would love me for it.

I felt hyperaware of myself as I moved through the house, as though my quiet declaration, while too hushed to pass the walls of the room, had reached the heavens. As though the Sun God had turned His gaze to this house. My mother and youngest sister still sat at the kitchen table, their plates mostly full. Idlysi had declared she wasn't hungry and was tucked away in our bedchamber. I wasn't hungry, either, for the spark inside me had burned up my appetite. I stood in the doorway, waiting for them to look at me and not at all surprised when they didn't.

"What would you think," I said, "if I were to go away for a very long time?"

Only my mother looked up at me. "Now is not a time for your antics, Ceris."

Her words didn't affect me. I felt as though I held a great, invisible shield. Like I was someone else, watching a play featuring myself. "These are not antics."

They did not reply. But that was fine. Once this was over, we would all remember our love for one another.

"The dress will fit Idlysi well," I murmured.

Mother glanced at me, one eyebrow raised.

I met her eyes, then Pasha's. Leveling my shoulders, I said, "Father will come home. I will be the star mother."

More than one plate hit the floor.

I left the house before anyone could argue with me. Truthfully, I *wanted* them to argue. I wanted some sort of proof that I mattered, that I was too loved for them to let me give myself up without a fight. The men had debated this long; they could debate a little longer and find someone else to answer the Sun's call.

But I also feared there would be only silence, or worse, congratulations, and so I left, allowing myself to be a coward then so I would not be a coward later.

Night had fallen, but it seemed to be early evening from the way the godly torch continued to burn, drowning out even the light of the stars. I walked away from it, nearly ran, for fear was creeping back into me little by little, and I worried that I would change my mind and forever suffer for what might have been.

But I did not go to the council meeting, nor the cathedral. I went to Caen's house.

I came around the side, planning to climb up the woodpile and knock on his window, but he was already out there, stripped to his shirtsleeves, quartering wood with a ferocity that revealed his own inner turmoil. Todrick was with him and spied me first, reaching over to swat Caen's ankle. He stilled his axe, glancing first to his brother, then to me.

"Ceris." He lowered the axe. I wonder what my expression must have been, for he dropped it and walked out to meet me. "What's wrong?"

Todrick silently excused himself and disappeared into the house.

I was short of breath, and not just from the excursion. I strained to keep my muscles from trembling, for even through my terror, I was aware that the only time I'd felt at peace in the last two days was after I had made my decision and spoken it aloud. If the Sun had heard it, I would be a fool to rescind the declaration. "I just wanted to see you one last time."

His brow, dotted with perspiration, drew low. "What do you mean?"

I gripped his elbows and stood on my toes, kissing him on the lips. It was a quick and modest kiss, but I had never kissed Caen before, and it startled him. "I wanted to tell you I love you," I admitted, my pulse racing with the confession, however obvious it must have been. "And I want you to be happy."

He stammered, "C-Ceris, what . . ."

"Remember that," I pressed. I was losing my courage, and even on the south side of the village, I could feel the heat of the torch pushing into my shoulders. Reminding me of my promise. "Remember me."

I let go of him and turned. He caught my wrist, confusion aging his face. Trying my best to smile, I gently pulled his fingers off one by one.

"Don't follow me," I pleaded.

I ran with all my strength. Or rather, I *outran* my doubts, my concerns, my fears. I ran clear to the tent erected at the village center, where the night air felt like midsummer day. Where our men still debated between the names of Gretcha and Anya.

My anxiety drove me to burst past the heavy flap of the tent door, drawing the eyes of everyone in the space. I was not the only woman present. Both Gretcha and Anya were there, along with their mothers and our wisewoman, whose nose had warts and whose hands were knobby with age.

Almost immediately, the blacksmith tried to turn me out. "You are not needed here."

And I countered, "I will be star mother."

The hush that bloomed around the statement was deafening. Gretcha looked at me with shock. Anya, with relief.

My father, his face long, asked, "Ceris? What did you say?"

Coming around the blacksmith, I met first my father's eyes, then the eyes of our priest. "I will be the star mother. I volunteer. There have been no others." It was a guess, but if the council still convened, then neither Anya nor Gretcha had accepted the duty. And since neither spoke against me, I suspected they, like Idlysi, were too terrified to say yes, and too afraid to say no.

Silence fell for nearly a full minute, until the priest repeated, "You volunteer, Ceris Wenden?"

"You're to be married soon." My father's voice scratched, as if he spoke through a throat half-closed.

I glanced at Anya, her eyes wide with fear and hope. "I suspect Caen will be wed before winter." I managed a small smile, and Anya clutched at her breast, her eyes glimmering with tears. Not willing to let my own emotions surface, I shifted my attention to the priest. "But I must be star mother. I will bring honor to Endwever and my family. I will have my name remembered and my face among the stars. I will dwell in paradise with my loved ones. I will sacrifice so that the others may not be persuaded." I swallowed, hoping my words sounded prideful and not desperate.

The priest shook his head. "You understand that a mortal body cannot survive the power of a star."

"I have been faithful all my life." I clenched and unclenched my hands in the folds of my skirt, where the others might not see them. "I know what I give, and what will be taken. How much longer will the Sun wait for us to decide?"

Others whispered to one another, and I realized I was not the only one afraid. Our people had kept the Sun, the greatest god of the sky, waiting three days already.

"Ceris," my father murmured, but he said no more. He felt the heat of the cathedral's fire through the heavy walls of the tent. He knew the god watched us. He knew what greatness I would bring to him, even if it meant losing me. And I hoped the strain in his voice meant that losing me mattered.

Softening, I moved to him and took his hand. "You will see my legend in the night sky, Papa."

The point of his throat bobbed. "But must it be you?"

"The first volunteer has claim." The priest turned to Gretcha, Anya, and their mothers. "You may return home unburdened."

All four women's eyes shone like Sunlit brooks. Gretcha's mother fled, daughter in tow, as though I would change my mind if she was not swift. Anya's mother bowed to me, and Anya mouthed, *Thank you,* before departing.

I hoped she would visit Caen first and foremost.

"You must go to the cathedral." The priest spoke reverently, and I couldn't help but feel he would have used the same tone at my wedding as he bound Caen's hands to mine, my body draped in a dress I now would never wear. Fear and pain stabbed my midsection, and I bit my tongue to keep them trapped there.

I would have to leave immediately, or I would never fulfill my promise. After the way Anya had looked at me . . . breaking my promise was something I could not do.

"You must enter through the front doors, despite the heat," he continued. "You must bear it and walk, unshod, to the altar in the eye."

For years I'd dreamed of being Caen's wife. Of keeping a house for him, of lying with him, of bearing his children. I'd dreamed of waking up to his face every morning and falling asleep to his hands every night.

As the priest spoke, those images became more and more brittle, until they began to crumble to dust at my feet. If I woke up to Caen's face, there would be no smile on his lips. If I lay with him, there would be no lust in his hands. For him, there had only ever been Anya.

Why should three hearts break, when it was needed of only one?

"You must kneel at it and offer a prayer to the Sun. Offer yourself. If you are accepted, He will take you up."

I held my tears until I left the tent. Now that I'd set my fate in motion, I felt a strong pull toward the cathedral. But my sisters and my mother stood in my path, leaning against one another, holding hands, connected in a way that was both foreign and heartwarming to me. Already I was bringing us together, and I hadn't even reached the cathedral.

Walking toward them, I embraced Pasha first, then my mother, leaving a kiss on her cheek. When I reached Idlysi, she threw her arms around me so fiercely she squeezed the air from my lungs. "Thank you," she whispered. "I love you, Ceris. I will never forget you."

I couldn't remember the last time someone had told me they loved me. "I love you, too," I croaked before moving away. The pull toward the cathedral intensified, overwhelming the sweet feeling that had begun to build in my breast. I felt *His* eyes on me now. I felt His impatience and His readiness as a heavy wool coat.

The others watched me as well. Streaming from homes, the council tent . . .

But I kept my focus on the cathedral and its wings of fire, burning as brightly as the Sun.

The air sweltered as I moved closer, unbearably hot as I approached the doors. Sweat puddled in my hair and the small of my back. I licked my lips and tasted salt. My hands shook as I lifted fingers to the door.

21

The handle burned me.

I bit down on a shriek and jerked my hand away, cradling it to my breast. Had the Sun rejected me, then?

Don't look back, I warned myself. *Let them be happy.*

I grabbed the handle with both hands and wrenched the door open, the searing breath of a god enveloping me.

I don't remember stepping forward, only the *thud* of the door closing behind me. The scorching onslaught of air made me stagger and fall, my hands and knees burning against the stone floor. The ends of my hair curled, and I breathed hard through my mouth as heat stole the moisture from my tongue, nose, and eyes. I felt I could not stand, but the stone blistered, and I had to.

Hurriedly, I removed my shoes and trekked farther inside. The air rippled as water. I felt faint as I passed through it, my hands and the soles of my feet throbbing.

There was no door to block me from the eye—the round lily garden at the center of the cathedral. Only an archway. The garden was burned away to nothing, the grass disintegrated, the flowers charcoal staining my feet. My sweat-drenched clothes stuck to me as a second skin. My pulse thudded beneath my skull. My body grew hollow and rough. I forgot my anguish, distracted by the scorching of my body. Of the marble pillars that glowed with heat ten paces away, standing like sentinels to the lily garden.

I dragged my legs, each heavy as a newly fallen tree. I fell into the ash, the grit sticking to my eyes, no tears left to wash it away. The skin on my lips split and dried as I crawled forward, regret burning up like tares after harvest.

I tried to pray, but my thoughts were on fire.

Take me, oh Sun. Make me star mother. I bow to Thy will.

I collapsed, skin charring and flaking away. I reached one burning hand to the altar. Touched it.

The light blinded me, and I was undone.

CHAPTER 3

And then everything was different.

There was no roaring fire, no blistering heat, no pain. I opened my eyes to a room that was not quite a room, with walls that seemed to stretch out forever on all sides and a bright, empty expanse above me. An enclosure that was there but not quite there. A place like a tapestry, its stitches not yet pulled tight. But it was calm, and the light was tinted a soft, rosy pink.

A luminous section loomed before me on one of those forever walls, like a window into the heart of heaven, and before it stood a man, perfected as though by the hands of a master sculptor, who put me in mind of a bonfire and a lion. He stood by the outpouring of light, or maybe *was* the outpouring of light, or both. He is so difficult to describe, and even now my language does not have words to do Him justice. But He was there, and He gazed into the brightness as one might gaze into a garden, peaceful and still.

I was . . . not lying down, but neither was I standing. Yet as I moved to right myself, I noticed I was not myself at all, but something else. Something that, like the room and the man, was difficult to describe. Like my skin was made of crystal, glimmering and hard, yet still pliable. I was not clothed, not exactly, but neither was I naked. As though this new, crystalline version of me were a carapace built to my body without emphasizing its subtle details. Unable to interpret them, perhaps.

"Come," said the being at the window. His voice was masculine, deep, and all encompassing, as though the very room we stood in was His mouth.

I oriented myself and walked toward Him, though I couldn't feel anything solid beneath my feet. The brightness should have hurt my eyes, but somehow it didn't. I stood beside Him and looked into His brilliance. His skin was made of flame, and His hair billowed like a lion's mane. The glory of His face made it hard to distinguish any individual features, but I thought He had a strong brow and nose, and eyes as white gold as the Sun.

The Sun. The *Sun*.

I thought to prostrate myself, and yet couldn't remember how.

Lifting a finger, He pointed above Him, where the walls that weren't walls gave way to open sky. "See there."

I looked, and the brightness wasn't mere light anymore, but a vast heaven brighter and more beautiful than any night sky I had ever seen in Endwever. Endless stars stippled a black velvet sky like hosts of angels. Never before had I seen the colors of the stars, but here, in this place, I could—white, red, yellow, even blue. So many colors and sizes, such utter majesty.

I should not have been able to identify where the Sun pointed—it was a simple gesture among millions of stars. And yet I could. An empty spot amidst the many pinpricks of light, spilled like glass beads. A tiny point, vanished.

A grave, an absence.

He was showing me the star that had died, the loss that had prompted Him to seek a means of replacing it. Yet *replacement* seemed cruel. One does not merely *replace* a child. Sorrow spun off the Sun as surely as light did. If anything, that was the most tangible thing in this place. I had never before considered that the gods might feel as we did.

"I'm sorry," I offered, feeling small.

The Sun merely nodded. "It is how the passage of time works. They are not meant to be forever." And finally He looked at me, His gaze penetrating and absolute in a way that struck both awe and fear into my core. He was the most beautiful and most horrifying creature I had ever laid eyes on. There was an ancientness to His face, and yet, if I were to stitch His likeness into a tapestry, He would not look any older that a man in his midforties. Not that I had the talent to capture the visage of a god, nor the dyes to try.

He was a *god*.

"There is purpose to all things, Ceris." My name sounded powerful on His lips. Of course He knew my name. Had He not watched Endwever all this time? Had He not reached down to light the torch? Had I not felt His expectations the moment I whispered, *I will be star mother*? "There is a balance in the universe, which is ever shifting. It is never easy and always painful. Your kind glimpses only a sliver of it."

I wasn't sure what to say, or if there could be any response to such a claim. So I simply nodded.

The Sun looked out the window again, then stepped back, studying me fully. I felt self-conscious, as though He could see more of me than I could of Him. As though He could see past skin, blood, and bone to my very soul. To my surprise, His lips curved up in a soft smile.

"You are unexpected," He said. "I know the burden the stars bring to mortals. Few volunteer, without persuasion."

A pain like a slender skewer pierced my chest as memories of my home, Caen, and my forsaken future fluttered to life. But the wonder of my surroundings, of *Him*, staved off my mourning. "I might be mortal," I tried, "but I am farseeing."

The Sun nodded, seemingly content with this answer. "Have you lain with mortal men?"

Were my body my own, it would have burned with the question, but this crystalline form did not react. "Does it matter?" I asked, feeling

every sultry daydream about Caen unravel in the back of my mind.
"N-No. Not yet."

He nodded, solemn, but the soberness did not hinder His light.
"Ceris."

I held my breath.

"If you wish to turn back, I will allow you to do so." He looked
away from me, at something that was there yet not there. Something on
a plane beyond my perception. "It will not be a slight to your people."

I swallowed, stiff with anxiety. My heart raced as though I stood at
the peak of the highest mountain, my toes lined up with its edge, my
body ready to jump.

Struggling for my voice, I said, "Do . . . I not please you?"

He shook His head, still not meeting my eyes. "I always give the
volunteers a chance to change their mind. Only one, but I give it."

I worried my lip and peered up at the glorious sky. "And if I don't
take the chance now, I won't be able to later?"

"No. The law must be honored."

I hugged myself and slowly drew my gaze from the stars.

"I will hurt you." His voice was hushed, but the words startled me.
"I do not wish to, but I will. Such is the manner of my existence."

My heart pounded. Not quickly as it had before, but hard, like my
chest was an unwanted wall in a cottage that needed to be torn down.

He was giving me a chance to leave. To go home. Surely I could ask
for a crown of light or some other favor to show my people that I was
not unwanted. To bring them honor without forsaking my life.

But honor wasn't the true reason I'd come.

"I'll stay." My quietness slid under His own. "I've made my choice.
I will stay."

He had no reaction to my statement beyond a simple nod. His
expression was bright and hard to read, but it seemed . . . sad? But why
would a god such as the Sun be sad that a mortal woman had willingly
answered His call?

"Come." He stepped away from the window light, and it faded behind Him. As we moved forward, the not-walls shifted around us. "This is the most I can withhold my power, the simplest form I can take."

He didn't touch me, but walked with the air of a king, as He should. I followed Him two steps before croaking, "Now?" I turned and peered up at the stars overhead, then curled in on myself, abashed for having been so bold with a god.

Thankfully, the Sun was not put out. "Time may be eternal, but it should not be wasted."

I swallowed against a dry throat. He was right. What reason was there to wait? The Sun would not court me—I was a mere mortal. I would be star mother, and I knew very little of what would become of me beyond that. But I knew there was no quaint cottage awaiting me, nor would there ever be a marriage wreath hung over my bed.

Feigning courage I didn't feel, I straightened, clasped my hands behind my back, and bowed. "I am ready."

His voice was not as encompassing when He said, "I wish to thank you for your service, and also ask your forgiveness."

I didn't entirely understand what He meant just then. The space changed—I sensed it, though I didn't *see* it happen. Were I to describe it visually, our surroundings would sound exactly the same as where we'd just met. And yet it was different. The silence was more complete, like a circle, and senses I didn't know I possessed came awake within me, noticing things beyond smells and sounds and sights. There was something deeply intimate about this place, and in my heart, I readied to complete my task. The Sun had waited days already. A star needed to be born.

I didn't grasp His request for forgiveness until He touched me. It was a searing touch against my arm, like hot iron pressed to my skin, but the instinct that told me to jerk away was muted, suppressed. My sense of direction faltered, and there was no up or down, no left or right. And then that touch was everywhere, *everywhere*, across every particle of my being, and then deep, deep inside me, lighting me like a pyre, scorching and peeling and crumbling.

I think I screamed. I must have. But it's hard to remember, even now. Neither can I recall the end of it, for after the consummation, there was only darkness.

CHAPTER 4

When the darkness ended, I found myself in another room much like the first two, yet very different. I was surrounded by not-walls and rested on a large not-bed. Everything was tinted crystal and pink. It took me several days to leave my bed and its canopy long enough to notice that even here there was no ceiling, only an endless night sky filled with stars.

I should have been ash. I should have burned to smoke and floated away into the heavens. But I was still me, the strange, crystalline version of me that existed in this place.

It was there in that room, in that bed, when I finally let myself mourn. I cried for Caen. For my love for him, for my sacrifice, for the future and family we would never have. I felt his loss most keenly of all, and though I had chosen this path *for* him, I anguished over what I had sacrificed.

Second, I mourned for myself. I mourned being alone in a strange place. I mourned my happy, playful self, because I was sure she had been scorched away along with my innocence. I mourned the emptiness of my room, for I had given of myself freely, and yet there was no man or god to lie beside me in bed, to stroke my hair and love me, to cherish me for what we had given each other. I saw no one but the servants—two unfamiliar godlings who gave me pitiful and sympathetic looks as they saw to my physical needs—and they did not speak to me. They did their work and nothing else. I had thought myself alone before, while surrounded by family, but I had never known true loneliness until I became a star mother.

My loneliness led me to mourn my family, however different we were from one another. We had loved one another, in the end. In the days immediately following my consummation with the Sun, I would have given anything to have my sister Pasha scowl at me, or Idlysi argue with me, or to be with my mother, even if she was apathetic to my presence. I thought of the way my father had reacted after I had volunteered, how unexpected his show of emotion had been, and I wept.

After that, I mourned my home. My friends, my forest, all the things that had been familiar to me since infancy. I would never see them again.

I craved company most of all, even the Sun's company, and yet I feared it all the same. What if His seed didn't take, and I would have to . . . *be* with him a second time? I didn't think I could bear it. The very thought of standing in His presence made my bones shake. Terrible anxiety punctuated by halved and quartered memories made me sick in my mind and my core, yet I felt as if He were some sort of lost limb, one I kept trying desperately to find and flex, only to discover it gone.

And yet my concerns about conceiving quickly abated. It seemed where there was a god, there was a way. By the end of my first week, I *felt* something unlike anything I'd ever experienced. A warmth inside me that wasn't my own, a *glowing* I couldn't see. I knew immediately, in all my ignorance, that I was pregnant, and that a star had budded to life inside of me. And with that budding came wonder, which turned into purpose, which shifted to hope. And that hope helped illuminate the darkness that had crept over my soul. It helped me return to myself, and I pulled the canopy from my bed so I could see the stars and remember why I was here.

I startled my first attendant when she came in with breakfast, serving me food that was entirely mortal but had a crystalline sheen to it as I did. Perhaps it was a sort of magic that let us exist in a world not meant for our kind. Perhaps this was how we really looked, away from the body of the Earth Mother. The attendant eyed me and set down my tray. Before she could depart, I asked, "What is your name?"

My words had astonished her.

She was an interesting creature, mostly humanoid. Predominantly pink in color, she had the body of a human, but there was no distinct separation between her long, thick neck and her head. Almost like a large thumb extended up from her shoulders, and her eyes, nose, and mouth were painted onto its pad.

It took her a moment before she answered, "Elta." Her voice harmonized with itself in a way that was mesmerizing.

I smiled. "How long have you been here, Elta?"

She eyed the not-door longingly, obviously eager to escape. But I was insistent.

She sighed. "Far longer than you can remember."

"I can count very high."

She *tsked*. "Five hundred and twenty-three years."

I whistled. Godlings were not immortal, but they were very long-lived; such was the benefit of having one godly parent. Or, I supposed, two parents who were both godlings. Still, I wasn't sure what that meant in terms of life expectancy, but I didn't think it appropriate to ask Elta when she expected to die.

She started for the not-door.

"I'm pregnant," I blurted, desperate for her to stay.

She turned toward me, compassion etching her features for the first time. "I know. It always takes. It is the way of the universe."

I placed a hand on my stomach. "How long?"

She understood my question. "Nine months, of course."

"Will it hurt?"

She tilted her elongated head to the right. "Not yet, my dear. Not yet."

My other attendant, Fosii, was not so willing to speak with me. I only knew her name because Elta told me. Fosii was short and wide, with skin darker than the space between stars. When she came to bring me food or water, she did not open her mouth once, and she avoided meeting my eyes, as though I were some hapless creature from the depths of Tereth's seas. I tried multiple times to befriend her, but each attempt seemed to push her further away. I felt myself mirroring her actions, withdrawing to make her comfortable, and I hated it. Hated feeling *more* lonely when she was in the room.

Two weeks into my pregnancy, I asked Elta why Fosii hated me so.

She shook her pink head. "She doesn't hate you, dear. But she is unused to mortals."

I picked at the bread Elta had given me—supposedly left on a shrine to the Sun—my legs folded under me, my room ever constant and never changing. "I thought all godlings were familiar with mankind."

Elta's smile was nothing if not maternal. "That's because the godlings you are familiar with are those who inhabit the Earth Mother. But there are others who dwell in realms beyond that. Like myself. I come from a space far away from here, but took up work in His palace."

"Far away?" Looking up, I took in the endless clusters of stars and space overhead. "Beyond where the Sun's light reaches?"

"His light reaches very far," Elta said. "So not as far as that."

Feeling bold, I asked, "Who were your parents?"

She blinked at me, and I wondered if I'd offended her. "You would not know them."

"I want to."

She fluffed the blanket atop my bed before answering. "My mother was a godling like myself. My father was the upward wind of the Broken Emerald."

"Broken Emerald?" Such a name fascinated me.

Elta merely offered me that same maternal smile. "I told you you would not know them."

Setting down my half-eaten meal, I leaned back onto my hands, watching the stars, my eyes drawn to the tiny gap where one had died. I stared at it, feeling as though I could fall into the open space and never return.

Elta opened my door, leaving. Hurriedly, I asked, "What about the children of the stars?"

But the godling shook her head. "Stars cannot have children." Then, before I could ask, she shrugged and added, "It is the way of the universe."

It was easy to grow bored in a place so far away from home, where only one creature was willing to speak to you. There were no books, no trees to climb, no music. Only me and my growing babe. I grew restless.

And so I passed through my not-door and decided to explore the palace that was not a palace.

The Sun was away; the not-walls changed with His presence. When the Sun was here, they were brighter, more translucent, and they dimmed when He left. I did not understand how the god could come and go when He, as far as I understood, perpetually hung in the sky, but He was a god, so it was done, somehow.

I learned quickly that the Palace of the Sun did not sit as an Earthly palace would, with stationary halls and rooms, stairs, floors. No, it unfurled like heavy swaths of brocade, forming itself where you stepped and where you looked. I wondered if turning too quickly would allow me to spy the not-walls ordering themselves, but I was never successful in that venture. The palace was too clever for that.

Everywhere I went, the sparkling night sky remained overhead. Every window I peered through was the same, and never once did I spy my home planet. I had no idea where I was, if it was even a *where* to be known.

But the place was not without décor. I eventually found a hallway that had what I can best describe as plants growing along its sides, with leaves like lily petals. Every part of them glimmered a pearly gold, bright and beautiful. Had I possessed thread that color, or even a pale echo of it . . . I would have been able to create the most beautiful tapestry known to man.

I found another place that looked like a pool, yet it was empty, and no one was there for me to question about its purpose. So I continued along, my path nonsensical, and happened upon other godlings who seemed, in one way or another, to be servants in the never-ending palace of crystal and pink. Some of the creatures were no higher than my knee, and others towered over me. For the most part, the godlings were not unlike Elta and Fosii, somewhat humanoid in appearance but distinctly *other*, and many of them noticed me immediately, like I was a blot of ink in the center of white linen. The first few I spoke with regarded me just as Fosii had, and many as Elta first did—with looks of pity. Perhaps because they knew I would perish, but it seemed more than that. By the time I wound my way back to my room, I was hugging my center, my child, if only to remind myself that I had a purpose there, and I was not alone.

Fortunately, I wore Fosii down.

I gave her space, always greeted her when she arrived and thanked her when she left. She became used to me. And perhaps Elta spoke kindly of me as well. I'd like to think so, anyway.

What surprised me was *how much* she let her guard down. By my second month of pregnancy, she treated me as if we were old friends. She talked like an old woman and sassed me like one, too.

"Child, you don't *need* to bathe," she told me when I requested it of her. My belly was still flat, but it was warm, and sometimes, under the darkness of my blankets, I could see a faint shimmer pulsing through the skin around my navel. "Not here. There is. No. Dirt."

I smiled at her. "I would like one, nevertheless."

She rolled her eyes, which were bright blue and very human in appearance. "You think the universe wants to conjure you a tub?"

Elta came in then, her arms full of what I immediately identified as string. I leapt from a not-chair and rushed her as she said, "It can't hurt, Fosii."

"You found string." I danced before her until she unloaded her burden into my arms. String every color of the rainbow and then some toppled against my chest, some of the bundles dropping to the floor. I had so much time and nothing with which to fill it and had asked on multiple occasions if I could start stitching something. I didn't think Elta had taken me seriously.

Fosii buzzed her lips. "From the mortals? What is wrong with you?"

Elta shrugged. "She is a star mother."

Folding her arms, Fosii looked away. As though she didn't want to be reminded. But she caught me watching her, and snapped, "Don't think I like you now, Ceris Wenden."

Thoughtful, I carried several spools of string to my not-chair and sat, thumbing through their colors. My fingers landed on a yellow so brilliant it was nearly white, the fine threads shimmering in the not-light. A familiar feeling pulsed in my gut, one of fear and wanting, a paradox warring with itself.

"When . . . When will I see Him again?" I had not so much as glimpsed the Sun since our night together. I should have been thankful for it, but it was hard to cast away the attachment of a first love, even if it hadn't *been* love.

Still, my skeleton shuddered at half-remembered pain. The song of those past sensations was etched into my very being.

Again, the godlings looked at me like I was something else, something beyond mortal. Like I was pitifully ugly or horribly injured. Elta said, "You'll see Him at your halfway mark."

Halfway? "Only then?"

She nodded.

A righteous anger bubbled up within me. "So He lies with a woman, only to ignore her for five months?"

Fosii warned me with "Child."

Elta shook her head, then tilted it back to look at the heavens. I followed her gaze, my eyes instantly drawn to the space where the star had died. I could always find it. "There are many stars," she whispered. "Many star mothers. One for each. It is . . . It is too much to bear, even for a god."

Her words pricked my heart. I hadn't even considered. Mortals . . . we were nothing compared to the gods. But did it hurt the Sun to know the mothers of His children had to die? Had He grown to care for any of them? Was that why He'd seemed so morose?

Did He care for me?

He hadn't given Himself the opportunity, and it seemed He didn't want to.

I understood then why Elta and Fosii had hesitated to speak to me. They feared befriending me.

I touched the warm spot in my belly and smiled. I felt a kinship with the child inside of me, though it was little more to me than a sensation.

"It's only three more months, anyway," I offered, setting down the string.

Fosii rose from her chair and, somehow, managed to start me a bath.

Whenever I grew restless or my fingers ached from too much embroidery, I would wander the Sun's palace. It was not unlike a cathedral, albeit far, *far* larger than the one in Endwever. The eternal architecture seemed to recognize the limits of my mind and attempt to adapt itself into something I could conceptualize. Windows—those bright spots of light—would simply appear when I got close to one of the not-walls, and I could peer out into the heavens, to the fantastic swirls of color and endless stars beyond.

Watching the stars, I would put a hand on my belly and wonder at the godling growing inside. All stars were godlings, or the third tier of celestial being. It was said godlings lived all over Earth, but they rarely revealed themselves to mortals. On the next tier there were demigods, like the moon. Demigods *were* immortal, although not nearly as powerful as gods. If mortals were mice, then godlings were dogs, and demigods were bears. But gods were storms, in a class of their own, with seemingly endless power and reach. Earth Mother was a god, too, but She was said to be sleeping, weary of the bickering of the sky, which was why She allowed so many to live upon Her. Only the demigod Tereth, who lived in the great ocean, could whisper to Her in Her dreams, for they loved each other, and thus were joined together, land and water.

I never saw the Sun in the hallways or through the windows. Only noticed how His presence illuminated the walls, or His absence darkened them.

I spent more time embroidering than I ever did back home. I had threads and strings of every shade, needles of twenty sizes, and long swaths of canvas taken straight from the hands of mankind. I worked with the fervor and glee of a lonely woman desperate for something to occupy herself.

The first image I stitched was Sun.

I tried my best to capture Him by this rudimentary means, using the brightest threads, whites and yellows, to capture His majesty, for He is where this new story started. Although His image was burned into my mind, it was almost impossible to re-create, and I unpicked my handiwork many times before it reached my satisfaction.

"This is your father." I found myself speaking to my belly, which rolled hot in response. "You are the child of a great king. Never forget it."

From there I created the dark sky, its swirling masses and stars of every color. "These are your siblings," I sang as I worked, calluses slowly returning to my fingertips. At first I sang songs from home, but soon I developed new lyrics and lullabies, songs more appropriate for a star. "You will always belong. Never forget it."

And then I stitched myself, mortal and delicate, long tawny hair down my back in a braid, gray eyes, mischievous smile. "I am your mother. And I love you. Never forget it."

My needle stilled as the confession sank in. I was wholly aware that the being growing inside me was not human. Was not like me in any way. And yet it was still *my* child, *my* offspring. I was a star *mother*, not a star host, or a star vessel.

Setting my growing tapestry down, I rubbed both hands over my ever-swelling belly. "Never forget me," I whispered to it, and wept despite myself, remembering that I would not live to see this star in the sky, that I had given up any real chance of motherhood for the sake of Endwever, for Anya and Gretcha, for Caen.

I wished the uncanny windows of this place would let me see him, smiling in his cottage, hand clasped in Anya's. Praying for me at night, his heart ever thankful. For it would be. I'd made a study of Caen these last years, and I knew he would always love me for making his desires real. Anya would be in his home and in his bed, but I would grace his dreams until his dying breath.

But I could not see him, for despite all my exploring, I still never found a window that looked toward Earth. As though they respected the slumbering Earth Mother too much to interrupt her privacy. Or they feared that I would miss my home so direly that I would jump and fall through the heavens just to return to it, taking my star with me.

At times, they might not have been wrong.

And so I continued my tapestry, hoping, somehow, my star would be able to see it from its place in the sky long after I was gone, and know me.

CHAPTER 5

I was practicing my calligraphy months later when Elta came into my room, wringing her small hands. "He will see you tonight, Ceris."

In this place, one never need ask who "He" was.

"Has it been twenty weeks already?" I asked, my fingers naturally grazing the bump in my abdomen. The time had passed so slowly up to that point, and yet in that moment, looking back on it, I could not see where it had all gone. The life inside me pulsed hot, as though eager to meet its father.

Elta rushed to the not-wall and moved her hands around in complicated patterns until she pulled a crystalline cape free from seemingly nothing. It trailed along the floors like the skirt of a wedding dress, and a pang of sorrow erupted in my chest as I thought of the one I had made by hand, only to leave it behind. Had my sister made a match? Would she wear it now? Knowing her, she'd want one of her own. Perhaps my mother would sell it.

"You'll have dinner with Him, right after western set." Elta laid the cape at the foot of the bed. It was always "set" and "rise" here, tagged with the relevant hemisphere of the Earth Mother. Though I had a suspicion such time markers were used only for my benefit, as the side of the Earth didn't matter to those not living on Her face. "I'll plait your hair and get you some shoes."

I looked down at my feet, which hadn't been shod since I removed my shoes on the scorching temple floor. "Why dress me up?" I lifted my hand. My nails were like thin gemstones.

"Because you are meeting with our Lord." Elta's tone was incredulous.

"I was not prepared like this when I met Him the first time."

She paused and glanced at me, blinking large eyes. "That was different."

I did not see how, but Elta was growing nervous, so I dropped the matter.

Were I meeting with a mortal lord, I would be bathed and oiled, my hair carefully coifed, my eyes lined with kohl, and my cheeks peppered red. I'd wear layer after layer of the finest clothes I owned, plus some lace or whatever other niceties we had to spruce them up. We'd massage butter into my hands and file my nails. I'd chew on parsley for my breath and rehearse every word I might possibly utter.

Here, I wore shoes and a long cape pinned to my shoulders. Elta braided my hair and saw to it that I was comfortable. And that was all.

Odd, that I would put in so much less effort for a god than for a man. But as I'd learned in a thousand different ways, the laws of the heavens were quite different than those of men.

"When the Sun doesn't shine on Helchanar," I said, trying to stave off nerves as I awaited my appointment, "He shines on the other side of the world."

Elta nodded.

"Then how is He ever here?"

She smiled at me like I was a child. Compared to her, I suppose I was. "*Satto* is a god," she explained, using a name common among the palace godlings. "His ways cannot always be comprehended by mortals." She put up both hands. "Not to insult your intelligence. But He can split Himself, in a sense." She paused, likely trying to simplify the explanation. "He can leave His brightness in the sky if matters must be

40

addressed elsewhere. He is fully cognizant in both forms, but He is not His whole self. It does make Him more susceptible to harm."

I sat straighter. "Harm?"

Elta clicked her tongue. "Do you think mortals are the only ones who suffer war?"

I mulled this over, imagining what a battle among gods must be like. Elta tidied the room and let me be.

It didn't take long for my nerves to catch up with me. I was about to sit down to dinner with the most powerful being I knew. A being I had slept with, and yet felt no intimacy with. But He was the father of my child.

I brushed thoughts of Caen away and walked to the not-door. The palace knew my purpose, and so it did not open to the usual long, contorted hallway, but to a large room seemingly without enclosure. A crystalline table about six feet long lay ahead of me, covered in serving platters. A godling set down the last tray of food, and I noticed it was all mortal—roasted pheasant, an animal I didn't recognize stuffed with apples and spices, pies and cakes, creamy soup, two different kinds of bread already sliced, a myriad of jams and spreads. It all had the same crystalline sheen as my skin.

My stomach rumbled, and the godling glided away as though made of cloud.

There were two chairs, one on each end of the table, and I sat down, gazing at the food. It smelled wonderful. My own wedding feast would not have been as grand.

The Sun did not keep me waiting, so thankfully my thoughts didn't linger on the life I had left behind. He appeared, utterly radiant and beautiful, His power as constrained as a god's power could be. He again had taken the form of a man, but something about Him, so regal and fierce, still reminded me of a lion. A lion on fire that didn't burn, and I wondered how utterly lucent He would be if He had not diminished Himself to meet with me. For surely He was divided as Elta had explained, else somewhere in the world, millions of people were missing their day.

I thought of His touch against my skin and shivered.

He didn't mean to hurt you, I reminded myself, but my body remembered the agony regardless.

The Sun took a seat at the other end of the table. "Ceris." He nodded to me.

I nodded back. Once He reached for a piece of bread, I began to help myself. Whatever I wanted suddenly became within my reach, and soon my plate was full of food. My stomach was tight with trepidation, but both my star and I were hungry, so I spooned soup into my mouth. It was warm and light and slid pleasantly down my throat.

We ate in silence for a little while, long enough for me to finish most of my soup and start on the pheasant. Hating the quiet, especially since I so rarely had company, I asked, "Do gods need to eat?"

The Sun looked up at me, His diamond eyes brilliant and mesmerizing. "Need, no. But We enjoy the same pleasures as mortals. I do, at least."

I nodded.

He considered me a moment. "I hear you've depicted Me in bundles of yarn."

Again, my new form kept me from flushing, but I felt the heat of the statement. "N-Not yarn, Your Majesty. Threads . . . an embroidery. A story for the eyes. For my star. *Our* star. So that she—or he—might one day look at it and know me, in a way."

The Sun nodded, His eyes cast down to the meal before Him. "I see."

Silence floated between us. I took a few bites of a honey cake before speaking again. "What were they like, the star mothers before me?"

He did not look up from His plate. "There were many before you, Ceris. The same number as the stars."

I looked up at the night sky, taking in the expanse of stars. The moon was never there—I hadn't seen the moon in five months.

"The last few, then," I pressed. "What were they like?"

The Sun set down His utensils and folded His fiery hands beneath His chin. "Must you ask?"

"Must I not?" I countered.

He pressed His lips together for a few heartbeats before speaking. "I would do a poor job of answering. I could tell you their names, but I know very little about them."

A new pang echoed in my chest. "Why?"

He met my eyes fully. "I do not revel in their deaths. Mortal life is so fleeting, but it is still life. It is still gone, when a star is born."

I studied His face, which seemed to become more human the longer I looked. My shoulders slumped. "Why must the stars be born? Why must their numbers always be the same?"

He investigated me like I was a book in a foreign language. Even from across the table, He seemed very close, like He could simply reach out and turn one of my pages. "Stars were one of the first things the universe created. They are the source of its power, and Mine. Starlight is the reason the worlds spin and move through the heavens. The reason the tides rise and fall, the reason rain falls and fire burns. Without stars, the rest of it ceases to exist."

I had never considered this, and my food went untouched for a full minute while my mind tried to grasp His meaning. "Does not the Earth Mother turn Herself? Or Tereth move the tides?"

"You asked Me if gods eat. No. Not in the way mortals do." He lowered His hands to the table. "But We, too, survive on starlight. The Earth Mother would not turn without the stars. The Sun would not burn. Even those who devour darkness would be unable to do so without the stars."

A heavy breath escaped me. "I see."

"When even one star dies, there is suffering. Thus it has been given to Me, and mortals, to keep the stars burning."

"If the universe made them"—I chose each word carefully—"then why not make them immortal as well?"

His lip ticked, like what I'd said was amusing. "If it had the ability to create an endless source of power, it would have done so. Stars are the most noble of godlings. They burn brilliantly and nourish everything around them. But everything we are given comes at a cost. In order for stars to give of themselves, they must be able to die. That is why they must be born of a mortal."

My mind traced back to our earlier topic. "How many star mothers before me?"

Any mirth the Sun felt dissipated.

I cleared my throat and took my questions another direction. "How often does a star die?"

The god looked away from me, taking another piece of bread that He didn't eat onto His plate. "It depends. Fifty years might go by, or two hundred. The universe is not cruel."

I took another sip of soup and washed it down with too-sweet wine. Once my palate was clear, I said, "The star mothers are mortals, but their passing hurts You. That's why You don't get close to them."

The Sun did not answer.

I picked at my food but didn't raise any of it to my mouth. "May I . . . May I speak freely, Your Majesty?"

His lip quirked. "You have not asked for permission before now."

"Then I have it."

He nodded.

"I think that is selfish."

His reaction was subtle: the slight lifting of His head, the tightening of the corners of His eyes. "Is it." It was more a statement than a question.

"We give our lives for the stars. For You." I measured each word carefully. "Our lives are fleeting, yes, but they are worthy. Is it so much to ask, to be remembered?" My throat closed, and I swallowed to force it open. "A gift of remembrance, from the greatest being in the universe."

"I am not the greatest," He whispered.

"To us, You are," I pressed. "When You dine with a future star mother, and she asks, 'Tell me about the others,' I want You to say my name and where I came from. I want You to tell her about me."

He studied me for a breath before asking, "And what would I tell her?"

I placed my fork beside my plate and folded my hands in my lap, reflecting on that. "You should tell her that I spoke out of turn often, and I made poor replicas of Your face in string, but that I was kind to Your servants and spoke my mind. You should . . . You should tell them what You think of me, Your Highness. You should speak of me fondly. As the bringer of a star. As the mother of Your child."

He considered this a long moment. Dropped His gaze. "You are right, of course."

"I am not stupid," I added. "I know You are the Sun. I know You have great responsibility and great power and do not have the time to learn every intricacy of who I am. But neither should You shy away from me because my death makes You sad."

For a moment, I thought the fire around His shoulders flared, and yet His color seemed darker, like the heart of a Sunset.

Several seconds passed, neither of us touching our food.

I traced the edge of the table with my thumb. "What is it like . . . to die?"

His diamond eyes found mine. "You are asking the wrong person, for I cannot."

"But You have seen death," I said, and He nodded. "Since the beginning of time—"

"I am hardly that old." He sounded almost affronted. "Time has no beginning, regardless."

I smiled. "For a very *long* time, then."

He straightened in His chair. "Why should you ask after it, Ceris?"

"Should I not be curious about my future?"

He frowned. "I suppose." He took a deep breath and let it out slowly. "There will be accolades for you, on Earth Mother and in the heavens. Your spirit will pass on to an elite hereafter where gods and godlings live only to serve you and your loved ones."

"My loved ones will come as well?" I interrupted.

"Yes. Those connected to you will be shown the road to paradise upon their passing."

Warmth not unlike my star's bloomed in my chest. So it was all true, the fate of a blissful heaven. I would see my family again. I would see Caen, too, if he chose that path. And why would he not?

"Your body will be sent back to your home, crowned with treasures of gratitude. You will be honored among your people. That is the way."

I clasped my hands together. I knew my fate, but it did not yet seem real to me. But His words were . . . comforting. "Thank you. May I postpone the end of our meal with one more inquiry?"

He waited for the question, ever patient.

"What will she be like, when she is born?"

Turning His plate a few degrees, the Sun said, "You believe her to be a girl?"

I shrugged. I wasn't sure if it was merely a desire for the child to be like myself or mother's intuition. I was new to all of this.

He considered for a moment, long enough that I took a few more bites of my meal. "I do not know if you will be coherent enough to know."

"All the more reason for You to tell me."

He almost smiled at that, but His diamond eyes shimmered in a sad way—not that a god made of fire would be able to weep.

"It will be bright and brilliant," He finally answered. "But it will be painful."

I set down my fork, my throat tightening once more. After a few heartbeats of silence, I asked, "Will she see my face?"

His countenance softened. "They always do."

I nodded and sliced into a piece of meat, but my appetite had waned. I expected death would come quickly—mortals were not made to survive such things. But I wished with all my heart that I would be able to claw on to life long enough to see my baby's face. To hold her. To know her.

"I will tell them," the Sun started carefully, pulling me from my spiraling thoughts, "that Ceris Wenden was wise beyond her years, brash, and yet oddly delightful. And that she loved her star with all she was."

A grin parted my lips, and I blinked back a tear. "I would be happy with that."

It is a woman's intuition to recognize labor, even when it's new to her body, so when the first, subtle contraction rippled across my abdomen, I stopped to listen. My tapestry was finished—I'd made quick work of it, with little else to do—and I was nearly done with an elegant border of honeysuckle wrapping around the edges when the first pain came.

The second was stronger, and the third even more so. By the fourth, I knew something was wrong. Not *wrong*, but not normal, for a woman's labor should come neither so fast nor so angrily. I had seen babies born in the village, and the midwife had chatted with me as she helped me make the linen for my dress, so of this, I was sure.

I stood, the contractions sudden and quick, each like a punch to the gut. With every tightening of my stomach, I felt a heat beyond my own, like coals dancing within my belly.

My star. My star was coming.

It panicked me so greatly I did not stop to think that I stood on death's door, or that the creature inside of me would rip me apart as its brothers and sisters had to their mothers before it. But I knew this being, this child, who had kept me company these last nine months, was ready to be known. And would, hopefully, see my face and hear my voice before my body released my spirit into paradise.

I made my way to my not-door, hunched, and opened it into the not-hallway that reached nowhere and everywhere, and cried, "The star is coming!"

Had I known those four simple words would give me such attention, I would have shouted them my first week in the palace.

Godlings descended upon me. Elta and Fosii were among them—they had been hovering for the last three weeks, knowing my time was near. Others were complete strangers. The great and bizarre palace moved and shifted around me, as though a womb in and of itself, and I found myself in a room not unlike my own. But this place felt more solid, the not-walls fully opaque, leaning in as though to better see me. And yet the space opened wide above me, no ceiling but endless stars and galaxies, colors and shapes I could not then, at that time, name. Not unlike the Sun's room, which I had only entered once.

Above me, the night sky sparkled with life, a blanket ready and waiting to catch its child. Twinkles of light danced in anticipation of meeting their new sibling. The empty space where the last star had perished seemed to yawn with wanting. In my delirium, I imagined a dark hand reaching down from it and grabbing my stomach.

The godlings barely had time to lay me down before I screamed.

I had been given bountiful time to consider my upcoming delivery. I had seen other women give birth. I had witnessed tears and bravery, trepidation and joy. I had spoken to my attendants and the Sun Himself about what to expect. I had thought I was prepared.

But there was no preparing for the vibrant pain that ripped through me, as though blacksmith's tongs had grabbed the skin of my toes and peeled it back to my forehead in one swift, cruel motion. As though my gut had been hollowed out for a cookfire, my entrails the meal. As though I had been piked upon the Sun Himself, my flesh forever charring.

I had thought making love to the Sun the most unbearable pain of my existence, but I was wrong.

This was far worse.

There was no question why star mothers died upon the birth bed. No mortal could survive this. Not even a godling could.

My world became utter agony, bright and unyielding, tearing me apart and remaking me only to pull me asunder once more. I was disembodied, and I was *fire*. I lost consciousness in the sense that thoughts ceased to process, but I never pulled away from the torture within me, blazing slowly, *so* slowly, toward my hips. I never broke away from the pain, not once. I screamed, unseeing, barely registering hands holding me down. If Elta and Fosii tried to comfort me, I couldn't hear them. If the Sun came to witness my death or His child's birth, I couldn't sense Him. I was locked in a world all my own, the bars smoking against my skin, closing in on me from all sides so I could not pull away. Not in body. Only in spirit. And I *felt* that pull, that need to break free from my own skin. I welcomed death with all that I was. I begged for it.

Time warped. I burned alive for years, decades, centuries, hours, minutes, seconds. I tore apart again and again and again, until finally, blessedly, the darkness swallowed me whole.

CHAPTER 6

When light again touched my eyes, it took me a very long time to process it. It was pale and unassuming, with the slightest touch of pink. My mind had to remember what *light* was. Blinking dry eyes, I stared at it, gaped at it, comprehended it. I lay there for a long time, trying to remember who I was, what this body was, and how we were attached. My thoughts were sluggish and ground together as two great stones, but they moved, and slowly I pieced myself together again.

Ceris. Star Mother.

The blessed hereafter.

And yet . . . the hereafter looked very much like the misshapen palace where I had spent nearly a year of my life. I gradually found the strength to move my neck, glimpsing the night and stars overhead and finding a not-pillar nearby, beyond the reach of my not-bed.

I was spread supine upon the covers, my arms stretched out to either side of me, my legs in a narrow V. I was dressed in white that shimmered with a light of its own, not unlike a star. A fabric unseen on Earth, unmade by man. Four glass roses lay across my breast, and I felt a metal crown at my brow, warm from contact with my skin.

I was dressed for a funeral, a burial. Dressed as the honored dead. And yet my spirit was still firmly in my body, which was stiff and tired but absent of pain. Or perhaps I ached terribly, but the comparison to my star's birth made it seem inconsequential.

Confused, I lifted my eyes to the sky above me, speckled with a million stars of so many colors. And somehow, *somehow*, my gaze was drawn to one in particular, a tiny white bead against the black, small and twinkling. A pinprick of life in a tiny pocket where life had previously gone out. Somehow I knew that was *my* star, though realistically I should not be able to tell it apart from any of the others. And I felt it watching me, looking back with . . . delight.

I let out a long breath and smiled.

Someone gasped near me.

"OH!" She dropped a pitcher, which vanished through the not-floor and reappeared in her hands. "Oh, by the Sun's watch, she's *alive*!"

Her cry rang against the not-walls. She backed away from me as though a dragon roosted in my hair, and ran from the room. I stared after her, my confused thoughts giving her a name. *Elta*. I tried to sit up, but my body was not quite itself yet. I could not so much as twitch my little finger.

Elta shortly returned with three others, one whom I recognized from earlier but could not name. They all stared at me with wide, incandescent eyes. The shortest, whose face reminded me of a bear's, came close and peered into my eyes for a long time. He then collected the glass roses and pressed his large hand between my breasts.

He drew back suddenly, like I was hot to the touch. "She lives." His words were airy, intangible as the wind. "She lives."

Another said, "Alert Satto at once."

Elta croaked, "Sh-She'll need nourishment."

And they all vanished, leaving me alone to gaze at my star, wishing desperately that I could reach for her.

I spent three days in my room, with my tapestry draped over the foot of my bed, recuperating from what should have killed me. I did not understand how I was still alive, and none of the godlings who waited on me understood it, either. One, the bear-faced being from before, thoroughly examined me, only to announce, "You are fully and undoubtedly mortal."

And yet I seemed to be recovering just as any mortal woman who'd had a difficult birth with a mortal baby would. Better, even, for there had not been a single drop of blood from my womb, and I knew most mortal women bled for weeks after childbirth. I wondered if it was a side effect of giving birth to a star, or if the act itself had somehow cauterized me.

I regained my strength quickly with rest and food. I'd seen the way people who had suffered continued to suffer in their thoughts long after the physical suffering had ended, and yet my memories of giving birth to my star seemed faint and distant, like they'd happened in a dream. Like my mind did not *want* me to remember them, though later I would realize my body recalled what I did not.

My arms felt too light, like there should be a babe cradled in my elbows to weigh them down. Something was missing, and I carried around the constant, nagging feeling that I had forgotten something. I asked if I could see her, but none of the godlings had the power to take me to that faraway place where my star lived, and I hadn't yet had an opportunity to ask Sun, for He was swept up in "critical matters," as Fosii explained. Indeed, the walls of His palace were opaque more often than not.

I spent much of my time looking up into the eternal night sky, peering at my star and all her siblings. Peace came easier that way.

The lack of blood wasn't the only peculiarity. My breasts didn't engorge, either. The only sign of my pregnancy was the droop of my empty abdomen, the skin thick like scar tissue. Strangely, that crystalline sheen I'd had since arriving at the palace was gone. I seemed remarkably myself, although my flesh sometimes, from the corner of my eye, seemed to glow with a subtle inner light, just as my abdomen had when it was heavy with a star child. My hair was streaked silver as well, like my aging mother's. A glimpse in a requested mirror told me the rest of me had not aged, but I thought I looked different. Like my soul bore more years than the rest of me did.

Most notably, I was alive and well. It was as if the birth never happened, and I was not the only one who found that unsettling.

After another three days, Elta and Fosii came to prepare me as they had nearly five months previously, when I dined with Sun, though I was given a dress beneath my cape since the crystalline spell was no longer on my person. I found myself oddly nervous to face Him, more so than I'd been at our dinner. I knew something was wrong. I knew it from the stories and the songs about star mothers, from the looks the godlings gave me, and from my own broken expectations.

Elta and Fosii worried over me so greatly. I loathed burdening them with my own trepidation, so I kept my anxieties to myself and allowed them to escort me through the palace to a great hall that looked very solid and very *real* to my mortal eyes. Within it was a throne that appeared to be made of marble pierced through with Sunset. It was tall and broad and glittered with gold, with golden rays jutting out from the back like swords, meant to mimic Sun spokes. He looked as He always did when in my presence, His power dimmed but remarkable, His body just as tall and wide as that throne, His face just as radiant and golden.

It was strange, how I could not quite remember the scalding and visceral birth of my star, and yet every inch of me still burned from the memory of Sun's body against mine, of the pain that had engulfed me inside and out, and of the way I'd felt *everything* and nothing at the same time. It alarmed me—not that I could recall the agony of our lovemaking, but that I could not recall the sensations of my own child coming into life.

"Ceris Wenden." My name sounded like a hymn in His deep voice. He strode toward me and stood close, utterly mesmerizing. His diamond eyes glittered with wonder. "Star Mother."

I curtsied low, pulling a few threads of courage from within myself. I dropped my skirt as soon as I thought it acceptable to do so.

His hot finger touched my chin and lifted my face. I flushed at that simple touch, not because it was arousing but because it stirred more memories of our night together. But the kindness in His face brought me forward just as it had at that dining table, where we had spoken so honestly all those months ago. We had parted on friendly enough terms.

It was then that I realized while His touch was blazing and hot, it did not hurt me. It shocked me to speechlessness.

He studied me for a long moment, eyes bright and white hot, His hand still holding my face. I scrambled for words. Part of me, the part I had left on Earth, wanted to utter, *Ta-da!* But of course I did not let those sounds pass my lips.

"You are an anomaly," Sun finally said. He studied His knuckle against my face for a moment, as though also realizing He did not harm me, before lowering His hand. "Never, throughout all the chords of time, has a mortal withstood the birth of a star."

I searched His face, finding wonder in its nearly blinding facets. He did not yet need to fulfill my request that I be remembered. Not when I stood before Him, whole.

He tilted His head to one side. "Have you nothing to say to Me?"

Clasping my hands together, I said, "I have been told I am very much mortal, Your Majesty. I'm afraid I cannot enlighten You." I paused. "The pun is not intended."

His lip quirked. He stepped back, then strode a small circle around me, making me nervous. When He returned to my front, He said, "You are remarkable."

I blushed from the praise. "Th-Thank you."

He glanced to the side of the not-room, to a few grand-looking godlings, far larger than the servants who graced my bedroom. One of them uttered, "What shall we do with her?"

"I know not," Sun replied, glancing back to me. Studying me as though He had not already done so. As though I had changed—which I had. Then, leaning close enough that I could feel the fire of His breath, He peered into my eyes. "Not entirely mortal, I think."

A hiccup pushed halfway up my throat at those words. *Not entirely mortal?*

My hand fell to my stomach, where a star had once been. My body *was* different. A body changed when giving life to a child. But what happened when that child was a godling? A *star?*

Sun hummed beneath His breath, thinking.

"If I may," I spoke quietly, and He nodded for me to continue. "I . . . I would like to return home."

Sun arched a bold, fiery eyebrow. "You wish to return to the Earth Mother?"

Another of the godlings at the side of the room said, in a voice like bells, "That is the home of mortals," as though we did not already know.

And yet, perhaps the god before me needed to be reminded.

Sun drew His bright fingers across His chin, considering. It was a very human gesture, which I found oddly endearing. Feeling bold, I thought to encourage Him. "I believe You've no further use for me, my Lord."

His lip quirked again. "I am not sure you are correct in that assessment, Ceris Wenden. You have broken the routine of millennia, and I am unsure how to proceed." He lowered His hand and gestured to the room around us. "You could stay here."

I did not look at the palace, but at Him, incredulous of the offer. "Here?"

He nodded. "You are a star mother. You have done a great service. Perhaps the greatest a mortal could do. You would be welcome. I . . . I would welcome you."

I swallowed, pulling my eyes from Him to look at the pink-lit not-walls around us. This place, as bizarre as it was, had become familiar to me during my stay. And yet, looking at it now, it was as though I saw it for the first time. It was strange, it was other, and it was uncomfortable. Not where I belonged. More importantly, not where I wanted to be.

But before I denied a god, I needed to ask a favor. "Our child. Might I see her?"

He paused. "You were right, of course."

My brow knit together.

"It is a *her*." He smiled at me and guided me to a not-wall, where a wave of His hand opened a porthole. It was as though the palace had shifted while my mind was elsewhere, for the stars I so often watched from my bed, looking up, I could now see through this porthole, looking out. There was my star, glimmering and beautiful, larger than she appeared from my bedroom, but still so far out of reach. I blinked tears away at her majesty.

"Can I go to her?" I whispered.

Sun's shoulders sagged. "I will take you, in due time. But I cannot now. Her power resides in wild space, and it is unguarded."

Disappointment and confusion swirled through me. "Unguarded?"

His mouth was a tight, dark line. "Matters of grave importance are threatening the balance of the universe. And *she* is taking advantage."

I stepped away from the porthole, and it spiraled closed. "You will have to be more specific."

"Moon." He rubbed the bridge of His nose—another human gesture. "She has always fought for power, fought to be counted among gods. But that is no trouble of yours."

I glanced back to where the porthole had been, my chest aching for it to reappear so I could jump from it and swim through the darkness toward our daughter. How long would I have to stay in this palace before Sun granted my wish?

If I had to wait, did I have to wait *here*? I was a star mother, and Sun ruled the day. Surely He'd have the power to find me, once the universe was well again.

"Promise me." When He met my eyes, I added, "That You will take me, when it is safe."

He nodded. "I promise."

I bowed my head to Him. "Thank You. I ask that You also grant my other desire, Your Majesty. I want to go home."

He did not answer, so I lifted my head, meeting His lionlike visage. Several seconds passed before He let out a sigh, and it was as though summer pulsed through the not-room. "I wish to speak with you further, but this problem must be seen to immediately. You have done Me and My kingdom a great service. I will see you returned home. If that is what you truly want."

My heart flipped in my chest. All that I thought I had lost—my parents, my sisters, my friends—would be mine again. Caen . . . Caen would not be mine in the way I had always wanted him to be, but he would be there, and he would love me in a way he could love no one else, even if it was not as a wife. And I . . . felt content with that. At peace.

I nodded, and Sun reached for a golden band crossing His broad chest, pulling from it a small loop of fire. He spun it between His fingers, the flames growing smaller and darker with each turn, until it formed a ring of deep amber with a scorched band running along its middle. It smoked in His palm when He offered it to me. Hesitant, I picked it up. Like Sun Himself, the ring was hot, but did not hurt me.

"Twist it," He said.

I did so, and the dark band glowed faintly.

"I will be able to find you when that band is lit," He said in answer to my unspoken question. "I can see the whole Earth Mother from My kingdom, but She is vast and mortals are many."

I slid the ring onto the middle finger of my left hand. "Thank You."

Sun reached out, placed His searing hand on my shoulder—

And I was home.

CHAPTER 7

I appeared at the altar in the eye of the cathedral, the spring air crisp around me. It had been summer when I left. The grass was young and green underfoot, speckled with a few clover flowers. The altar stood resolute. Reaching out a hand, I ran my palm over its cool stone. This place had been hot as an oven when last I traversed it.

My dress was the same I'd worn when I volunteered to be star mother: a simple gray linen with the embroidery of green leaves running down the skirt in two rows, remarkably undamaged. Leaves I'd stitched myself. I had nothing else with me, not even my embroidery—but that was my star's now.

I peered up toward heaven, seeing for the first time in ten months blue sky and wispy clouds looking back at me. Daylight. Dawn. I marveled at it for a full minute before turning back to the cathedral, to the archway that led into the main vestibule.

A smile split my face. What would the others say, to see me alive and well? What would my parents and sisters think? Perhaps we would be able to recapture the closeness I had glimpsed before stepping into the Sunlit cathedral. My stories and the honor Sun had promised me would bridge the gulf between us.

I wanted to see Caen again, to witness his happiness. Part of me would always love him, but nothing could jolt or destroy my new sense of peace. There would only be joy in our reuniting, nothing else.

Picking up my skirt, I hurried into the cathedral. I heard someone deeper within it, despite the early hour. Was it Father? He was the one who swept out the church. Heart racing, I turned past the main doors and wrapped around to the back, finding a man wearing a cap, sweeping the floor. But it wasn't my father.

"Oh," I said, and the man looked up at me, his face completely unfamiliar. He was about fifty years old and wore a white stole embroidered with gold. I'd never seen the like before. A pair of dainty spectacles rested on his nose.

"I-I'm sorry," I said. "I thought you were someone else."

He smiled at me. "I am only myself." Taking one hand from the broom, he adjusted his spectacles and squinted at me.

Suddenly embarrassed, I asked, "This is Endwever, is it not?"

"Yes, of course." He took a step closer to me. His expression went slack suddenly, his skin pale. "By the gods."

Uneasy, I asked, "What?"

"You . . . But it can't be."

I repeated, "What?"

He let the broom drop from his hand. "My dear woman . . . what is your name?"

I answered, "Ceris Wenden," only to have him recite my last name along with me. He gawked, and I smiled. "I know—no one was expecting me to come back. You must have met my father." A sudden rush of fear prickled down my spine. "Is he well?" I didn't know this man, and it was my father's duty to take care of the cathedral.

He hesitated a moment before replying. "Oh, I . . ." He rolled his lips together, thinking. "Here . . . come with me."

He left his broom and moved deeper into the temple. He had a slight limp in his right leg. Despite my eagerness to return home, I followed him past the ambulatory and out a small door that opened onto the cemetery. My heart leapt into my throat and squeezed my windpipe, making it impossible to speak or breathe. The grounds were larger than I remembered, but I didn't visit them often.

He paused once, then continued walking, leading me to a row of large graves, notably higher and more ornate than the other tombstones. They were weathered and worn, their writing nearly illegible, the Sun spokes carved atop the stones short and rounded from wind and rain.

"These are the Wendens." He pointed them out with a weak gesture.

"Wendens," I repeated, emphasizing the *s* at the end. I glanced to the row behind them, to a row of even older graves. Weren't *those* the Wendens? I had thought my grandparents were buried in that corner . . . but perhaps I was mistaken.

Reaching forward, I brushed the top of the highest tombstone. I could make out an *A* in the engraving, a faded Sun above it. I shook my head. "These stones must be centuries old. My family was in good health when I left."

The man didn't answer, so I turned to look at him. Sadness dipped his eyes and confusion thickened his brow. I straightened, waiting for an explanation, but all he said was "You really are Ceris Wenden of Endwever."

He spoke like he was announcing a queen. I nodded.

He wrung his hands together. "Come." He headed back into the cathedral.

I jogged to catch up with him. "What is it you're not telling me?" I asked. "What is your name?"

"I'm Father Aedan, Your Highness." He covered his mouth to cough. "Star Mother. Forgive me, I don't know what to call you."

"Ceris is fine," I assured him, but he shook his head as though he didn't agree. We stepped back into the cathedral, Father Aedan leading me closer to the eye, but I stopped in my tracks, spying a sculpture that had not been there on my last visit, standing directly across from the apse. It was life-sized, made of marble, and stood atop a three-foot-high pedestal. A woman draped in billowing clothing, skirt running past her toes, a crown of Sun spokes gracing her brow, a five-pointed star in her outstretched hand.

The face was undeniably mine.

Gaping, I dragged my feet forward, moving closer. I touched the ends of the stone dress, which were smooth from the passing of a million fingers. I studied my face—it was reverent and wise, chiseled into an expression I don't think I've ever actually worn, but it was lovely and inspiring, nonetheless.

No wonder Father Aedan had recognized me.

"Beautiful, isn't it?" he whispered.

I nodded. "Who carved it?"

"Alas, I do not know."

My gaze dropped back to the hem of the skirt. The sculptor must have made quick work of it, to capture my likeness so perfectly, to have it put in the cathedral already. How could anyone who worked here not know his name?

Why was the stone so worn, like it was . . . old? Just like those tombstones . . .

"Father Aedan"—I enunciated every syllable of his name—"how long have I been gone?"

He swallowed and looked around, searching for something. I now realize he might have been searching for a place for me to sit. "Our scripture says you left in 3404, Star Mother." He gestured weakly to the pedestal, and I saw the same four numbers etched there.

When he didn't continue, I pushed another question through my tight throat. "And what year is it now?" My thoughts cried, *3405. Please say 3405.*

His blunt answer was, "4105."

I reeled back from the statue as though it had stung me. My breath rasped. Not enough air. For a moment, I was back beneath the torch of Sun, burning in its light, crawling across stones like embers.

Then I blinked, and everything was cold and gray. The stone, the air, the rising light filtering through the windows. My feet, still bare, were ice. "4105?"

Father Aedan nodded.

I gripped the hem of the statue's skirt, lowering myself to the floor. "Seven hundred years? I've been gone *seven hundred years?*"

He reached toward me. "Star Mother—"

I shied away, uncaring that my skirt rose halfway up my calf. "I was just there. Ten months, the same as it would be with any mortal child. I wasn't supposed to live, but I did. I *lived.*" My volume raised with each word. "I lived, and He sent me back. How could seven hundred years have passed?"

The poor father looked ready to weep. "I-I don't know the ways of the gods, Star Mother. Not beyond what They've revealed to me. Please . . . let me get you some water and bread. Something to settle your stomach."

But I was on my feet again, shaking my head as though I could dispel the truths he spoke. I ran through the cathedral, past the eye, down the nave, to the heavy double doors of its entrance. I rammed my shoulder into the one on the right, forcing it open.

Spring air engulfed me, and for a heartbeat, Endwever was exactly how I remembered it. But small wrongs ticked in my vision one by one. That house, and the one behind it, hadn't been there when I left. The Farntons hadn't had a fence, and their vegetable garden was missing.

I walked, cutting across the village, stepping around a stray sheep. People were rising to start their chores and their day. A man hooked his plow to an ox. A woman carried a laden bucket in each hand. A girl tied her apron tight around her small waist. All of them, strangers.

Panic rose in my breast, and I moved faster, as though the exercise could burn away all the unfamiliarity of this familiar place. The path wound toward my own home, but as I neared it, I noticed an addition had been put onto it, and a plump woman nursing a babe sat in the window, glancing up at me with unfamiliar eyes. I changed direction, running toward the tree line. Passing a man who called after me, another who stared at me the way Father Aedan had. All of them wore strange fashions, the women with lower necklines and fuller sleeves, bright aprons over their skirts. The men had heavy folded cuffs and sharp collars. My dress alone made me stand out among them, a blue jay in a flock of cardinals.

I ran until I came to the cottage Caen had been building for us. It was entirely finished, with a fenced-in vegetable garden beside it. There was no thatching on the roof, but dark tiles. Bird droppings highlighted the walls. A new walking path cut a rivet in the Earth, heading toward the village square. And the village . . . it was much too large. Far larger than it had been . . .

I stopped, staring, trying to catch my breath. With each exhale, my thoughts screamed, *Seven hundred years. Seven hundred years. Seven hundred years.*

This was not the Endwever I had left behind.

These were not my friends, my neighbors, my family. No, they were all long dead, and I was the only one left. The only one left.

Alone.

I sat by the fireplace, sipping yarrow tea, clasping the cup to warm my fingers. I was inside Father Aedan's house. He had found me in my despair and, with the help of his wife, coaxed me inside. The house was centuries old, but it had not stood in Endwever during my time.

My time. I took another sip of tea, feeling the warmth drag down my throat, and peered out the window at the afternoon sky. At the Sun. Did He know what He had sent me back to?

The ring on my finger was lined amber. Would He try to find me?

A face appeared in the window and startled me. An adolescent boy, peering in, going wide-eyed at the sight of me.

Shila, my hostess, noticed as well. Clucking her tongue, she strode to the window and shut its thin curtain. "She's not a show hen."

"What she is is a miracle," Father Aedan replied. He smiled at me from his seat across the room, at a short wooden table. "A miracle. They are bound to be curious."

Frowning, Shila moved to another window and peeked outside. "There's already a dozen of them out there."

"I haven't exactly been clandestine," I managed.

Shila turned, perhaps to speak to me, but she studied me instead, her eyes glistening. She recognized me from the temple statue, too. They all did.

"There's a scripture about you," Father Aedan said, as though hearing my acclaim could soothe my confusion, my shock. "About how the Sun God favored you and kept you."

I swallowed a hot mouthful of tea. "Because my body was never returned."

He nodded.

But that answered nothing, and I neither confirmed nor denied the assumption.

Shila worried her hands and stepped into the kitchen. "I'll make us a fine meal, and you a bed. Take the day to relax, my dear. We'll sort it all out tomorrow, when you're feeling yourself again."

But a day couldn't make me feel like myself.

Only seven hundred years would.

There was a crowd waiting for me when I departed for the cathedral in the morning.

The popularity was strange. Once upon a time, I would have enjoyed it, but my thoughts were too rattled and thin to take the attention. Villagers of all shapes, sizes, and ages had been outside the Aedans' home since dawn. Some, I suspected, had camped out all night to get a glimpse of me. I was more than a show hen—I was a prize bull.

I thought back to how I'd likened myself to an old cow in the backyard, before becoming a star mother. The irony was not lost on me.

Father Aedan and Shila walked close to me, as though their bodies could give me some privacy. I smiled and nodded at those we passed, igniting whispers like fire in my wake.

At the cathedral, I returned to the cemetery, taking my time with the tombstones. The Aedans didn't leave me, but they did give me some space, watching over me from a distance as though I were a bird that might flit away at any moment. But where would I go? Although I had a growing feeling the Aedans saw me more as a scriptural phenomenon than a living and breathing person, I did not know of any other who would have me. Every last human being I had known was long dead.

A comment in an unfamiliar voice marked the arrival of a third party.

"How did she survive?" the man asked, as though I could not hear him.

I glanced over my shoulder to a man of about forty, wearing worn but well-made clothes and a hearty jacket. Father Aedan gestured for him to follow, and the two came out to meet me.

"Ceris, this is Toder, the stonemason who carves all the tombstones. We thought he could help."

I glanced at the man, then back to the weathered grave markers before me. "Did he carve them seven hundred years ago as well?" I couldn't help the bitterness in my voice, but I did regret it instantly.

"No," Toder replied, crouching beside me, "but my father and his father before him worked this place. I know it well."

Hope sparked within me. "You have records?"

He looked abashed. "N-No. Not records that old, my lady."

"Ceris," I corrected him. Turning back to the tombstone, I ran my hand down its length. I could make out a few letters of *Wenden*. Had my family still gone to the paradisiacal hereafter Sun had promised me, even though I had not been there to greet them? "And I don't know why I survived, to answer your question." That more or less denied what had been written in scripture about me.

Behind us, Father Aedan said, "Perhaps many have, only to come back in a different time—"

"No." I corrected him, firm. "They all perished with their stars."

Silence fell around us like snow.

Clearing his throat, Toder stood and moved to the next row of graves. "These ones are from the 3800s," he explained, and I followed him, light-headed from crouching so long. He walked a little farther. "These are more recent."

I could tell, for they were still legible. I read the one he stood beside. "I don't think the Parros family will help me here."

Toder shook his head. "The placement . . . most likely a Wenden woman married into the Parros family. That's why the Wenden graves dwindle in number."

That ember of hope reignited, and I read the names on the Parros family tombstones. "Are they still here? Their descendants?" I might have family after all, just not family I've met yet. One of my sisters, at the very least, had married. She'd had children, too, if there were tombstones on the Wenden plot from the 3800s.

Father Aedan worried his hands. "I-I'm afraid not."

Toder said, "Let us ask Jon. He might know."

They took me to Jon Ellis, who was the oldest man in Endwever at seventy-four. A crowd traveled with me when I departed for his home, but the glimmer of hope in my belly softened my disposition, and I grasped hands with many of the bystanders, nodding when they said my name or asked if my story was true. Many acted like I was some holy demigod. A few looked at me skeptically. Fortunately, I had no desire to prove anything to anyone.

To my surprise, we went to my cottage. Caen's cottage. The cottage where I would have birthed mortal babes, had my life progressed as expected.

"Is this a family home?" I whispered to Father Aedan. "Or did the previous owners move on?"

"The Ellis family has been here longer than mine has, certainly," the father replied. Caen's last name had been Allyr. Perhaps the name had evolved over time? I wondered at it, suddenly eager to check the graves for a possible change of name by marriage.

I took in the doorway as I passed through it, the fireplace, the kitchen, and the backrooms, trying to imagine myself the woman of the household. I found it very difficult to do so.

Jon sat in a rocking chair near the dying fire, his hair thin and white, his face narrow except for his cheekbones. It took a bit of explaining, and a bit of remembering, before he could answer our questions, but his eyes lit up, and he tapped his index finger on the chair's armrest.

"I remember. Parros . . . He was in metal trade. Blacksmith. Married that skinny girl and moved on for an apprenticeship, wasn't it?" He nodded. "Headed to . . . Nediah."

Nediah. I clung to the familiar name. Nediah was a city northwest of Endwever. The merchants who traveled by Endwever were always either coming from or going to Nediah. It was said they had a library and their roads were all cobbled with stone.

"Do you remember how long ago?" I asked.

Jon shrugged. "I was but a lad. Younger than you." He waved at me.

Some fifty years, then. But that was not too long ago. Two or three generations. The young man who'd left might no longer be alive, but his family would be.

"Then I must go to Nediah," I said.

A restrained sob broke from Shila's throat. "Oh, say you won't, Ceris. We have need for you here."

I gaped at her. "What need?"

She didn't answer. Father Aedan put a hand on her shoulder, his gaze finding me. "You are a symbol of hope for us. For the people. You have been for . . . centuries."

"I am merely a survivor," I insisted. "I am no god."

"But you've been touched by one," Shila whispered.

My cheeks warmed. "That means nothing." But my hand flew to my belly, as though I could feel the warm pulse of my star there. However, my womb remained cold, and a hollowness gaped within me when I remembered that fact.

As we offered our thanks and stepped back into the spring air, I said, "Everything I had . . . it's long gone now." I glanced in the direction of my old home. "I don't have anything for the journey."

Shila and Father Aedan exchanged a glance. Sweetly, Shila took my arm and wrapped it through hers. "Don't worry, Ceris. We'll see to it you have everything you need."

Shila kept her promise. She and the rest of Endwever provided me with everything I could possibly need. But not what I wanted.

I had hoped for a bag in which to carry supplies. A few morsels for the road—if memory served me right, the next closest town, Terasta, was a full day's journey away, and I could possibly restock there. I had no shoes, nothing in the modern fashion, and no money. I was willing to work for those things, but Shila and Father Aedan would hear nothing of it. They gave me a warm room in their home. One of the local women insisted I take her best dress, and Shila worked on another for me while also finding me a pair of shoes that were just a hair too big. The villagers provided me three meals a day, offered me fine bath oils and prettily carved hair combs. It was all so very gracious.

But the more I spoke of going to Nediah to search for my sister's descendants, the more the villagers closed in around me. They wanted me to stay, badly, and it became increasingly hard to be alone. I felt guilty for wanting to leave, until someone nailed my window shut one night. That was when I understood: no one in Endwever was going to let me leave. Despite all the charity offered to me, I was a prisoner. Even Sun's palace hadn't stripped me of freedom.

Father Aedan coerced me to the cathedral every day so that I could be seen, touched, even prayed to, which alarmed me to the point that I refused to leave the house unless the prayers stopped. So the villagers sang to me instead.

> She came amidst the tempered fire
> The bride that was to be
> And offered up her tender heart
> Between the oaken trees
> Hers was a gift of peace and honor
> Given to the town
> Children, at night, when you look up
> Her child is looking down

The scriptures had promised I would be immortalized in song, but I'd never imagined I'd be able to *hear* the song. It was a lovely, haunting melody that played in my dreams at night.

My eighth day in Endwever, I watched my stone likeness as I stood in the apse of the cathedral during a service. The song, like a lullaby, echoed all around me. And I realized I was no different than the statue that had been carved in my honor. Unmoving, unchanging, and completely subject to the whims of those around me.

I had sacrificed myself for the good of those whom I loved. And, admittedly, for somewhat selfish reasons. My departure had been spun into songs and stories, stretched and emboldened over generations, idolized to the point where I was placed above the Sun. It felt wrong.

I hated it.

The only thing I wanted was family and a place to belong, and *if* such a thing existed for me, it was across the country in the city of Nediah. But I would never have it if I could not leave the place of my birth. I glanced at the amber stripe of the holy ring on my finger. The Sun could find me as long as it was activated, but *when* would He find me? He had mentioned trouble with the moon before I left. How long would those celestial politics take to resolve?

What if it was another seven hundred years?

And so, as the song finished, as I smiled at the congregation and thanked them, I made a plan to leave, with only one thing certain: once I ran away, I could never, ever come back.

CHAPTER 8

The villagers had given me enough supplies and clothing to keep me more or less comfortable for a few days' journey, though I would need to steal food from Shila's cupboards. So much had been donated to her on my behalf, I felt only minimal guilt for doing so. Yet I had to plan the timing of my escape carefully. My door wasn't locked at night, but the house doors were, and I didn't know where either Shila or Father Aedan kept the key. My tenth day in Endwever, I faked sick and stayed in bed all day. Shila was kind enough to bring me my meals, and I stowed away crusts of bread and winter-wrinkled apples for my journey. On the eleventh day, I managed to sneak some cheese from the cupboards at night without waking anyone. On the twelfth, I turned my old dress into two bags I could carry on my shoulders and loaded them up.

And then I did what might be considered blasphemy. I told Father Aedan I needed to talk with the Sun and could only do so at Sunset. He took me to the cathedral, and I knelt at the altar for so long my knees and belly hurt. The first night, I did offer a prayer, though I'm not sure if Sun heard it. The next two nights, I just knelt there, thinking, planning, once dozing off. It didn't matter, so long as I established a pattern. So long as Father Aedan believed the ruse and grew tired of waiting for my hours of "supplication" to end.

On the fifteenth night, I again went to the cathedral to pray at Sunset, and once more knelt at the altar past nightfall. Father Aedan had taken to sweeping the floors, just as he had at our first meeting. And when I could no longer hear the broom, I dared to rise early from my knees and peer behind me.

I was blessedly alone. Taking off my shoes to minimize noise, I hurried deeper into the cathedral, easing open the door that led to the cemetery. I slowed only long enough to touch the Wenden graves, offering a final, silent, and heavy farewell before moving on. The walls surrounding the burial ground were short and easily scalable. I bounded over them and, under the cover of the waning crescent moon, cut through Endwever back to the Aedans' house. This was the riskiest part of my plan, but I hadn't been able to conceive of anywhere else to hide my bags.

The two parcels waited just behind the woodpile en route to the privy. I had stashed them, one at a time, under my skirt and tucked them away there. To my relief, both still awaited me. I pulled their straps crosswise over my chest and darted into the wood. It was the wrong direction for Terasta, but I would change my route later. Right now, I needed to get as much distance between myself and Endwever as possible. I needed them to lose me.

These were my woods, where I had spent so much time with Caen. They, too, had changed over seven hundred years, but I knew these trees. I knew where to go.

I hurried through the forest for an hour before the excitement of my escape loosened, as did the added energy it had given me. I slowed, picking my way carefully. The hairs on my arms stood on end. Had things gone my way, I would have hired a guide. Not only to prevent me from getting lost, but because it was dangerous to travel alone, especially for a woman. I severely doubted that fact had changed during my extended time away.

I ate some of my pillaged cheese to keep up my strength and peered up at the moon as I walked, trying to gauge when it would be safe to turn toward Terasta. The spring branches were not full, but dotted with tiny budding leaves still discovering their place. I tried spying past them to find my star, and in my strain to do so, stepped on an uneven bit of ground and toppled into moist, weed-ridden soil, bags swinging around my hips from the fall. Pulling my foot free, I rotated my ankle carefully, and said a prayer of thanks to all gods that I hadn't hurt it.

Then the first wolf howled.

My spine went stiff as an icicle. The sound was high and sorrowful, and not very far away.

Swallowing, I slowly stood, adjusting my bags so their weight wouldn't throw off my steps. I changed direction, walking away from the howl. Its answer came seconds later, from the south.

That one felt closer.

I forced my breaths to stretch up and down my throat. Forced my mind to think. I'd had little real exercise for nearly a year; I could hardly outrun them. They might not know I was there, but I knew better than to hope I could slip away unseen. Moving as quietly as possible, heart thudding, I shifted from scanning the shadowed way ahead to searching the trees, looking for one I could climb without injuring myself.

I spied a promising pine when another howl sounded. Was it closer, or did my fear amplify its call?

Setting my jaw, I reached the pine and grabbed the rough bark of its lowest branch, heaving myself up, adjusting my bags, and then heaving myself up again. Needles prodded my skin, but I ignored their discomfort. I would gladly take pine needles over wolves.

I leaned against the trunk as I tried to stand. The next branch was almost directly overhead. I took off both bags and hung them from it before climbing up and up again, grateful I'd disobeyed my mother's rules about the "boyish" pastime of tree climbing in my youth.

The howls stopped, but I heard movement in the forest now, the soft kind that stands out in the quiet of night, when birds and bugs are silent. I straddled a branch, the bark scraping my thighs, and hugged the pine's trunk. Sap stuck to my arms and clothes. I blindly twisted my Sun ring on and off, hoping the change of power might alert Sun that something was wrong.

I never saw the wolves, but I heard more than one beast pass under my tree that night. Even when the forest quieted again, I didn't move from my spot, enduring the needles and the cramps. I think I dozed at some point, letting the bark imprint against my forehead in uneven patterns. It wasn't until after dawn, my limbs and back sore and shaky, that I finally climbed down.

Using the Sun as my guide, I oriented myself as best I could toward Terasta, constantly on alert for pursuers, both of wolf and human make.

It took longer than I had planned to find the main road. Looking back, I think I overshot it by a couple of miles and ended up walking parallel to it for a few hours instead of perpendicular. Needless to say, I did not find a road through the wood until midafternoon, and I was so exhausted I found a thicket not far from it to lie down in, the brush thick enough I was sure anyone searching for me would pass on none the wiser. I wrapped my second dress around me for a blanket, and used my elbow as a pillow.

I dreamed of my infant star, her body human and glowing like Sun's, her fiery fingers tracing my palm. I whispered her name to her, but when I woke, I could not remember it.

My eyes opened to dimming Sunlight and three unfamiliar faces lurking over me.

I startled, thinking a search party from Endwever had come to drag me back to my worshipful duties. But though the town I had returned to was unfamiliar to me, I had seen its inhabitants at the cathedral every day for two weeks, and none of these men had been among them. They were well built though thin, with mismatched, travel-stained clothing. One had tied a strip of fabric around his head.

The other two held my bags.

"Told you she wasn't dead." The man with the fabric headwear stepped on my foot and slowly eased his weight onto it.

My eyes darted to my bags. "P-Please, I don't have any money." My mind raced to name what few valuables I had planned to sell in Terasta. "I-I have a compass, some woodwork, and—"

"Oh, we know." One of the other bandits held up his hand, which clutched my compass. The tombstone maker had given that to me as a gift.

The first said, "We'll help ourselves to all of it." His eyes roamed up my legs. "Hold her down."

Fear slammed into me the same time the third bandit did, rushing at me while the first held my foot. I screamed and jerked away from him, but he pinned my shoulders down with a forearm and used his other hand to cover my mouth. I writhed under his weight and clawed at him, digging my nails in.

He screamed and released me, cradling his arm. But it was not my nail gouges that had hurt him; an angry, long welt had seared his arm where his skin had touched my collar.

"What *are* you—" the first asked as I wrenched my foot free and scrambled back. His eyes widened suddenly, and he tripped over himself to put distance between us. For a fraction of a second, I thought Sun had returned to save me.

It wasn't until the man croaked, "Specter!" that I realized I was glowing. All of me that was uncovered: my nose, collar, hands. It wasn't a harsh, fiery light like Sun's, but a soft halo, feathery and pearlescent.

"Godling!"

I didn't hear which of them had said it, but I wasn't about to dispel the notion. If I *was* a godling, I would be more powerful than they. My assailants dropped my bags and ran for the road, cursing as they went, leaving me in a half-terrified stupor. I heard the retreating of horses moments later.

My hands trembled. I stared at them until the glow receded and I was myself again, confused and cold and wrought with panic, feeling hungry in a way I couldn't explain.

A dry sob scraped up my throat. I threw myself onto the ground, picking up the things they'd thrown in their haste and shoving them back into my bags.

The bandits had taken off east, toward Endwever. I ran west. I ran, and ran, and ran, until my lungs scorched and my legs ached. The darkness came on so quickly I didn't even remember the Sun going down. But still I ran, my mind delirious, my body numb. Had it not been for the candle in its window, I wouldn't have noticed the farmhouse off the road.

Sweat-streaked, limping, and panting, I dragged myself to the door and banged my fist against it. I don't remember who opened it, but I recall begging them to help me.

And then I passed out.

CHAPTER 9

I woke slowly, groggily, my body sore and stiff, my throat as dry as paper. I stretched, and my legs ached with the movement. My knuckles were slow to bend, and my neck popped when I turned my head.

The walls weren't lit a soft shade of pink, and it took me a minute to recall where I was. The room was small, barely large enough to fit the bed and trunk that were its only furnishings. I did notice a glass filled with water on that trunk, and I slid my sore self from the covers and hobbled to it, drinking greedily, my stomach protesting at the cool weight. Stretching, I glanced out the small window fitted with only a twine grating. It looked to be afternoon, the Sun shining brightly in a white-blue sky. My ring was still lined with amber, and I wondered what was happening beyond that sky and how dire it was. I hoped Fosii and Elta were all right.

The creaking floorboards under my feet must have given me away, for a soft knock sounded on the door, and it opened, the face of a middle-aged woman poking in.

"Oh good," she said, "you're awake."

Unsure of myself, I clasped my hands together and bowed to her. "I am so sorry for disturbing you. Thank you for giving me a refuge for the night . . . and most of the day, I see."

To my relief, the woman merely smiled. "That is all right. What's your name?"

My tongue started the sound of an *S*, but I paused, thinking twice. Father Aedan would have noticed my absence from the cathedral. Someone had likely been sent to Terasta to search for me. If they'd taken a direct route, they would have reached it before I did.

I was not yet in Terasta itself; this farmhouse seemed to be on the outskirts of the small town. But that promised me nothing.

The woman's face softened. She stepped inside and shut the door behind her before taking up a seat on the trunk. "My name is Telda. I live here with my husband, Jude. We've three sons who have all moved on to their own houses."

Taking a deep breath, I said, "My name is Ceris."

Telda nodded. "I thought so."

A worm of fear wriggled up my sternum. "Then you know me."

"Some riders came by yesterday asking after you. Claimed you were in great danger. And when you came pounding on our door, you looked like you were. Jude stayed up guarding the place, but nothing else followed you here."

I thought of the bandits, their hands on me. The strange glowing of my skin. "Did the riders say what the danger was?"

She shook her head, but her eyes drank me in. "They said you were a living star mother."

I sat back on the bed, the single worm of fear becoming three. "Please. I don't know why I survived, but I was granted permission to come home. Only . . . time must pass differently here. The home I knew, the people I knew"—my throat constricted, and I coughed to loosen it—"they're gone. The riders you saw are strangers to me. They wish to keep me against my will. I only want to find my descendants." Or, rather, my sister's, but such was an unnecessary detail.

To my relief, Telda nodded. "I don't understand, not entirely. But you seem like a capable woman. You must be, for Him to choose you. If you went out on your own, I expect you had your reasons."

A long sigh escaped me and fled through the twine screen of the window. "Thank you, Telda."

"Of course. I've had my share of hardships. Sometimes all a person needs is a hand." She stood. "I insist you stay one more night. We'll tuck you away, and I'll make sure Jude knows. I packed some lunch in case you woke."

My stomach grumbled and my eyes watered. "Thank you."

I went downstairs to eat. Telda told me more about her family and current events, patiently stopping each time I wasn't familiar with a name or term, which was often. I helped her with her chores—any that didn't involve me going outside—to show my gratitude, and the work loosened my sore muscles. When Jude came in from the farm, I greeted him warmly, and he offered to go into town in the morning to sell what little I had for coin. The most valuable item I'd brought with me was the compass, although I couldn't decide which would benefit me more—to sell it or keep it—for it could also help me find Nediah.

When I asked if there was anyone in Terasta who might let me hire them as a guide and guard, both Jude and Telda looked doubtful, but he promised he would ask around. I felt terrible taking any more from the kind couple, but when Telda began packing me food for my trip, I couldn't refuse. I had so little, and even if Jude successfully sold my few wares, I would need to be careful with my coin, especially if most of it would go toward a guide.

That night, I waited until the rest of the house quieted down before I took a candle and, holding the shoes Shila had given me in one hand, crept down the stairs and into the kitchen. I snuffed the candle and set it aside, then slipped on my shoes and slid out the back door. The scent of horses was heavy, even with a chilly breeze. I started walking, letting the light of a waxing crescent moon guide me. Its silver bands fell over a small shrine, about hip high, set a short ways from the house, made of carefully woven twigs and yarn, filled with tiny dolls carved from wood and a stale loaf of bread that had already made meals for at least one mouse. The shrine to the Earth Mother was not too different from the one that rested outside Caen's home, and I paused to bow to it, showing respect to a goddess so critical to us, yet so easily overlooked.

Short clover covered the ground in abundance. A crooked fence to my left marked the grazing field for the animals. I walked straight ahead, ensuring I wouldn't get lost, though the area was fairly open, the forest a narrow, dark swath in the distance. A lake shimmered halfway between the house and the woods, reflecting the moonlight.

Tilting my head back, I studied the stars, holding my breath as I searched, my hand twisting the ring on my finger. The sky was not as deep here on Earth. The stars were numerous and uncountable, but not in the way they had been in Sun's domain. I couldn't see their separate colors. I couldn't see—

There. My eyes moved toward a tiny prick in the heavens, almost of their own accord. "Found you, little one," I whispered.

The tiny star twinkled back.

I stared at my daughter a long time. The air grew cooler by the minute, but I wasn't ready to return to the house. The walk had helped tire me out after my rest, but I still wasn't sleepy. My emotions being pulled like taffy had done little to help ease my wakefulness.

"One step at a time," I whispered to myself as I walked, grateful only a few clouds marked the sky, allowing me ample light from the moon and stars. It was strange. I had already given up my friends and family. I had made peace with that decision up in Sun's palace. It was the hope that had awakened after I survived, and the death of it, that ached the most—and now that I wasn't surrounded by worshipers, I felt it keenly. That, and the distance between myself and my child, though I had always known I wouldn't hold a mortal babe in my arms. But a woman cannot help what her heart yearns for.

"You are a star mother."

I started at the deep, crackly voice and turned back to the house, expecting to find a local, or perhaps someone from Endwever. But I was alone in the field, surrounded by wild grass and clover.

"I have never met one," the voice continued.

I turned again, this time facing the lake. The water rippled as though a stone had been tossed into it, and as I watched, it shifted upward like clay in a potter's hands, taking on the impression of a face. It surprised me, but I did not run. I had been around enough godlings in Sun's palace not to fear this one.

"Godling of the lake." I offered a curtsy.

"Not an inaccurate name." The watery mouth moved as he spoke, but the voice didn't stem from it. The risen water shifted left, then right, as though studying me. "He wouldn't let you walk the Earth Mother . . . but no, you've already had your star. I can tell."

His voice took on a pitying sound that reminded me of the looks Sun's servants had given me so often after I arrived in their heaven. I touched my braided hair self-consciously.

"Is it so obvious?" I asked.

"You are bright," the lake confirmed. "Starlight burns within you. But your shell is still mortal."

Starlight. So that was what had scared the bandits away. "I was told I was not quite mortal."

The lake nodded. "How interesting. Will you stay long, Star Mother?"

"Ceris," I corrected, though once upon a time, I never would have had the audacity to correct a godling. Or a god, but I had already done that as well. "And no, just the night. I'm on my way to Nediah."

"Nediah, Nediah," the godling repeated, and his voice sounded like a trickling waterfall. "I have rested here too long. I do not know it."

"It is northwest of here. A larger city where my sister's kin may be." I wondered how many, for I might find dozens of Parroses across generations, or I might find only one survivor. Anything was better than more graves.

"Hmmm. Sounds tiring." The lake's appendage shrunk into itself. "Take care, Star Mother. Use your light well."

"Th-Thank you. And may the rain keep you full."

I sensed a smile at that, and then the lake grew still, the godling either slumbering or gone entirely.

I woke after Sunrise the next morning and dressed quickly. I repacked my bags, ensuring everything had its place, and gently set in the wrapped meals Telda had given me. After making the bed, I came downstairs to help Telda with breakfast. I was churning butter when Jude came home with a small pouch of coin for me. I was thrilled he had managed to find buyers for my things, but I did not miss that he had returned alone.

To this, he shrugged. "We're a small town of farmers, Miss Wenden. No one can leave their work long enough to journey to Nediah and back. If you want to wait out the season, there may be some merchants passing through."

But I couldn't wait. If I stayed in this farmhouse, I would likely be caught, and I couldn't inconvenience Telda and Jude for so long. I would simply have to follow the road, perhaps not walk it, but keep it in my vision, and set up a camp each night before it got dark. I could avoid most dangers that way. And who knew—in the next town, I might find someone on their way to Nediah and be allowed to ride with them. Hope was not lost.

Part of me also whispered that the starlight could protect me. It had once already.

I tapped my nail on my ring. Perhaps Sun would come for me soon and take me to my star, and then politely drop me off in Nediah Himself.

I thanked Telda and Jude profusely before stepping outside, ensuring the road was clear before running across it and slipping into the forest, where I could follow its guidance without being noticed. After only half an hour of walking, I heard horses in the distance, and tucked myself behind a tree to watch the riders pass. They were heading toward Endwever, and I wondered if they were the same horsemen who had visited Telda.

When they'd gone, I continued ahead, trying to keep a good pace. Trying also to calm my thoughts. *If a star mother had returned alive before Endwever's torch had been lit, how might I have reacted?* Surely I would have believed it a miracle. Surely I would have been fascinated by her. I could not disparage the people of Endwever for feeling that way, even if Father Aedan and his wife were . . . overly enthusiastic. I wouldn't bow to their will, but neither did I want to carry any fear with me that was not necessary for my survival. I was a woman alone in an unfamiliar world, but I desperately wanted to be happy in it.

The road turned; I thought it was away from Nediah, but surely it would right itself eventually. Nediah was too big a city for any main northbound road not to lead to it. Following the turn, I had to step away from the trees for a while, which made me uneasy, but I'd already left Terasta behind. I spied one more farm, but it was too far north for anyone to notice a lone woman passing by. I dared not wander too far from the road, for villages in Helchanar were so few and far between I could travel for days and easily miss them.

I looked skyward, twisting my ring so its center line flashed from amber to black and back again. I wondered how much I could sell such a ring for, or what it was even made of. Yet I had so few allies; I did not want to barter away my only connection to the one with actual power.

"Could You just pick me up and plop me down where I need to be?" I asked, chin tilted back. But I had the distinct impression Sun wasn't listening. Likely He wasn't able to. Perhaps He was divided again, and the light in the sky was only a portion of Him, while His other half

Charlie N. Holmberg

dealt with the moon. Perhaps this ring was useless, merely a parting gift meant to make me look pretty.

Maybe I *would* sell it.

I took a few deep breaths and tried to orient myself. Nediah was northwest of Endwever. I would follow the road and wait for it to angle northwest. If I crossed paths with someone friendly, I could ask for directions.

The road straightened, and after a few hours, I found myself again enveloped by trees. I ate some of Telda's bread, constantly scanning my surroundings and listening for sounds of human or predatory life. The small creatures of the forest I passed seemed completely indifferent to me, which came as a relief after the wolves and the bandits and the people of Endwever. Different though I may have become, in my mind I was still a mortal woman, nearly twenty-one years of age, misplaced in time. I was no god, demigod, or godling. I was nothing to worship. I had not conquered some great feat by surviving what other women had not. I had no idea why I had woken to the glass roses on my chest when I could have sworn I looked Death in the eye. Then again, I had always been a fanciful person, much to my parents' chagrin. Perhaps my fancies had simply gotten the better of me.

I shuddered involuntarily, my hand again touching my stomach. An unpleasant feeling went up my spine, almost like a chill, except it burned hot, similar to the fiery contractions I'd felt before going into labor. Leaning against a tree, I waited for the sensation to go away, and relaxed when it did.

I had not gone far—perhaps a mile—when I heard a clamoring of horse hooves in the forest. I turned toward the road, only to realize I'd wandered away from it and the hoofbeats were coming from the trees to the south. Unsure if the rider would prove to be my salvation or another bandit, I stowed away behind an old oak, peeking out in the direction of the sound. It came closer, closer . . . and I spied a horse without a rider. It didn't even wear a saddle.

84

It was possibly the loveliest creature I'd ever seen.

The stallion was dark and large, what I imagined a warhorse must look like. Its mane and tail were like midnight, with faint purple hues. Its body was strong and lithe. But as soon as it passed beneath a ray of Sunlight, I realized it was no normal horse, for the light passed *through* it, highlighting its spectral quality. It was then I noticed there was no trail for it to gallop on; the trees clustered in too many places. Yet it passed right through them, as though it ran in a field and not a forest.

I gaped, no longer hiding myself as I should be. *What sort of godling is this?*

The horse grew close and almost passed me, running about thirty feet to the south. But it slowed as it neared me, rearing its head silently, nostrils flaring as it sniffed the air.

Turning its head, it looked right at me.

In the distance, I heard a new commotion. I couldn't tell what it was, but it came from the same direction as this steed.

In an instant the dark horse was before me, flashing through the trees with barely a twitch of its legs. I stumbled back and would have fallen, if not for the trunk pressing into my shoulders. The stallion was nearly twice my height, and though it was magnificent, it frightened me.

"You are a star mother." Its voice was like the wind, its tone incredulous. Male.

I swallowed. "I-I am."

The commotion grew louder. The stallion looked over its shoulder, ethereal muscles twitching.

His attention flew back to me. "Hide me. Please."

I gaped. When I didn't respond, the godling moved as though to nudge me, but his muzzle passed through my arms just as his body passed through the trees. The motion put me at ease—if the creature could not touch me, surely it could not harm me.

But that caveat likely did not pertain to his pursuers.

"Hide you?" I asked. "From *what*?"

I recognized the commotion as running, though I could not identify the animal. A small flock of ravens burst from the forest a short way to the west.

"They won't hurt you. Please help me," he begged, crouching and dropping his head. "They are looking for me. Your starlight will mask me."

His pursuers rocked the forest like thunder. The horse godling whinnied.

I spoke through my fear. "I need a guide to Nediah," I hurried, hushed. "If you will take me to Nediah, I will hide you from your pursuers."

I didn't know *how* I would do it, but from his confidence, I assumed he did.

The godling lifted his head. "Done."

The body of the dark horse dissipated into a midnight breeze, swirling around me and billowing my skirts before spiraling into a tight ball that disappeared into the pocket of my dress.

There was no time to fret. The commotion tumbled toward me, and three godlings—two large and one small—burst into view from the trees. The small one looked like a gremlin wearing a clay mask, and the two large ones appeared to be twins. Their big bodies, covered in thick fur, resembled bears with equine legs, but they had upright torsos and humanoid faces. Mostly. It was as if someone had grabbed the bottom halves and pulled them forward to mimic a muzzle. They each had a pair of long white horns growing out of their skulls, pointing backward. The only difference between them was that one's horns had blue stripes and the other had silver.

I clung to the horse's promise that they wouldn't harm me. They actually looked remotely familiar, and I wondered if I had glimpsed them at Sun's palace during my bored wanderings.

"Ho!" the blue-striped godling called, lifting a hand as they neared me. Even after they stopped, their speed sent a gust of wind over me, whipping my hair and skirt. I lifted an arm to block debris from my eyes. The gremlin godling did not halt with the others, but bolted in a wide circle around me like a dog before heeling at Silver Stripes's side.

"What are you?" asked Blue Stripes.

"I am Ceris Wenden." I thanked my time at Sun's palace, for otherwise I would have cowered before these creatures.

Silver Stripes said, "I know you. You are the living star mother." He studied me from head to toe.

"I am. Returned to the mortal realm by the Sun Himself." I could not feel weight in my pocket, but I was acutely aware of a presence there, and it took all my self-control not to see if my skirt leaked midnight.

Blue Stripes replied, "We are looking for a runaway. A shapeshifter. He came this way."

"It is only I, and I travel alone. You are close to the road. Be careful; there's a mortal village nearby. You'll scare them."

Blue Stripes snickered as though that would be a delight, and the gremlin godling echoed him.

Silver Stripes tipped his head and whispered under his breath, "He's used it again."

I followed his line of sight, noticing nothing out of the ordinary . . . except for a single orange leaf falling from an overhead branch. It stood out among the growing green buds, a taste of autumn in the beginning of spring. A leaf that had somehow held on through the winter, only to give up beneath the glare of a godling.

Blue Stripes gritted his teeth and scanned the forest. To me, he said, "Call the names of Yar"—he pointed to himself—"and Shu"—his finger swung toward his companion—"if you see him. He is a ghost and a trickster."

Trickster. I would have to be careful with him, then. To the godling before me, I only nodded. "I shall."

The godlings turned about and barreled back the way they had come. The gremlin hesitated for a moment, interested in me, but then took off after his companions. They vanished among the boughs as though they had never been.

"I am no trickster." The runaway godling poured from my pocket, taking again the form of a horse, but this time his head came only to my hip, as though the chase had stripped him of courage. "They don't even know what they hunt."

"A trickster would say the same thing." I planted my hands on my hips.

He lowered his head in a bow. "I gave my word, Star Mother. I will take you to Nediah."

My body softened. "You know it?"

"I know all mortal cities."

I paused at that, impressed, but Yar and Shu had put doubt in my mind. "Why are they hunting you?"

The horse looked away and did not answer.

Pressing my lips together, I looked skyward and twisted my ring. I desperately needed both a guide and protection. What better protection could I ask for than that of a godling?

Unless he was indeed a trickster. He *seemed* harmless, but appearances could be deceiving.

"I want an oath," I said. "A covenant. That you will do as you say and bring no harm unto me."

The horse looked alarmed. I did not know if it was from my requirement or from my assumption that he might be villainous. Either way, he bowed his head. "I give you an oath that I will see you to Nediah in return for the aid of your starlight. I will not hurt you."

"Thank you," I whispered, and he shuffled back, as though I had uttered something far more shocking.

Curiosity bloomed. I had many questions, but I started with the easiest. "What is your name?"

He shifted, still a horse, but even smaller than before, his ears reaching midthigh. From the way he cowered, he couldn't possibly be dangerous . . . unless he was a magnificent actor. Godlings lived a long time; they could easily master such a skill.

"Ristriel." He spoke so quietly I barely heard him.

"Ristriel," I repeated, holding my bags close. "We best be on our way."

Nodding, Ristriel walked ahead of me, starting me on the long path to Nediah.

CHAPTER 10

We walked for a long time. It was like I indeed traveled with a small horse and not a godling, for our conversation was limited, interspersed with long stretches of silence. But the silence soon became comfortable, and I found I didn't mind the quiet. I was simply happy to have a companion.

Lagging a few paces behind, I studied him. He was the blue of early night, but whenever we passed beneath the shade of a tree, he took on a more violet hue, sometimes darkening to black. He slowed every now and then to ensure I kept up. His gait was fully equine. His ears twitched on occasion, but he stopped only once to scan our surroundings. I wasn't sure if that was to reassess our direction or to listen for his pursuers. When I asked, he didn't answer. When I pressed, he said, "I am making sure we are not being followed."

Yar and Shu. I mentally repeated their names in case I should need them. Celestial beings have always been more honor bound than mortals, or so they seemed in scripture and my own experience, and Ristriel had given me an oath.

I could trust him, for now.

Ristriel never took me to the road, or to any man-made paths. We stayed in the forest, once crossing a wide pasture that must have belonged to a rancher, given how the grass had been cut, but I didn't see him or his herds.

We slipped into the woods once more, and I asked, "Why are those godlings chasing you?"

He looked at me with large, dark horse eyes as deep as a well. When I did not look away, he confessed, "Because I ran away."

The strangeness of the answer pricked me. "Ran away? From what?"

The godling turned his muzzle forward.

"Will you not tell me?"

"You will be safe from harm." His voice was soft as a midnight breeze. "Especially with that ring on your hand."

I glanced at the golden band Sun had given me. When had he noticed it?

Seeing that I would not get much conversation today, I hummed as we walked to occupy myself, calling up folk songs and lullabies from memory. Even the song sung to me in Endwever came to my lips, and it softened my heart toward those people. My people, however misguided.

When the Sun began to sink in the sky, I took a break on a fallen log and stretched out my calves. "Will we make it to a town before dark?"

The forest's shadows were growing long. Ristriel was small enough to be swallowed in one. His color darkened again, and his shimmering stilled, making him appear solid. I squinted at him, surprised, but it must have been a trick of the light. When he stepped out of the shadow to peer at the way ahead, orange-tinted Sunlight fell over him, and he was just as ghostly as before. "There is a glade three miles from here where we can camp. The closest mortal village is seven miles south."

I chewed on my lip. I had been afraid he'd say that. "There are wolves." And who knew what other creatures. I'd never been this far from Endwever. I wasn't sure if there were new predators to be watchful of, or perhaps an unfriendly godling.

But Ristriel simply answered, "They will not bother us. I will keep my promise, Ceris."

It struck me that he had called me by my name rather than "Star Mother." I had not yet asked him to. I hadn't even told him my name, but he would have heard it when I announced myself to the godlings chasing him.

"Will I be safe if your pursuers return?"

He nodded. "But they will not return. Not tonight. They will not sense me if I am close to you."

I shook Earth from the bottom of my skirt. "How close?"

The ghostly horse glanced at me. "We should continue on."

Agreeing, and accepting that this was yet another answer I would not receive, I stood and followed him. I would have to bandage my feet before setting out in the morning, because my shoes were chafing. Spending so long in a not-palace had softened my calluses.

I wondered if the godling truly knew the Earth Mother well enough to find a particular glade, but sure enough, we found one, and I took out a small blanket given to me by Telda and spread it over the wild weeds. The spring was new enough that the night would be chilly, so I sought to build a campfire before darkness descended. Ristriel did not help me; he couldn't pick up sticks or build them up, but he did point out some to me.

Fortunately, I had a flint among my supplies, and I managed to get a fire going. I rummaged through my sack for the rest of Telda's bread, knowing it would spoil fastest and should be eaten first. I offered some to Ristriel, who shook his head.

Night swallowed the wood whole and completely. As I chewed my bread, I lay back on the blanket, looking for my star. I watched the sky for nearly an hour before she popped up over the tops of the trees. I smiled.

The blanket shifted as the dog-sized horse stepped onto it. I glanced over, shocked to see a very solid animal beside me. His coat glimmered like the sky above, shimmering violet where the firelight touched fur.

"You're solid," I murmured. I had an impulse to touch him, to test my words, but decided better of it. Ristriel seemed a mellow-minded being, but I didn't want to test his temper.

He smiled ever so faintly—at least, as much as a horse could. "Not for long. Not if we stay in this glade."

I sat up. "Why? Is it . . . enchanted?"

The horse gave me a wry look. "No. Only open to the sky." He tilted his muzzle upward. I tried to see what he saw, but there was nothing special in the heavens tonight except for my star, who twinkled merrily among her siblings. I wondered if she'd seen my tapestry.

The first-quarter moon peeked over the tops of the trees, and I caught a shift of colors from the corner of my eye. I looked to see Ristriel ethereal once more. Everywhere but his tail, which was situated close enough to the trees' shadow that the moonlight didn't touch it.

He sensed my question before I asked. "Moonlight and Sunlight." He peered up at the moon, and the longing in his face was evident, despite its lack of human features. "In truth, they are one and the same."

I tilted my head. "How so?"

"She stole it from Him." He gazed at the moon the way a poor man might gaze at a loaf of bread. "Long ago, when she was still young and first came into her greed, she entered Sun's domain, posing as a loyal servant. Once she earned His trust, she snuck into His room while He rested and stole a portion of His light for herself."

I thought of Sun and realized I had never seen Him sleep. Did He? Had He stopped sleeping after the light was stolen from Him? "Was He angry?"

"Of course. She was only strong enough to take a portion, which is why she does not glow as brilliantly as He does. That is why her light does not have as great of an effect on me."

He shifted his tail, which was out of direct moonlight. Unlike the rest of him, it was solid. And yet, during the day, if even a tendril of Sunlight touched him, his entire being became as ethereal as a ghost.

I gazed up at her. "I wonder why."

"I think"—his voice was soft—"that she wanted to be seen. She was born in the realm of shadow, watching the world, and the world didn't notice her."

I thought of Endwever. "Sometimes it's better not to be seen."

"But it is lonely," he countered, and his next words sounded far away. "It is very lonely."

I considered this. Before becoming star mother, I had wanted to be seen. Unlike my sisters, I'd always loved attention and sought it out. I wondered how my childhood might have been had I been invisible to those around me.

I watched him watch the sky, his expression eerily human, and my thoughts turned another direction. "You look at the moon the same way I look at the stars."

He glanced at me. "You were looking for yours."

I nodded and pointed, sure he would not be able to determine which of the thousands of dots of light I referred to. "She is there."

"What is her name?"

I paused. "I told my attendants I wanted to name her Phinnie. I might as well have told them I wanted to bathe in mud." I laughed, but my humor died like a wilting rose. "I . . . I never asked what name Sun chose. I'm not even sure whether stars have names." Would I see Him again, and have the opportunity?

"All life has a name, even if it is an unkind one," he whispered.

I wondered if that meant he didn't like "Phinnie," either.

We were quiet awhile, watching the moon slowly climb the night sky. I added a few sticks to the fire. Ristriel moved to the shadows, leaving the blanket to me, becoming solid once more.

I wasn't sure I wanted to share my blanket with him; I'd known him for only a matter of hours, and he was a godling on the run from . . . something. Instead, I asked, "Are you cold?"

Ristriel didn't reply.

Reaching into my bag, I grabbed a piece of bread and offered it to him. He gave it a longing look but then shook his head once more.

"Are you hungry?" I pressed.

"I do not need to eat."

"But you still can." I recalled the lavish feast I'd had with Sun. He was a full god, and even He could eat.

He hesitated, then reached a hoof into the moonlight. It shifted into the shape of a hand, which he then pulled back so it would turn solid. I gaped at the human-shaped hand jutting from the leg of the miniature horse. Trying to behave as though that were a normal thing, I leaned into the shadows to give him the bread. He looked at it with a sort of wonder only a toddler might have, then nibbled away, his expression thoughtful.

When he finished, I asked, "How did you know I was a star mother?" For every godling I came across, on Earth and in Sun's palace, somehow knew me immediately. I had figured it was some sort of godly sense they had.

"Because of your starlight," he said. "And because of your scars."

I started. "S-Scars?"

He nodded. Then saw my face, and shrunk. "I've upset you."

"I . . ." I didn't know how to answer. I pulled up my sleeves, examining my arms in the firelight. "I . . . I don't have any scars." Stretch marks, certainly, but those were tucked away beneath my clothes.

"They're not on your body but your spirit," he explained, watching me, gauging my reaction.

I glanced over myself as though I would be able to see the marks. "Why do I have scars?"

He took a moment to answer, and I could tell he was choosing his words carefully. "If you thrust your hand into that fire, would it not hurt you?"

I glanced to the flames.

"You are a mortal woman who lay with the Sun and carried a star. Of course you have scars."

It dawned on me then, the pitiful looks I got from Elta and Fosii and the others within the Palace of the Sun, even after my star was born. They could see the mutilation that I could not. I hugged myself, wondering what I looked like to them.

"Do not be ashamed, Ceris." Ristriel spoke gently. "They are marks of your journey and your sacrifice."

I supposed he was correct, but it was strange, knowing I was so marked beneath my skin.

"Look at the moon."

I did. It hovered overhead, pocked in a way that almost formed a face. I had once likened demigods to bears, but the moon was a bear who could swallow cities whole if she so desired. The stories said that many godlings found refuge in her kingdom when they were cast out from Sun's. And so the moon was the most powerful demigod of all. At least in all the lore I knew.

"She, too, is scarred. But she is beautiful."

I lowered my arms. "She is."

Ristriel stepped onto the blanket, turning half-ethereal. "She was once much larger than she is now, but the war has whittled her down."

"War with whom?"

He looked at me, surprised I didn't know. "With the Sun, of course. They have always battled over the heavens. Sun is older, and He resented her for stealing His light and encroaching on His territory. She resents Him for being what she is not, and hates Him even more for shrinking her, scarring her. But He is of the law and must enforce it. Such is His nature. The moon does not like being disregarded simply because she is young. Since she is *less*. They have warred and peaced for millennia. Like you, her scars mark her journey."

I glanced up again, studying the gray splotches of the moon. I tried to imagine her as a flawless orb of silver light. Truthfully, there was beauty to her dimensions, despite the violence with which she had received them.

I shivered, my body remembering the pain of my spirit's scars, and for a moment, I relived each and every one of them.

"Rest, Ceris." Ristriel crossed the glade, ears pricking as he listened to the forest. "I will watch over you as you have watched over me. Nothing will harm you under my protection."

As I lay down, using my second dress as a blanket, the fire warming my back, I realized that I believed him.

One would think that sleeping out of doors would make for a restless night, but I slept soundly beneath the stars. Ristriel, wholly solid and once again the size of a warhorse, roused me with his muzzle just before dawn.

"We should go. It isn't wise to stay in one place for too long."

Rubbing sleep from my eyes, I nodded and gathered my things, noticing with disdain that the little bit of dried meat I'd had with me had suddenly spoiled. I cast it aside and hefted my bags onto sore shoulders. It would have been nice to put them over Ristriel's back, but Sun was quick to reclaim His kingdom, and my godling guide again became as the air, translucent the moment a Sunbeam touched his broad back. If last night had given me any clues, I believed he could change shape only when he was ethereal. It seemed, unless we found a building of some sort to enter, he would be ethereal for most of the day. I also wondered if his ghostliness would help him keep his promise. He could not hurt me if he could not touch me, though lack of physicality did not mean he couldn't trick me.

Thinking of his pursuers, I reiterated one of my earlier questions. "How close do you have to be for my starlight to conceal you?"

I could tell my prodding made him uncomfortable, but if we were to travel together, I wanted to know what I had gotten myself into. Several seconds passed before he answered, "Very close. Like before. If it isn't shining."

I flashed back to the bandits' terrifying attack, and the pearlescent glow of my skin. "What if it *is* shining?"

He paused before answering. "You will attract attention."

I might not have been a well-traveled or well-studied person at that time, but I could tell he was hiding something from me. Purposefully slowing my steps, I let two extra paces stretch between us.

Ristriel led me to a narrow river, and we followed it for a time, blue dragonflies darting across our path. The day was a warm one, and I fanned myself as the Sun grew high. His light was almost at its peak when I found a large boulder alongside the water and sat upon it, kicking off my shoes and searching through my bag for a bit of cheese.

The dark horse stopped and looked over his shoulder, flicking his tail as though he could feel the flies on his skin. "Why are you stopping?"

"For lunch."

He glanced at the sky. "Already?"

I found a wedge of cheese and pulled it triumphantly from my bag. "I may be the mother of a star, but I am still mortal. We walked far yesterday."

He turned around, his large body oddly graceful. "You are not entirely mortal."

"You are not the first to say so."

"You will be long-lived, like the godlings. The starlight will make it so."

I lowered my treat, contemplative.

"I've offended you."

"No." I dug the toe of my shoe into the moist Earth. "No, you haven't. Just given me something to think about."

"Your years?"

I nodded. "There have been . . . several changes, since I became what I am. I hadn't really considered what I'd do, oh, next century.

Here I am, trying to find my sibling's descendants, but even if I succeed, I suppose I'll have to watch them die, and their children die, and their children's children die." I considered Sun's reaction to my question about past star mothers. Did He feel this same heaviness in His chest when He thought of them?

My thoughts turned toward the paradisiacal hereafter Sun had spoken of at our dinner together. What was it like? No bandits, no wolves, no blisters, surely. All those I loved around me, instead of buried in the ground, far away. I was grateful to have lived where others had passed, but was not life in the hereafter still life? My spirit would still be thriving. My way would be easier than it was now. Had I perished and passed on, I wouldn't have felt so . . . lost.

Ristriel lowered his head. "It can be a lonely existence."

The admission did nothing to bolster me. My existence had already become lonely. How much worse would it get if I lived for centuries yet?

I studied him, noting subtle things about him that were not entirely equine—the curve of his ears, the spark in his eyes, the shape of his hooves. "Ristriel, how old are you?"

His ear twitched. "I am very old."

"As old as the Sun?"

He snorted. "Not as old as that."

I hesitated with my next question, but my thoughts were heavy. "Are you . . . lonely?"

He glanced at me, his eyes deep and never ending. They reminded me of the night sky.

He did not answer, and sorrow planted itself in my heart. I took a bite of cheese, then slid the rest into my pocket and stood, needing to guide my mind elsewhere. "If you're going to hide yourself in the mortal realm, you'll need to start acting more like a mortal."

He tilted his head, obviously taken off guard. "Petulant and toilsome?"

Charlie N. Holmberg

I turned to rebuke him, but there was mirth in his expression, and I realized he'd meant to tease. It was the first moment he'd been anything but withdrawn and elusive. I smiled. "Many of us are, yes. But you can't, oh, run through trees and the like. Not if you don't want to draw attention."

He nodded. "Your kind have always been very superstitious."

"When you are short-lived, it is safer to be." I raised a finger. "So, lesson number one, be more superstitious."

He snorted again. "Fear the uncanny and the unexplained without searching for enlightenment."

"You're a fast learner." I peered up and down the river, half expecting a farmer to come by with a pail, or a godling to jump from the water, but saw no signs of intelligent life. "And perhaps don't call us petulant. You can't treat mortals like they're peasants."

"But you are peasants."

"I—" I paused. "Not all of us are."

Touching his muzzle to the ground, Ristriel acquiesced.

"And if you're hiding, perhaps you should be something smaller. Or more commonplace, like, I don't know, a goat."

He tilted his head. "Horses are much more esteemed than goats."

"They are also more noticeable."

He pawed the Earth, leaving no print, then changed into a goat, long horns growing from his head. But he still looked like the shadow of a distant galaxy, swirls of dark and violet in his coat. No one would believe he was normal livestock, even if he were solid.

"Can you change your color?"

The goat frowned and shook, fur turning more solidly black, eyes gaining a slightly amber hue, enough that horizontal pupils showed within them.

I leaned in close, mesmerized. "That's quite the talent."

"Have you met many shape-changing goats?"

100

Straightening, I put my hands on my hips. "Not with a sense of humor, no. Though my . . ." *What to call Caen, now?* "A friend of mine once had a goat that enjoyed head-butting children's backsides. I suppose that was a little funny."

He looked himself over. "It will take me three and a quarter times as many steps to travel in this form."

"Do you grow tired?"

He considered. "In a way." His fur shifted back to midnight, and his shape melted and grew until it was a hand's breadth taller than I was, taking on the form of a man. I don't know why it surprised me—most godlings were human shaped—but perhaps having met him as a horse, it was strange seeing him so much like myself.

Like before, he shuddered, and his colors shifted and muted into less celestial tones. His clothes were still dark with a purple hue, but his skin paled to the same shade as mine. His hair, whisking over his forehead like orchard grass, was the blackest black I'd ever beheld . . . or so I thought until I saw his eyes. They were blacker than the darkest spot of night, yet bright as polished obsidian. They were as black as the Sun was bright.

"I've found this is the least obtrusive form." This time, his mouth moved with the words. "Unless I am in a place where mortal men ought not to be."

I nodded dumbly, feeling a little warmer than I should. He certainly hadn't modeled himself an *unattractive* mortal.

"If I am to act more like a mortal"—he gestured up the river, insinuating we should walk again—"then you must act more like a god."

Adjusting my bags and slipping on my shoes, I followed his lead. "I am hardly a god."

"You will meet those who do not agree with you."

Thinking of Father Aedan and Shila, I sighed, feeling every bit as petulant as Ristriel had claimed mortals to be. "All right, I'll humor you. How do I act more like a god? Glow at people?"

His lip quirked. "Yes."

I shook my head, pinching my lips to keep from smiling. The river curled south, but this time Ristriel kept moving straight ahead, utterly confident in his direction. We'd be in the woods again in half a mile.

"You must act superior." He was quieter, watching the ground pass under his feet. "Like you are better than those around you."

"Better than mortals?" I retrieved the cheese from my pocket and chewed and swallowed another bite. "Do you think you're better than me?"

"You are not a true mortal."

"But if I were?"

He didn't answer for several paces. "I might make an exception."

Something about the answer warmed me. It was a comfortable warmth, like curling up by a hearth with a new thread and needle. It was the most at peace I had felt since returning home. It was easy to forget myself, to forget this godling's secrets, when he was charming. Yet I did not think he was aware that he was.

We stepped into the forest, though the trees were thinner and farther apart than they had been before, as though a fire had swept through some hundred years ago. The terrain was flatter as well, which made for easier travel.

"How much farther?" I asked.

"To Nediah?" Ristriel was about to step through a tree, then stopped himself and walked around it instead. "Two hundred forty-three miles and a third."

My pace slowed. "That's incredibly specific." He didn't have so much as a compass on him, let alone a map.

"I have watched Earth Mother turn for a long time."

There was no mirth in the statement. It was as though he were remembering something unhappy, like the death of a loved one or the loss of a home. I wondered at it, but he closed into himself, shifting back into a horse. Though, by his size, he was more of a pony.

He didn't appear to notice he had shifted. And for some odd reason, it felt cruel to point it out to him.

CHAPTER 11

I found some spring tubers along our way and pulled them, explaining to Ristriel that while I had some money, it was best to be self-sufficient. I showed him what edible plants I managed to find, and for the rest of the day, he pointed out any he saw as we walked, for in his Sunlit state, he wasn't able to pick any of them. We made camp in the evening, and when night fell, he shifted into a midnight wolf and raced out into the forest, returning an hour later with a hare. I thanked him, and he watched me in wonder as I pulled out a knife to skin it.

Preparing animals for meals was something I had done often in Endwever—rabbits, squirrel, or fowl. But when I pierced my knife through the hare's hide and drew it down, that same burning shiver from days before coursed up my spine, and I dropped both tool and catch together, my hands shaking.

It had felt like that. The birth of my star. Like someone had stabbed me with a knife and cut me open head to hip.

"You're hurt." The wolf stepped closer. He sniffed my hands, but the only blood on them was from my dinner.

"No." I wiped my fingers on the wild grass and then hugged myself. "No, I'm not. I just . . . remembered something."

Ristriel lifted his head, eyes meeting mine. "Remembering can be the worst kind of hurt."

I rolled my lips together. Swallowed. "I think you are right."

"I will keep you safe, Ceris."

I smiled and, forgetting myself, reached out to scratch behind his ear as though he were any tame dog. He dropped his muzzle, silent, but leaned into my touch.

After a moment he pulled away into a band of moonlight, and suddenly there was a human hand reaching for the knife. "I can do it," he said, every bit the man he'd been before, but this time he was solid through and through. So close, so physical, I noticed he smelled like a winter storm. Like the stillness and cold before the snow fell.

"I can manage," I insisted, but I didn't reach for the hare.

He glanced at me with those ever-dark eyes, waiting for me to resist. When I didn't, he took the hare and made quick work of it. His cuts weren't the neatest, but it didn't matter—the pelt was too thin to sell, anyway.

"You can manage it," he said softly once he'd finished with the hare, set it over the fire, and washed his hands with collected stream water. "Manage it, escape it, or grow with it. Pain, I mean." I noticed the fire didn't reflect in his eyes. "But you can't forget it. Even if you could, you would lose the strength it gave you. There is always strength in pain. It's small and it's hidden, but it's always there."

My lips parted, but no sound passed them. I felt like the hare once more—opened up, the excess stripped away to reveal what lay underneath. It hurt, but not like a wound. Like a balm that stung once applied, but would hasten healing.

Shifting close to me, Ristriel gingerly took my heel in his palm; I'd taken off my shoes while he was out. When I didn't protest, he pulled off my wool sock and turned my foot so we could both see the red spot on my heel, where the shoe had chafed during our long walk.

"Our souls are like blisters," he said, a whisper of smile flavoring the words. "The irritant, the hardship, the pain, will make your skin tougher. Stronger." He delicately touched the sore spot. "But take that away, and you take away the growth."

He set my foot down like it were made of glass. Reaching forward, I grasped his hand. He studied my fingers for several heartbeats before he met my eyes.

"Thank you." I swallowed to keep my emotions at bay, though tears threatened the corners of my eyes. I would remember the metaphor of the blister for years—centuries—to come. "Thank you, for saying that."

We finished roasting the hare in silence. I had no salt to season it, but it was warm and filled my belly. And this time, when I offered a portion to Ristriel, he accepted it, marveling at the glistening meat as though I had bequeathed him a bar of gold.

I woke on my own to early morning birds chirping in the boughs overhead. The sky was still dark, but the dawn seemed close. Ristriel was awake, a wolf again, prowling around our campsite, standing guard. He rustled through uneven patches of long grass in the small glade, the blades towering over the shy grass of early spring.

I grabbed my second dress and a bar of soap. "I'm going to wash in that pond we passed."

The wolf nodded, and I stepped carefully through the trees, my path still dark. I got turned around once, but managed to find the pond. Bowing to it, I asked, "Does any godling claim these waters?"

When I received no response, I stripped out of my dress and submerged into the water, biting down on a gasp for how cold it was. Working quickly, I scrubbed the hem and then the underarms of the dress I'd shed, then hurriedly ran the soap over myself, pulling my hair out of its braid to get at my scalp. I slowed in my scouring only once, when my fingers passed over the stretch marks on my hips. I imagined a little babe tied to my back, crying for the chill, comforted on my breast. The longing for it bit harder than the icy pond did.

Teeth chattering, I waded out of the pond, wrung out my hair, and pulled on my second dress, tight muscles slowly relaxing as the dry fabric warmed them. I had just finished braiding my hair when the Sun grew bright as noonday over the pond, although the woods around me remained basked in shadow.

I turned toward the brightest light, pulse quickening. It was either a godling come for Ristriel, or—

Sun.

"Hello, Ceris." The grass curled at His feet. Swaths of celestial fabric looped over both of His shoulders, coming down into a golden belt before splaying over fiery legs. The way it hugged and flowed would be any sculptor's dream.

He seemed so radically out of place in the forest. His presence did nothing to stir the sleeping Earth Mother, but Her trees seemed to bow to Him.

I blinked as my eyes adjusted to His brightness. "H-Hello." I remembered to bow, but a burst of excitement stuck my spine up straight again. "Is it time? Now?"

Sun frowned, diamond eyes gleaming. "I am sorry, Ceris. I have very little time, and the way to her is more dangerous now than it was before."

Hope evaporated from my skin. "Oh."

"I wish to speak with you."

"Is that not what we're doing?" I stepped closer to Him, drawn to the heat of His presence. He was a bonfire that would not burn me, and the cold touch of the pond quickly receded from my limbs. "What has happened?"

His shoulders slumped. "The battles again." He sounded tired. "They are bothersome."

"That's how I always think of war. Bothersome."

I'm not sure if He grasped my jest, for He simply nodded. Then His jewellike focus narrowed on my face. "Ceris, I've come to ask you to return with Me."

My mouth went dry. "To the heavens?"

Another nod.

I caught myself wringing my fingers and forced my hands to drop. "But You said it was too dangerous to see her." Our star. Our child.

He appeared uncomfortable, which oddly made Him look more mortal, if I were to ignore the brilliance of His person. "It is, but I wish you to come to the palace. I wish you to be with Me."

My jaw hit the mud ringing the pond, or it might as well have, with how I gaped at Him.

"You would be as a queen, until your years ended." He held out His hand as though the promise were a tangible thing He could show me. "You would be able to return to Earth as often as you see fit; I would of course give you that freedom. I only ask that you be at My side in the interim."

I stared at Him a moment longer. Then another moment.

Was the Sun God trying to . . . court me?

Oh stars, what would my mother think of this?

"W-Why?" I dumbly sputtered.

He pressed His lips together, glancing skyward a moment. "Because I think of you. Because you are different."

"Because I survived."

"It is not just that."

His presence made me warm, and I stepped closer to the trees. "I . . . I don't know how to answer that."

"Come with Me, and I will show you."

My spine tingled like someone drew a spent match over the bumps. "Sun—"

"It would not be the same," He added, quieter. "You are no longer purely mortal."

It took me a moment to realize He meant lovemaking. That it wouldn't hurt me. Just as His touch no longer hurt me.

My chest flushed at the thought. His hand was still outstretched, and I came toward Him, reaching past it to take His wrist. It was hot, just on the cusp of burning, but not enough to do me any harm.

I pulled away. "Every time I came back, the world would be different. I'd lose every friend I'd made. I'd—"

The furrowing of His brow made me pause. "Time is constant, Ceris. It would affect you, as a mortal, the same in the heavens as it would in any other world."

I froze, jaw half-open. The sincerity in His face made my knees weak. "Wh-What?"

He cocked His head, confused.

"No." I shook my head. "No, that's not right. I was there, with You, for . . . almost ten months? But when You sent me home, *seven hundred years* had passed since my departure."

Sun went so still even His flames ceased to move. "What did you say?"

"This isn't my Earth. Not the way I left it." I gestured to the forest around us. "Everyone I knew is dead. Their children and their children's children are nothing but bones—"

My voice thinned, and I stopped, struggling with my own emotions. Swallowing hard, I said, "How did You not know?"

His features hardened, making them even more radiant. "Time is constant, but it affects celestial beings . . . differently." I could tell there was a tome of information behind the statement, but one He did not wish to share. "That is how we are long-lived. The chords of our songs play differently than yours."

I shook my head, trying to grasp His meaning. "But then I would have been seven hundred years in the heavens."

"You are not quite mortal," He repeated, and yet He sounded doubtful.

Regardless of my mortal or nonmortal state, one thing was certain. "I've been displaced."

All the god had to say was *So it seems.*

Deep breath in, deep breath out. "Sun, can You return me to my time?"

He didn't even consider it, only shook His head. "Time is constant, Ceris. I cannot travel it, even with My power. It is against the law."

I was ready to weep. "What law?"

"Eternal laws." He held up a finger. "Time cannot be altered." Another finger. "A god's reign cannot be inherited." A third finger. "Death cannot be reversed." And His little finger. "A mortal cannot be forced to do a god's will. Only convinced."

Like the star mothers. He had given me a chance to change my mind.

I hugged myself and glanced at the forest behind me. Even a god could not fix what had happened, and yet I didn't understand *why* it had happened. Had I slept so long before opening my eyes to the glass roses on my chest? But if that were the case, I would have been sent back. Elta . . . she was still there in the room with me. As though she hadn't left. As though I hadn't been displaced in time until Sun sent me home.

Nediah sprung to mind. If Sun could not take me back to my time, surely He could pick me up and place me in that city. But then I thought of Ristriel, of his oath to me. He had pledged to guide me to Nediah, to protect me, if I would protect him in return. While I had not sworn with words, I was part of that oath, and abandoning him now sang of wrongness. I knew keenly what it was like to be alone, to be afraid, and I couldn't go back on my word to force him to suffer the same fate. We would part at Nediah, yes, but such was expected for both of us.

My hesitation must have concerned Sun. "Consider Me. I cannot stay any longer, so I ask that you consider Me."

I managed to nod. He began to brighten, readying to leave, but I stopped Him with, "Wait." The hope on His face almost silenced me, but I had questions and didn't want to lose the opportunity to ask them. "How are Elta and Fosii?"

If He was disappointed I wasn't running into His arms, He didn't show it. He thought a moment, perhaps trying to remember whom I spoke of. "Your attendants? They are well enough."

"Enough?"

"Whispers of war unsettle most." A flame licked His shoulder.

"And, Sun"—I stepped closer to Him, and His fire shrunk, as though He was trying to make it more comfortable for me. I smiled at the simple gesture—"our daughter . . . what did You name her?"

His eyes softened. "She is called Surril."

"Surril," I repeated, the name godly and perfect. "Surril."

He moved toward me, the heat stronger but not unbearable, and tucked a knuckle beneath my chin. It heated me down to my toes, as though I had submerged into a steaming bath just on the brink of being too hot. "Consider Me," He repeated. "I will return."

Retreating, Sun flashed so brightly I had to turn away. When I looked back, He was gone, and the dawn had broken, illuminating the pond and crowning the trees. To my surprise and delight, all of the threads and needles Elta had given me in Sun's palace rested on the Earth where Sun had just hovered, along with an empty canvas. I knelt and picked up the bundles, whispering my thanks to the dawn before tilting my head back to the blue heavens.

"Surril," I whispered, and smiled. "Dearest Surril, I miss you."

And though I could not see the stars, in the back of my mind, I heard the faintest tinkling of laughter, like a child taking her first steps, and my heart was full.

When I returned to camp, Ristriel was nowhere to be seen. I searched in the woods for him, then retraced my way to the pond and back. Not even a pawprint gave him away.

"Ristriel?" I asked, quieter than my normal volume. I didn't think shouting his name in these unfamiliar parts wise, in case those godlings came looking for him again. I hadn't the faintest idea what they might do to a mortal, or mostly mortal, who got between them and their quarry, but neither did I care to test them.

I escaped. That was what he had said, when I asked about his pursuers. Escaped from what? Surely this softhearted godling was no great criminal.

Unease stirred. What if he had been captured in my absence? But the pond was not far from the camp. Surely I would have heard it. Or there would be some sign of a struggle.

But what else could have become of him? He could not have gone hunting again, not in the day.

I searched the nearby woods once more, but found not even a broken twig.

As I wandered back to the still-empty camp, the chill I'd accumulated from the pond rushed into my bones.

I had just been in the presence of the *Sun God Himself*, and I had not asked Him for help because I felt indebted to a stranger who had made an oath to me. And now Sun was gone, and so was my guide.

Trickster.

I fell onto my blanket, the hard forest floor jarring my knees. He'd left me. He'd *left* me. He'd left me in the middle of nowhere, with no roads, no people, no means to protect myself. He'd lied to me, used me, and now I was worse off than I had been before, utterly lost with only the rising Sun to tell me which way was east.

I had never felt more alone than I did in that moment.

Eyes burning, I leapt to my feet and grabbed the edge of my blanket, whipping it into the nearest tree as hard as I could. It didn't even give me the satisfaction of a good *whoosh* in response, and the tree was, of course, unharmed. Dropping the blanket, I dug my hands into my hair. Twisted my braid. Paced the camp back and forth. Turned toward the Sun and shouted, "Come back! Please!"

I might not have known a lot about eternal law, but I was sure it dictated something about Sun's eternal patterns and His abilities to help me. He had told me He had little time to speak, and from what Elta had told me, He risked much by splitting Himself, especially with an ongoing war. If He returned to me, I was sure it wouldn't be soon.

Grinding my teeth, I picked up my blanket. The wood around me suddenly seemed so vast, the trees taller and closer together, their branches jagged. A rustle behind me made me jump, but it was only a shrew.

My hands shook as I packed my bags. I couldn't control Sun. I couldn't control Ristriel or anyone or anything around me. Only myself. I knew which way Ristriel had been leading me. I would simply have to continue in that direction until I found help.

Unless Ristriel hadn't been taking me to Nediah at all. Perhaps he had led me in the direction *he* needed to go, using me as a shield for those who would capture him.

I escaped, he'd said. From what, a prison for godlings? What awful things might he have done to wind up there?

I shuddered, remembering the bandits. At least Ristriel had kept that part of his word. He hadn't harmed me.

Stay calm, Ceris. This far from the road, the chance of running into bandits was slim. I could be loud as I walked in case I'd reached bear country, and then find a good tree to rest in at night as a protection from wolves . . . but they hunted during the day, too. I would have to always have a good tree in sight.

I wished very badly I had nicked a knife from Shila's kitchen before leaving. There was my starlight, I supposed, but I wasn't entirely sure how to ignite it, let alone wield it.

I started walking, wending my way through a forest that gradually grew thicker, keeping an eye and ear out for predators, constantly planning where to run, climb, or hide, just in case. I relaxed somewhat after an uneventful hour of travel. I started checking the sky, praying for chimney smoke, and searched the ground for a hunters' trail. Perhaps fortune would smile on me and there'd be a village nearby.

A little deeper in, I thought I spied an old chimney ruin in the forest, which might have meant a village was nearby. Diverting from my path, I picked my way over the uneven forest floor until I reached it, then paused, gaping. This was no chimney, but an eroded stone pillar standing as straight as the trees around it. Coming closer, I noticed another, shorter pillar toppled nearby, covered with years of debris. Triangulated to those two was a third pillar, its base upright but the rest of it broken into several pieces. I walked over to it, running my hand across one of the pieces. It had the same texture as my family's gravestones.

But this was no grave marker. I'd never seen a moon circle before, but I understood that this was one. An abandoned one, left to decay long ago, perhaps even before my time. If there was once power here, it had long since dissipated.

I left the wayward worship circle behind and continued to pick my way, alone, through the woods.

After the second hour passed, I began to sing to myself again, under my breath. I hadn't realized how accustomed I'd grown to Ristriel's presence in so short a time. Even when we didn't converse, I liked having someone beside me. One who let me think when I needed to think, one who didn't judge or worship me. I passed an herb and thought to point it out to him, only to be reminded that I was alone, and my anger kindled anew. Picking the plant in silence, I tucked it away into my bag and let the heat of betrayal fuel my pace. Soon enough I'd be craving even Father Aedan's presence.

My energy waned by the third hour, and I slowed, only then remembering I should break my fast with the last of my bread. My thoughts drifted back to Sun as I chewed. My heartbeat grew heavier as I recalled His simple and straightforward request.

He wanted me as a lover.

His offer would have been utterly scandalous, were I the Ceris I once was, and were He a mortal man. Even *I* would have found it scandalous. But now I was only surprised and . . . thoughtful. I had seen and heard things most humans would only dream of. I had partaken in fairy stories and lived to tell them, not that I had anyone to tell them to. I felt like I'd already lived an eccentric lifetime and was halfway through the second.

If I told Him yes, I would return to the palace, to the friends I had made during my pregnancy. My bed wouldn't be empty at night. Yet the idea of Sun being fond of me . . . I supposed He had seemed to like me well enough, despite my forwardness, after our meal together halfway through my pregnancy. He might have been intrigued by me when I faced Him again, before He sent me home. Part of me desperately wanted to read His thoughts, peel back the flames of His hair and know His every secret concerning me. Another part of me wanted to stay far, far away.

I did not, and still do not, blame Sun for the pain of being a star mother. I had consented to all of it. I had known the sacrifice, as far as a naïve mortal could understand such a thing. And I loved our child—Surril—even though she was far away and bodiless, a star in a sea of so many. As Sun would say, our union was the way of the universe. It was no more His fault than it was mine.

But that could not change how it had affected me, changed me, aged me. I believed Him when He said it would not hurt were we to . . . perform that act again. It might even be enjoyable. But His offer was not merely about sex. And I could not comprehend how an all-powerful god, a being I had worshiped since childhood, could want *me* with any sort of romantic fervor. Indeed, I was not certain our brief conversation had not been a fever dream.

Surril. I pushed away the confusing thicket of thoughts to focus on my daughter's name. *Surril.* It was strange and beautiful, and I could not wait for night to fall so that I might say her name to her face, regardless of the miles and miles between us.

I wondered, Did she know my name as well?

"You are going the wrong way."

The voice scared me so much that I jumped and fell to one knee, only to leap up again and spin, my bags carrying my momentum and turning me too far.

Ristriel was there behind me, ghostly indigo, in the shape of a human man, though his features were not as sharp as they could be.

He added, "You are headed toward Terraban, though it would take you three months to get there, and you would have to swim."

I had never heard of such a place. For a moment I could find no words; my voice lost to the waves of shock and anger and betrayal warring within me, so deep and wild I was drowning in them, swimming in every wrong direction possible.

His color lost opaqueness. "You are angry with me."

I gaped, choked, and sputtered out, "Wh-Where did you go?"

Shoulders slumping, he knelt in the foliage before me. "I did not mean to break my promise. But I am here now, and you are unharmed."

"Ristriel, *stand up.*"

"I had to flee when I sensed Him coming. He is powerful. He cannot find me from the sky when I am like this"—he lifted an ethereal hand—"but down here, I feared He would sense me. So I ran."

I stared at him for several heartbeats.

He feared Sun? But then, I supposed on this end of the universe, Sun lorded over everyone. He was the ultimate judge, the ultimate penalty.

"Ristriel."

He looked up at me.

I pressed my lips together. He looked so pitiful like that, so afraid. "What did you escape from?"

Lowering his eyes, he again did not answer me.

I let out a frustrated sigh. "How can I trust you if you will not trust me?"

His gaze lifted up enough to fall on my hand. Or, perhaps, on the ring on my finger, lined with amber.

Speaking so softly I could barely hear him, he said, "My oath is intact. I will take you to Nediah. I will protect you. I am sorry."

He was still kneeling before me, head slightly tipped. Even the people of Endwever had not genuflected so lowly.

Anger dissipating, I approached him and crouched down to his level. "Do you remember your lesson to me yesterday, about being godly?"

He slowly met my eyes.

"You tell me to behave as though I am better than the people around me, but what about you?"

He blinked at me, confused.

I lifted my hand to his arm, but my fingers passed through him. "I was confused, and scared, and angry. Yes. But you are a *godling*, Ristriel. And as you said, your oath is intact."

He didn't respond.

Taking a more direct approach, I said, "Do you not know your own worth?"

His lips parted as though he wanted to answer, but no sound came from him. He looked into my eyes, his expression almost childlike, and my heart sank as I tried to picture what sort of place he had escaped. What torments would it take to convince a powerful godling that he was something less than a celestial being? For it was evident from the way Ristriel spoke, the way he moved, the way he transformed, that he did not understand his own greatness. No mortal should ever have to be convinced they were worthy of every breath they took, and no celestial being should have to, either.

I had seen Yar and Shu in Sun's palace. I did not think they were prison guards.

Ristriel did not answer, so I asked another question, one that stemmed from the unease in my gut. "The Sun knows you?" Sun did not know half of His own servants, so why should Ristriel stick in His memory?

Ristriel looked away. He began to shift into something equine.

"Ristriel, you are safe with me." Perhaps using his own words would inspire trust.

His shifting reverted until he was a man-shaped spirit once more. "Yes."

I studied his eyes. "Do you know how to lie, Ristriel?"

He leaned back, surprised, and color firmed his features, almost enough to make him appear solid. "I have never lied to you, Ceris."

"Then tell me, will you hurt me?"

He shook his head. "Never. You have been . . . kind to me."

Those simple words struck me like a well-aimed mallet. "Will you not tell me where you came from?"

He set his jaw.

My fists tightened on the straps of my bags, then relaxed. "I believe you. And I will not hurt you, either."

He glanced up at the bright orb in the sky. "He wants you." While his deep, endless black eyes were childlike, the question was nothing of the sort. We both knew what kind of *want* he meant.

"That doesn't matter right now." I stood and adjusted my bags, rolling my shoulders beneath their weight. "Right now, I want to go to Nediah, and I want you to take me."

He stood as well, studying my face. "You are not like most mortal women, Ceris."

"I'm told I'm not quite mortal."

His lips quirked into half a smile, a handsome expression that punctured the heaviness of the moment. "You wouldn't be like the others even if you didn't have starlight in your hair. You are not afraid as you should be." He glanced westward. "But sometimes it is safer to be afraid."

I chewed on my lip. "Are *you* afraid, Ristriel?"

"I am. But I am also free, and freedom is worth the fear." He turned back to me and held out his hand. "We can still make good time today. We'll find your kin. I swear it."

Reaching for his hand, I wished dearly that I could take it. Instead, I let my fingers pass through his, getting the impression of distance and coolness. He gestured in the direction we should go, and as we started walking, I said, "Is there a meadow along our path anywhere?"

He paused a moment before saying, "I can take us through one, if you'd like."

"Please." His brief words on freedom had burrowed themselves into my blood. "I have the very strong desire to run."

CHAPTER 12

We came across a field in the late afternoon, and I dropped my bags, hiked up my skirt, and ran through the new grasses and small violet flowers, pushing my legs as fast as they would go. I'd run from the bandits earlier, but this was different. This wasn't desperate or terrifying, but liberating and peaceful. Running pulled me out of my gloom and threw me back seven hundred and ten years to my childhood, when I'd darted around the village and climbed trees without a care in the world. I could almost hear my mother screaming after me, telling me I was being immodest and unladylike, and what if Caen's parents saw?

Even though the memory wasn't necessarily a happy one, it made me miss her. It made me dwell on all the unanswered questions that danced inside me. Had my mother found some happiness in the end? Had both of my sisters married? How many nieces and nephews did I have? And Caen . . . had he remembered me the way I'd wanted him to?

I would have to wait until I died to find out. But when I died, because I had lived . . . would we even end up in the same afterlife?

I stopped midfield, catching my breath, letting the questions unravel like slipped stitches. "I simply have to believe the best will pass," I chided myself. Try my hardest. Barter with the gods themselves, if I needed to. I couldn't undo what had already come to pass. Sun had made that much clear.

"Are you all right?" Ristriel hovered nearby. He stood in full Sunlight, and I could see the forest line through his torso.

Straightening, I tucked loose strands of hair behind my ears. I smiled, stretched. "I'm trying to be."

He glanced back toward my bags, barely noticeable above the grass at the other end of the field. "What are you believing the best of?"

I flushed. "Oh, you caught that?" Leave it to a godling to have impeccable hearing. "I was thinking about my family. The ones I left, when I became star mother. They're all deceased now."

He nodded solemnly. "I'm sorry."

"Thank you." Leaning back, I stretched my spine. "But it's been a long time." *Longer for them than for me.* "I'm hoping to find my sister's descendants in Nediah. Stories get passed down in a family, so they'll be able to tell me about the relatives I never got to meet. They'll be my stories, too, in a way, and I'll become part of their tapestry, and everything will feel right again." I laughed, though it wasn't particularly funny. In truth, it hurt. "That's the plan, at least."

"Mortals have always been fond of stories," he supplied.

"Of course." Turning about, I hiked back toward my bags. "We don't live long enough to remember who we are without them."

Ristriel followed my path, lingering about two paces behind me. "What are *your* stories, Ceris?"

My steps slowed. He didn't mean *the* story, the one that drew attention from everyone else. The one that had made me "important." He already knew that story. He'd discerned that story the moment we'd met.

It was strange, and somewhat alarming, how long it took me to reflect beyond that, to the person I was before that star died. Like it really had been several centuries. Like I was an old woman scraping up her past.

"I liked to play in the forest," I finally said, turning around. I was on an incline, making me a hand's breadth taller than he was. "I liked to pretend I was a wolf or a fairy, and bound around like a wild thing. My mother hated it."

A smile bloomed on his mouth.

"I liked jokes. Pranks. The setup was almost better than the reveal." I chuckled to myself as memories surfaced. "I often dragged my sister in on it. It was never as fun by myself. I'd switch neighbors' cows, or put peppers in our breakfast . . . Once I moved an entire woodpile to the other side of my betrothed's house."

He seemed impressed. "That sounds like a lot of work."

"It was certainly a lot of splinters."

Ristriel seemed to consider this as he resumed walking. "I was very much like you, when I was young."

I laughed. "Leading milk cows around in the middle of the night?"

He looked abashed. "Unfortunately . . . I was not so tame."

I watched him, imagining what sort of mischief a godling might get into. Wondering if that's where he'd earned his reputation as a trickster. "Oh?"

By his body language, I could tell he did not want to answer, and I considered whether or not I should push for information. However, he did relent, "Did you know the Earth Mother used to have rings?"

"Rings?" I glanced at the gold band on my finger.

He shook his head. "Not like that. In the sky." His head tilted back as he scanned the blue-and-white expanse. "Rings across the heavens, circles of dust that lit up the sky."

I tried to imagine such a thing. "And you . . ." I wasn't sure how to finish the sentence.

He shrugged, and I sensed him closing off.

"But," I interjected, stepping around a large stone, mirth dwindling, "that's not who I am anymore. I grew up too much. And I have a suspicion that's not who you are anymore, either."

"Has your joy changed so much?"

I had nearly reached my bags, but his question made me stop completely. "What?"

"Your joy." He stepped beside me, hands clasped behind him, eyes endlessly dark and curious. "Is that not what all mortals—all creatures— live for? That which brings the most happiness?" He glanced heavenward. "Did she change so much? Or did He?"

I opened my mouth, closed it. Contemplated. With anyone else, the silence might have been awkward. But Ristriel waited patiently, taking in the landscape around us while I sorted my thoughts.

"Surril *did* change my joy," I said after a minute. "She *became* my joy. I was never able to hold her in my arms, but she means more to me than anything. And without Him, I would not have her. As for the rest . . . I haven't been able to hold still long enough to know how much of *me* has changed. I'm still trying to swallow the changes of the world around me. Does that make sense?"

He nodded.

I tilted my head. "What brings *you* joy, Ristriel?"

The corner of his mouth ticked up. "I am still learning that as well. But you have given me something to think about."

"Have I?" Pulling my eyes away, I picked up my bags, securing them crosswise over my shoulders. As I turned back to him, I said, "Will you start moving firewood to—"

Not two inches from my nose stood a massive black-and-violet scarecrow.

I shrieked and jumped, the weight of my bags pulling me rump first to the soft meadow.

"Hmm," the scarecrow hummed before melting back into Ristriel. "I could see the draw of that."

Hand to my racing heart, I laughed. "When did I tell you about Farmer May?"

He regarded me. "Farmer May?" He reached a hand out as though to help me, but the Sun made him as tangible as the fog, so he dropped it.

I gaped at him a moment. I hadn't told him about Farmer May, had I? The last prank I had pulled with Idlysi before becoming a star mother. Ristriel had chosen a scarecrow all on his own.

It was such a small and silly thing, really, but I felt it like a plucked string right between my breasts. Pulling myself to my feet, I agreed with him. "Perhaps we aren't so different."

He seemed confused by my statement, though in truth he had been the first to suggest it. I did not explain—I didn't know how well I could—so we continued our trek, sometimes in silence, sometimes with easy conversation.

The field gave way to another, and then another, the forest opening up like a great maw. The Earth began to rise and fall in soft hills, upon which grew the emerald stubs of wheat and other plants. I spied a farmhouse off in the distance and suggested we journey there. We reached it midevening, and the tenants agreed to let me shelter in the stable overnight in exchange for a few coppers. I wondered if I'd gotten them wet at the pond for them to tarnish so, but a copper was a copper. They seemed a little suspicious of me until Ristriel approached from behind. The Sun had just dipped below the gable of the house, rendering him solid, and he looked perfectly human. I introduced him as my husband, and Ristriel smoothly explained we were from a village I'd never heard of to the north, passing through to a town I'd never heard of to the south. They believed the story and offered us a few spare blankets. Ristriel waited until they returned inside before walking to the barn, as Sunlight streaked the path. Like he had said, mortals were a superstitious lot. It was better to play it safe.

I stayed outside when the darkness descended, swift and sure, but the sky was clogged with clouds, and there was not a star to be seen. My chest tightened at the lack of light, but I reminded myself I needed to wait only another day to see her. So I sang a lullaby to Surril, one of the songs I had repeated often during my pregnancy, slipping her name in wherever it could fit.

When I returned to the stable, Ristriel had lit a lantern and hung it from the ceiling. There were two unwalled stalls available, filled with dry hay leftover from winter stores. Two horses and an ox watched me as I passed, the latter mewing softly under its breath. I dropped down onto a bale and loosened my hair, which had gone wavy since I'd braided it wet.

"You have a lovely voice." Ristriel watched the light on the ceiling as though it were the moon's, like he yearned for something he could not reach. He looked remarkably human.

I flushed at the compliment. "Th-Thank you. My sister Idlysi was always the talented one in my family." I could carry a tune, but her voice was angelic.

"I have heard many mortals sing," Ristriel went on, finally pulling his eyes from the light, "in different tones, styles, languages. The way you sing is simple and genuine. It's . . . calming."

No one had ever described my voice in such a way. "Thank you."

A thought struck me, and I rummaged through my bag for my thread, needle, and canvas, scooting closer to the light to hold up my limited supply. I chose a deep-purple thread, looped it through my needle's eye, and leaned back to get to work.

Embroidery had always helped me relax before bed. It was a rewarding task that let my thoughts work out on their own, unless I was doing a particularly difficult design. I hadn't had a pull to work a needle since finishing the tapestry for my star, but I felt that itch now. Pushing the first stitch through the small canvas relieved it. The work felt firm and solid, like Ristriel was at that moment. It felt *right*. It was him I wanted to create, as best as I could in such a limited space. Ristriel had many forms, but it seemed right to stitch him as a man, for he was intelligent as one and, truthfully, it was the form of his I liked most.

I had just finished his outline when Ristriel stiffened and stood, heading toward the edge of the stable to peer out into the darkness. I set my work aside and followed him. "What's wrong?"

He didn't answer right away, so I touched his shoulder. He flinched before glancing back at me and relaxing under the faint pressure of my fingers. It raised sad questions in me, but he distracted me by answering the only one I'd spoken. "I sensed them."

"Godlings?"

He nodded. "Moving away. We are safe. They were not very close to begin with." He paused. "They're being followed, by hers."

"Hers?"

"Moon."

I wondered what that meant. Were the moon's godlings spying on the Sun's? Did they mean to attack? But Ristriel did not appear worried, so I forced my concerns to shrink.

"You have far-reaching senses," I said.

"I was very far away, so I had to."

Lifting my hand from his shoulder, I pulled at my pocket, offering to hide him, but he shook his head. He really did believe we were safe, then.

"Where, Ristriel?" I asked. "Where were you, before I met you?"

He offered me a weak smile. "It is better that you don't know. It is a place I have risked much to forget." He ran his palm over a splintering wooden post. "I should go outside. They'll have a harder time finding me if I'm incorporeal. And if I'm moving."

I could understand how becoming a ghost would make him harder to find, but I failed to see how pacing outside the barn would be beneficial. If anything, he should hide. "Why moving?"

His fingers curled inward, away from the post. I could see him struggling to find an acceptable answer. "It is the way of things."

I scoffed. That was the sort of answer Sun would give. Hooking my thumb into the pocket of my dress, I asked, "Can I not hide you?"

He dipped his head, but his features were uncertain. "I do not want them to find you again. It will raise suspicion."

And he'd promised I wouldn't come to harm, though I still didn't think Yar and Shu would harm me. Then again, when it came to things celestial, Ristriel would know better than I.

Further prying would have to wait until morning. "I'm going to rest, then."

As far as I knew, Ristriel did not return to the barn until Sunrise.

We left before the farmers rose, making our way northwest. We moved farther and farther from the forest, until I couldn't see the shading of its trees any longer. After a day of traveling, the hills began to mellow, giving us flatter ground dotted with smatterings of trees not quite large enough to be considered a wood. We slept out of doors, and I sang my song to Surril while Ristriel, malleable in the moonlight, shifted into a wolf and curled up at my feet, listening. That night and the next, I worked a little on my new tapestry by firelight, my stitches so small in my attempts to capture the intricate play of darkness and light that was my godling guide that my needle threatened to tear my canvas, which I'd had to trim twice, because it had started yellowing on the edges. It was not handling the shift from heaven to Earth as well as I had.

"Why do you create that way?" the wolf asked late the second night. I had thought he was slumbering, but of course Ristriel did not need sleep the way I did. Fatigue weighed down my eyelids, but I'd wanted to finish some violet highlights before turning in for the night.

My hand paused, and I looked at my tapestry. "It's art."

The wolf tilted his head almost like he was offended by my obvious answer. "Why thread? Why not sculpture, paint, storytelling?"

I smiled. "This is much easier to carry."

"Storytelling is not heavy."

Chuckling, I pushed another stitch through the tapestry. "It is if you write it all down." I paused at my next stitch. "Can you create, Ristriel?"

"In the celestial sense, no. But I can hold a paintbrush, when I'm whole and have given myself hands."

"Do you paint?"

"I have never tried."

Stifling a yawn, I rolled up my tapestry and put it aside. I could work on it again tomorrow. "I could show you needlework, if you'd like."

His canine ear twitched. "I have seen many things in my lifetime, Ceris. Needlework seems one of the dullest. That is why I asked why it is your preference."

I laughed out loud. "If I'd had the universe at my fingers, perhaps I would have taken up another hobby. Just spinning and dying the string alone is toilsome, I'll have you know. There is a great deal of accomplishment in a finished tapestry."

Ristriel grinned as much as a wolf could, and laid his muzzle down again.

I lay down as well, supporting my head on my elbow. Thumbed the edge of the tapestry I'd lowered beside me. "Have you seen so much?"

He hummed an affirmative.

I chewed on the inside of my cheek. Rolled over so I could see the stars. "Have you seen the hereafter?"

His fur rustled. "The hereafter is not one place to behold. It is many, it is always, it is . . . difficult to explain."

"But you've seen it?" Hope pulsed behind my breastbone.

"I know of much of it."

"The star mothers' hereafter?"

He shifted again. "I understand it is a beautiful place, where those who sacrificed, and their lines, are treated as gods."

"And if a star mother does not die?"

He didn't answer for several seconds. "I am not sure. It is a place I cannot see. A place I cannot go."

I pressed both hands to my chest, trying to soothe my dying hopes. "But can a soul move from one hereafter to another? When I perish, will I still live with the other star mothers? Will my line still follow me?"

A long breath came from his muzzle. "I do not know. I wish I could tell you, Ceris. Even your Sun would not know. It is not His domain."

Two tears, one for each eye, blurred my vision, and I blinked them away. "If they have gone where I cannot follow, I will be alone when I die, too."

I hadn't meant to say it aloud. I barely did; it was more breath than whisper, a plea to the stars overhead. But Ristriel heard me. He shifted again, paws padding as they grew closer to me. His body lowered to the ground again, close to me but not touching, his breath stirring the baby hairs lining my forehead.

"You will not be alone." His voice sounded like the wood around us, distant and deep. "You will be worshiped, and if that does not please you, we will find your family in Nediah. And if they do not love you, I will be your companion as long as you wish. As long as mortal paths allow me to follow. But I would not worry, Ceris. You are a being that is easy to love."

More tears filled my vision, and when I blinked, they ran down my temples and into my ears, but I did not wipe them away.

All I could think to say was "Thank you."

We rose early the next day. I took a quick wash in a nearby creek and ate a breakfast that was half-foraged. My thoughts were still tied into knots, so I was not good conversation until after noon, when I finally let questions of family and the afterlife and Ristriel slip away and found myself rambling about how wool was spun and various dying methods, as well as merchants I remembered who'd come through town with more rare supplements like indigo and turmeric. Ristriel listened contentedly enough, though I don't think I succeeded in furthering his interest in needlepoint.

We were still walking when night fell suddenly, not yet to the town Ristriel was hoping to give me shelter in. It was my fault, for I had taken an extra break and slowed us down, foraging for elderflower and chokeberries. Ristriel, ever patient, had not complained once about my dawdling. Indeed, he'd begun to make me feel guilty for ever doubting him or his intentions.

"It isn't far." He walked a step ahead of me, cemented by darkness into the form of a man. "Just over that rise."

I could barely make out a rise up ahead, and knew it was solid land and not sky only because it was a piece of uneven blackness without a single star. The night was so absolute, so dark, that while searching for Surril, I tripped on something and stumbled into Ristriel.

He steadied me with cool hands, then wrapped one of them around one of mine. "It isn't far," he repeated, and I sensed a smile. "I forget that you cannot see in the dark."

I gripped his hand tightly, grateful for the anchor of his presence. "I'm not entirely incapable," I countered, but it *was* very dark. As Ristriel led me across the field, toward the rise, I looked up at the sky, searching.

Pulling back enough to make him slow, I said, "Where is the moon?"

He stopped, scanning the heavens himself. Not a single cloud marred our view; half the world was filled with stars. But it was not time for a new moon—last night the moon had been at her third quarter.

I was marveling at the beauty of the star scape when I heard a clamor somewhere . . . I couldn't pinpoint where. Like the crashing of two bodies, but it echoed across the field, followed by the scraping of metal and a distant shout.

Ristriel's grip tightened. "We need to go back." He spun me around and began running back the way we had come, using his free hand to relieve me of one of my bags. "Hurry."

I didn't doubt him and ran as fast as I could, but a full day of travel and my bags made me slow. "What? What's happening?"

Another clamor, like hammer against anvil. Or sword against sword. Distant voices made me think of the crowd of people outside Shila's home after my return to Endwever had been made known.

Only, these voices were angry.

Ristriel didn't answer, only tugged at my arm, urging my legs to move faster. Putting my head down, I put all my energy into my legs as we flew back the way we had come—

I saw a flash of blinding light before I heard the *boom*. It was the loudest thunder I'd ever heard, so violent its percussion pulsed through my body. I turned back not to see storm clouds, but light falling from the heavens like the petals of a wilting flower. Like some great god had ground lightning into dust and thrown it as though rice at a wedding.

The Sun's words surfacing in memory made my breath catch. *The battles again.*

The clamoring, the shouting, was growing louder, closer. And I remembered what Ristriel had said in the barn. The moon's soldiers were following Sun's. And Sun's soldiers . . . they were following *us*.

"Gods help us," I whispered.

Ristriel tugged me to the Earth, and I hit on my hands and knees. Still holding my hand in a desperate grasp, he bowed his head, and darkness even thicker than the night around us began to ripple from him as dye dropped into water, blacking out the stars, the fire in the heavens, and the deep hues of night.

"Don't move," he whispered against my ear.

He was trying to hide us. Hide us from the violence in the sky, the clamor that was nearly upon us. The Sun had mentioned battle. Ristriel had spoken of it, too. And the moon was gone.

We had walked into the middle of a war, and my mortal eyes could not even see it.

Panic, sharp and cold, crawled up my legs and arms, raising goose-flesh in its wake. I could hear a cacophony of people—*godlings*—swarming around us, thrusting their weapons and igniting their powers, screeching at one another in a language I did not understand. I could see none of it, but I could hear it, smell it, *feel* it through the rumbling Earth beneath my hands.

And just like with the bandits, I began to glow.

"Ceris, no!" Ristriel cried, but I could not control the light. My starlight spread, and his darkness evaporated like windblown smoke. He ripped his hand away from mine as though I'd burned him. Just like the bandit had.

With starlight in my eyes, I saw the soldiers—creatures silhouetted against the sky, creatures on the ground, creatures in every space in between as though the pull of the Earth Mother meant nothing to them. Some were manlike, others were monsters, even more were spirits or mere shadows I could not identify. Many of them turned toward the beacon I had created. One charged for me, tall and red with the horns of a bull and the snout of a pig. Another just like him but stouter. A green godling noticed me as well, but something large mowed him down before he could reach us.

"You!" The first godling pointed a great spear at me, the tooth of some legendary monster bound to its haft. "Do you fight for the day or the night?"

Ristriel stepped between him and me, even as more godlings charged toward us. "We are not here for war. We only wish to pass!" he shouted back. He had to shout, or else not be heard over the crazed orchestra of battle haloing us.

The godling's spear shifted to Ristriel, hovering inches from his nose. "You must fight. Or have you no loyalty?"

Gritting my teeth, I urged my body to darken, to cool, to *extinguish*, and slowly, like a Sunset, the starlight dimmed. That same strange hunger from before—a sensation I hadn't been in the right mind to dwell on—crept up my limbs. It was not a want for food, but something . . . missing.

"We have no qualms with you." Ristriel didn't even flinch as the stout godling turned around and cut through another creature sneaking up on him. My view of the beings grew dimmer and dimmer as I sucked in my starlight. "She is blessed of the Sun. Let us go."

The last thing I saw before my light vanished was a cruel grin on the red godling's face. "Ah, but I see her darkness in you."

And he struck.

"Ristriel!" I cried as his body knocked back into me, sending me onto my backside. Another explosion lit the heavens, a battle too far away for me to see, let alone reach. My thoughts flashed to Sun. *He* was up there, wasn't He? Fighting for His kingdom, His powers, His people. Did it make Him weak, battling within the moon's kingdom?

I did not have long to wonder. The trailing, mystical light from the explosion helped me make out two silhouettes—Ristriel and the red godling—grappling with each other. Ristriel was smaller by half, but he was not easily thrown aside. He shoved away the godling only to intercept another, and another, until I could not tell his shadow from the rest.

My heart raced inside me. I pushed onto my knees, only to cower when some sort of enormous bird cawed over my head, diving into the fray. I could not leave Ristriel to fend for himself, but neither could I fight.

Desperate, I scrambled over the Earth, searching for stones to throw. My fingers grazed a palm-sized one when a shadow whisked across my hand. I thought it was another flying godling, but when I looked up, the shadows all around me warped, gray against black, coming alive, defying the light of the stars. The shadows surged into the fray, lassoing around the necks of godlings or whipping at their legs. Warriors turned around to strike, only to be engulfed.

Another explosion rent the sky, this one like a full bloom, orange and blue like true fire. I saw Ristriel speed away from the godlings faster even than his war stallion form could move, then rush back in so swiftly he blurred. A horned godling took off after him.

Fear-fueled energy pumping through my limbs, I wheeled my arm around and threw my rock. It sailed true, striking the horned godling on the back of its head.

Behind me, a snakelike voice hissed, "Do you fight for the day or the night?"

Grabbing the handle of my bag, I whirled around, letting its heavy load smash into the head of a gargoyle-like godling that reached no higher than midthigh. It flew two feet and hissed, shaking its head, trying to orient itself for a counterattack.

I ran.

The field lit and darkened over and over with the battle of the gods, all the while festering as godlings rained from the sky or wriggled from the ground, some armed with weapons, others wielding their own hands and feet. My starlight pressed against my skin, urging me to unleash it, but I forced it down. I needed to see what warriors stood in my path, yet I dared not draw attention to myself.

There were so many of them, I couldn't find a clear way out.

A godling noticed me and rushed for me. Biting down on a scream, I darted in a different direction until he called, "Ceris!"

I wheeled around as Ristriel crashed into me, his arms enfolding me and pulling me tightly to him. We fell and froze, the ground inches away.

And everything changed.

The grasses shifted with a dozen breezes. The sky brightened and darkened, colored and blackened, all too quickly to be natural. The shadows and faces around me distorted, blurring or disappearing entirely, only for new ones to appear, shrink, and vanish. The Sun whisked across the sky in a fiery streak again and again, until noon daylight washed over the field, the battle was over, and everything went still.

I hit the ground, dazed and confused. Ristriel, ethereal and looming over me, stared wildly into my eyes.

My breaths came deep and sharp, my body still recovering from its run. I stared back at him, so many questions pulsing in my mind. His ghostly nose hovered inches above mine. His chest heaved like any man's would, even without solid lungs, blood, bone. Had his hair been solid, it would have brushed my brow. And his eyes—his eyes were wide and fierce, darker than new ink and as insubstantial as cloud.

What had just happened? Where were the other godlings?

Why was it midday?

But Ristriel, still as shadow, whispered, "It's . . . yours."

It took a moment for his words to register, for his presence to make sense, for my body to feel mine, and the world to feel whole. "What did you do?"

He pushed away from me, curling into a crouch, still staring at me, the emotions on his face very much mirroring my own. His body warped for a moment, like it wanted to transform, but he snapped it back into human shape again. And me . . . My nails were long, my *hair* was long, reaching past my hips. The grass below me was dead and curled like it had been cast into a fire and hastily pulled back out. The blades beside it were as tall as my shoulders, while the rest of the field was just as it should have been.

"Ceris," he spoke carefully, "how long has it been since the Sun lit your torch?"

I sat up, blinking away a wave of dizziness. "Seven hundred years."

He hesitated, then nodded, as though he'd known it all along. Again his body rippled, but after a moment, it settled on his human form, though he was so faint he was only translucent shades of gray. He found his feet without effort and moved toward the ridge he'd indicated earlier, every step soundless, his gait that of an old man.

I hurried to his side, wanting to grab him, but my hand passed right through him. "What did you do?" I asked. "What happened? Ristriel, *what did you do?*"

His face lost definition. "I did what I had to to get us away." He paused as though out of breath, but Ristriel had never shown any signs of mortal fatigue. "It's over now." He met my eyes. "I couldn't let them hurt you."

I looked him over, searching for signs of injury, for *he* had been the one fighting. If he was wounded, they weren't the kind of wounds that could be seen. But he was very shaken. We both were.

His answer didn't satisfy me. I wanted to know what had happened on that field. What had happened to me, to *us*.

But he spoke before I did. "Will you sing, Ceris?" A breeze slipped past us, carrying away the question asked in such a sad tone my frustration simmered down to a thick syrup.

I swallowed it, steadied myself with a breath, and started the song of Surril's first lullaby as we walked, and for miles all around us, it was the only sound to be heard.

CHAPTER 13

I sang for a while, until my throat grew too dry, and then we passed the ridge and came upon a tiny village along the river, one that made Endwever look sizable. Ristriel did not insist we travel farther, so I found us a place to stay in another barn. The kind people who owned it didn't charge me, and even fed me a helping of stew and traded with me so I could have some deep-blue thread for my tapestry and thicker socks for my shoes.

Ristriel did not come into the town, which was for the better. I needed to sort through my thoughts, my feelings, and determine what my next steps would be. Ristriel had, indeed, kept up his side of the bargain. He'd even seemed genuinely concerned for my welfare, which was touching.

Yet I struggled with trust again. I did not know what he was. I did not understand what he could do. And the godling he'd spoken to in the battle . . . The soldier's words had stayed with me.

I see her darkness in you.

He could only have meant the moon.

I was of the Sun. All my life I had worshiped Him. My parents had worshiped Him, my grandparents, and all my ancestors before us. I had shared His bed and birthed His child. He had touched my face and asked me to love Him.

Trickster.

I rubbed a chill from my shoulders as I explored the small village, my thoughts interrupted by questions from curious locals. I passed along the story I'd arranged with Ristriel—that I'd come with my brother to find our relatives but he was still off hunting. And I asked about events going on beyond the town. Many people told me what I already knew—the gods had been angry last week, so they'd dedicated a day of prayer to both the moon and the Sun, supplicating them for peace.

What caught my attention in these stories were the words *last week.* Because for me, the battle had been last night, and morning had simply vanished. And yet my hair and nails had grown as if a year had passed.

None of this should have been possible, and yet he had done it. If Ristriel were merely a man, a guide I had hired, I would have had no reason not to trust him. And yet he was not a man. I had seen him call shadows. I had seen him walk through trees. I had seen him lose part of what he was when Sun's light stole it from him.

What did it all mean, and what did it mean for me? It might be safest to dismiss Ristriel and continue on my way. And yet, I couldn't bring myself to do it. Not only because I needed to make it to Nediah in one piece, but because the thought of leaving him behind drowned me with guilt.

Because if Ristriel were simply a mortal man, I would have cared for him. And despite my better judgment, I was starting to. He was kind, clever, temperate. But he was as intangible as the secrets he carried. My mind would not settle until I knew what they were.

After my wanderings, I returned to the farm to dine with my hosts. Our talk was pleasant, and before I left, I assured them my "brother" would be fine with the supplies we already had. When I reached the barn, it was empty save for a couple of lambs. I wondered where Ristriel had gone. What he was doing. I climbed a ladder into the hayloft and pulled out my tapestry, needing the focus of needle and thread to orient my thoughts. I sensed Ristriel when he appeared, the way one senses an oncoming storm or a passing cloud.

"What kind of godling are you?" I asked quietly, adding a stitch to his leg.

He hovered below me. Eager streaks of western Sunlight reaching through the barn window kept him ghostly.

"What do you mean?" he asked. He knew very much what I meant, but I let him play coy.

"What is your domain?" I tucked the needle away and smoothed the tapestry across my lap. "Most godlings who stay on the Earth Mother have a domain." I thought of the being I'd encountered in the lake on my second night in Terasta. "What is yours?"

"My domain is not linked to any location. It is me. Myself." He looked around the barn, taking in the common tools, the rusted hinges, the smell of animals. "I was once among mortals, but not anymore."

"Are you not among us now?"

Instead of reminding me I wasn't quite mortal, he said, "It is different."

Sighing, I set my work aside and scooted to the edge of the loft to better see him. "We need to talk about last night."

"Your starlight weakens me." He didn't meet my eyes. "That is why we were seen. Why I left your side."

My lips parted at the confession. That was not what I had meant, but the information was valuable. I remembered how his cloud of inky darkness had dissipated the instant my starlight surfaced. I remembered the fear of watching his shadow merge with so many others. Of being alone, and unable to help.

I rubbed my hands together to warm them. "You used time."

I remembered what Sun had said to me. *Time cannot be altered.*

When Ristriel did not reply, I added, "It's a universal law, isn't it?"

"There are laws not of this universe that are broken every day, with much more far-reaching consequences." Sharpness laced his tone. "Acts that create only suffering among your people and mine, and yet they go unpunished." His volume squeezed down to a whisper. He looked up at me, hair black as soot swishing over his eyes. "Do you believe what I did was wrong?"

Did I *know* it to be wrong? Yes. Only he hadn't asked what I knew, but what I felt. "No."

He pressed his lips together, dark eyes shifting from me as though I had scolded him. As though something I couldn't see weighed on him, and I watched as it slowly crushed him. He breathed slowly, deeply. The rays of Sunlight coming through the window turned ruddy.

"What can I do for you, Ceris?"

I hadn't expected that. In truth, he had done so much for me already, but I couldn't let the opportunity for an honest exchange wither. "You can answer my questions."

The way his mouth drooped told me that was not the response he had wanted. Gathering my skirt in one hand, I came down the ladder. When I was on solid ground again, I asked, "Who are you?"

He didn't meet my eyes. "My name is Ristriel."

"Why are Yar and Shu hunting you?"

He took longer to respond this time. "Because the deity who gave you that ring ordered them to."

I glanced at the ring on my middle finger. Reaching down, I twisted it, the amber line at its center turning black.

Ristriel visibly relaxed. I hadn't realized how tense he'd been until his shoulders slumped and his expression unwound. In that moment, I switched places with him. Empathy overwhelmed my fears, and I imagined myself in his position. Alone, on the run, afraid, only to have a star mother constantly barrage me with questions I feared answering. Questions that could send me back to wherever I came from, and it was clearly an unpleasant place. Questions asked by a woman courted by my . . . nemesis? Enemy? As professed by the ring on her finger.

I wanted to touch him—to feel his presence so I might remind him, and myself, that we were not alone. But a sliver of Sunset still grazed him, and I could not.

"What's wrong, Ristriel?"

Now he looked at me, as surprised as he'd been the first time I thanked him. He didn't answer, only studied me. Had he been solid, had he been as any other man, the moment would have been intimate. We stood very close, alone in a barn away from prying gazes, eyes locked, searching each other's depths.

It *was* intimate, but in a way new to me.

When he spoke, he answered my question with one of his own. "If you could have anything at this moment, Ceris, what would it be?"

The enormity of the question made me pause. *Anything?* Would I rip open all of Ristriel's secrets? Fly back seven hundred years and pick up life as I knew it? Go even further back and turn Sun's eye away from Endwever, or turn Caen's heart toward me? Yet those things felt unreal to me, like pieces of a complex dream I was forgetting more of by the day. I did not have to search my heart long to know what I truly wanted more than anything else.

I moved toward the barn doors, stepping outside as the golden tip of the Sun dropped below the horizon. "If I could have anything, I would want to meet Surril."

"Your star." He had followed me.

I nodded, looking upward as the stars began to poke through, waiting for her face to shine. "I carried her, gave birth to her, but when I opened my eyes again, she was already among her sisters and brothers." I turned, watching the sky. I found her twinkle easily and pointed. "There she is."

"You want to see her?"

I pulled my gaze from the sky to Ristriel, who stood solidly before me, dressed in his inky clothes. "If I could have anything, that is what I'd ask for."

Ristriel held out his now-solid hand to me, a soft smile on his lips. "Then let me take you."

My heart surged enough that the faintest silver glow danced across my skin. "What? There? You can . . . do that?"

He nodded, hand still extended.

I stared at his outstretched fingers, my pulse a drum in my ears, my breaths quick. I had been waiting and waiting for this war to end, for Sun to break away from His responsibilities for long enough to safely traverse the universe to our child's home. Could this godling really accomplish such a feat now?

Did I trust him? Did it matter?

My own fingers trembling, I slipped my hand into his. He grasped it firmly and pulled me to him, embracing me tightly like he had on the battlefield, when time had rippled around us, and I felt strangely safe, like he was a shield against this strange world I'd become lost to.

We flew, weightless, the Earth and the night sky blurring around us. Not as it had after Ristriel broke the law of time, but in a whimsical way, the way of gods. I was a falcon diving into the heavens, I was a falling star, I was a baby's first breath. The sky opened to my eyes, the stars becoming large and *real*, their light warm and cool all at once, soft and blinding, dazzling and mesmerizing. Matter of all sizes and shapes flew around them in dark rings, and when I asked about it, Ristriel answered simply, "Their power attracts the unmade things of the universe."

He flew with skill and ease, weaving through the halos of dust, speeding among the stars. As we soared past them, they became streaks of color. I could hear their interest, their laughter, their singing.

Time seemed to warp. I was everywhere and nowhere, flying through seconds and years. And then I saw her in the distance, silver and white, small and precious. I pointed, and our direction shifted, until I was surrounded on all sides by velvet nothing, yet with Ristriel's arms around me, I did not fall.

Before me shone an effulgent being smaller than myself, a child enveloped in a massive halo of starlight. Her skin was starlight, and her hair and eyes shone like diamonds. She smiled at me, and my heart grew too large for my chest to hold.

"Mother." She reached for me.

Tears fell from my eyes, one after another. Extending my arm, I clasped her hand in mine. She was warm and soft and everything a child should be, though she seemed more a girl of ten than a newborn.

"My dear Surril," I whispered. Ristriel's arms released me, but I floated into hers, my skin glowing as she did, our light combining into something even more beautiful.

"I saw your picture," Surril sang. "I watch you every night."

I wept into her hair and clung to her, giving her all the love I had within me. "I watch you, too, my dear girl. I love you."

"I know." She giggled and pulled her fingers through my hair. "I know, and I love you, too. All of us do."

Pulling back, I looked at her face. "All of us?"

"You are a star mother," she chimed. "You have stayed with us when others could not. You are mother to all of us."

She gestured outward, and the stars around us twinkled and shifted, as though waving to me, reaching out with pearly fingers. At that moment, with my daughter clasped tightly to my chest, I was the happiest I had ever been. Never would I wish to go back and be what I had been—a mortal girl with a normal life ahead of her—for it would mean Surril was not mine, and she was my everything.

Surril grinned at me and ran her soft hand across my cheek, then shifted her gaze to Ristriel. "You should not be here. They'll find you."

Ristriel had floated some distance away. He seemed thinner, and his skin was ashen as though he were sick. But of course he was—Surril beamed with starlight. Expression serious, he nodded. He looked behind him to a place I could not see, but what I assumed was the Earth Mother. "I believe they already have."

My light dimmed. "Who? Your pursuers?"

He nodded. Such a spectacular show of power—taking me up into the heavens themselves—could not be easy to hide. It was the same reason Sun could not risk Himself, not when the court of the moon battled against Him. Ristriel must have known it, and yet he had brought me anyway, simply because I had asked.

I swallowed. "Does the starlight not hide you?"

Surril answered, "Not here, Mother." She kissed my chin. "I will watch over you always and burn in your heart. But if you want him, you must go."

I turned to Ristriel. He shook his head, as though telling me to take my time. Acting as though it would not hurt him if I did.

I did not want to leave this place. I did not want to peel away from my daughter's side. But even absent the war and Ristriel's pursuers, I could not stay forever. I was still mortal enough that I could not live among the stars.

If you want him.

Ristriel was shriveling before my eyes. Sacrificing himself for me, for these brief moments of happiness with my daughter.

Quieting my own light, I kissed Surril and released her. Floating toward Ristriel, I outstretched my hand. "Let's run, Ristriel."

His too-thin fingers wove through mine, and we were flying again, stars streaking past us. I clung to him as our surroundings shifted, as we fell back toward Earth, my face tucked against his neck, his arms tight against my back. The farther we moved from the stars, the more whole he became, filling out, solidifying, until he was the only real thing around me. An anchor in the gaping expanse of space.

Our deal had been my protection for his guidance. And yet he had risked his safety, his life, to make me happy. He was more than kind. He was inspiring. Loyal, thoughtful, mysterious.

I clung to him as the Earth rushed up to meet us, never once doubting that we would land whole. Because I *did* want him. He had promised I would never be alone, not while he existed, and I wanted to believe it—and was terrified it might be a trick that would break me. For Ristriel was a godling I did not yet understand, and although I wasn't wholly mortal, I carried in me the fears of one.

But one thing was becoming certain: the thought of Ristriel leaving me behind, in Nediah or elsewhere, roused a misery in me I did not think I could face.

CHAPTER 14

We landed in the shadows behind the barn; a long strip of clouds had covered the moon. In my mind, I heard the distant galloping of otherly creatures coming for us, a sound like a bad taste on the back of my tongue. It was something I was sure I would have missed, had I been wholly mortal.

They were coming for him.

"Get your things, quickly," Ristriel urged.

"But the moon will come out soon." I gestured to our right, away from the barn. "You can conceal yourself in my pocket again."

He hesitated half a heartbeat. "If they are the same hunters, they will find it odd that they've crossed your path a second time. You might be putting yourself in danger."

I swallowed. "But I'm a star mother."

Grabbing my hand, Ristriel twisted my ring so the amber stripe shone again. "And the Sun is not here."

I looked at our entwined hands. At my ring. At his strained expression.

Throwing my skirt over my arm, I ran into the barn and scaled the ladder to the loft.

I shoved my tapestry supplies into the lighter bag and practically jumped back down. Ristriel was there, looking out the barn window.

"This would have worked better if I were a horse," he mumbled before turning his back to me and crouching, "but let me carry you. We'll go faster."

"But the moonlight—"

"I will not drop you."

Taking a deep breath, I secured my bags across my shoulders, stepped behind him, and put my arms around his neck. Where Sun was hot and fiery and all encompassing, Ristriel was cool and firm and steady. Hands grabbing my thighs, he stood, jerking upward once to situate me above his hips. I flushed, both from the touch and the embarrassment of being carried like a little girl.

When he turned to speak to me, I kissed his cheek.

"Thank you for taking me," I whispered.

He had tensed when my lips touched his skin, but his rigidity fell away at my words. "Hold on tightly."

I did, and he ran.

Ristriel moved faster than a mortal man could, though not quite as swiftly as he had when fighting off those godlings. Godlings who, I was sure, fought for the day. I wonder how Sun would have taken it, had they killed the woman He'd propositioned. I wondered, too, if He had tried to find me again during the week Ristriel and I had skipped. Or if He'd tried to come when I'd turned the ring to black, and Ristriel had taken me from Earth entirely.

Would he stop Ristriel's pursuers if I asked, or was that, too, bound by some complex law?

Ristriel dashed in a roundabout way until a cloud passed over the moon. Under the cover of darkness, he soared in a straight line, and I had to close my eyes against the wind that repelled us. We came upon a wood, and he angled toward it, perhaps to avoid his captors, or to gain cover from the moon, or both. I held tightly to him, legs and arms, focused on staying as calm as I could manage, for surely Ristriel would be forced to break his promise and drop me were my starlight to rise.

But what sort of creature could not withstand starlight? Was it not what powered the universe itself? Was it not so important that mortal women died for it? Was it not *good*?

Did that make Ristriel . . . ?

I gritted my teeth and pushed my forehead into his neck. There was nothing I could do about it now, short of let go. And had he not just taken me to see Surril, despite the harm that came to him?

The clambering of our otherworldly pursuers grew louder, and Ristriel zipped east and west so suddenly I nearly lost my grip, but he never once loosened his hold on me. Gradually, the sound of the chase lessened, though Ristriel ran on even after it had faded, running for his freedom wherever the shadows would let him.

When we finally stopped in a place utterly unrecognizable, he set me down gently and fell to his knees, breathing hard. Even godlings cannot exert themselves forever. Our pace had been so punishing my breath was labored, too, and I had not been the one sprinting.

I rested against a young tree, watching a cloud pass over the stars. A cool breeze smelled of rain, but we remained dry, for now.

I had not quite caught my breath, but I had to know. "How do you live, if starlight hurts you?"

Lifting his head, Ristriel looked up through wind-tossed hair. "I was not made by the stars."

"But the stars power the universe."

He shook his head and stood shakily. "Are you powered by the stars, Ceris?"

I opened my mouth, paused. "No. I get my strength from what grows in the Earth."

Leaning against a tree, weary, Ristriel said, "Stars power the great things of the universe, and great things power other things. It is a never-ending cycle."

I stepped closer to him. "Are you all right?"

He nodded. "I will be."

Guilt soured my mouth, but if he was talking, I needed to get as many answers as possible. "But you are a godling."

A soft smile touched his lips. "Where there is light, there is shadow. I get my strength from the darkness cast when the starlight shines. It has always been that way."

I studied his face. I was sure he did not need sleep, just as Sun didn't, but his eyes drooped and his neck hunched. I touched his face, cool as rain, and moved hair from his eyes.

"You pass," I murmured.

Ristriel tilted his head. "Pass?"

"Your next lesson for passing as a mortal." Pulling away, I touched my chin, tracing the unseen mark Surril's lips had left there. "It is a rule unspoken but always heeded among the good. Always care for those weaker than you. You pass."

He shook his head. "I am the one putting you in danger."

"No, Ristriel. You are the one taking care of me."

To my relief, he didn't argue further.

Despite uneasy sleep, I was more than eager to start out with Ristriel at dawn. Our chase had put us off course, but not terribly so. In fact, with luck, we'd be in another town by nightfall. With that thought in mind, I did my best to keep a good pace. If given the choice, I would always choose a bed over camping on the ground.

We'd not gone far when Ristriel flashed into his dark colors and dived into my pocket. He'd said nothing, but I knew there had to be a godling nearby. I searched the trees as I walked—they were strange ones, much thicker around than those back home, almost like they'd grown so weary of being tall they'd melted into themselves. Their trunks reminded me of spent candles, their branches of spider legs. They had no leaves yet, only green buds still growing.

I'm sure the lurking godling noticed me—I tended to be noticeable then—but it never presented itself or called me Star Mother. After several miles of walking, Ristriel curled out of my pocket and became a hart at my side, flicking his ears to listen just as the real animal would.

"I suppose my next lesson in being godly is to hide whenever the opportunity arises." I slipped rabbit jerky from my bag and took a bite.

The hart blinked at me. "It's safer that way," he spoke without moving his mouth.

"But it's not just you. Whatever godling we passed was hidden. In fact, I'd never seen one down here until, well . . ." I gestured to myself, to the scars still invisible to my eyes. "A godling in a lake spoke to me before I met you, but I'm sure it wouldn't have done so were I not the mother of a star."

Ristriel nodded, his hoof-falls soundless. "This is true. Many godlings prefer to live in peace, if they choose a *domain*, as you call it, on the Earth Mother. Else they might attract unwanted followers."

I understood that.

"Some want the followers, however. There are godlings who make themselves very well known. People build shrines to them and give them offerings, often without asking for anything in return. There is something peculiar about human beings and their need to worship. Their need to find hope outside themselves."

I rolled the jerky between my fingers. "It isn't a bad thing, to seek hope when you cannot find it within yourself."

"No, it is not. We have both done so."

I glanced at him. I understood my hopes, but I did not yet understand his. Not entirely.

"What do you hope for?" I asked.

He gave me that curious look again, which I could read even on the face of a deer. Like he was surprised anyone could possibly want to know.

Before he could answer, his ears pricked.

"Another godling?" I whispered.

He shook his head. "No. Mortals."

I followed his gaze through the trees. We were nearing a narrow road, a good sign that we would approach a town before the day was out. But I saw nothing.

It took a quarter hour before I heard hooves on the road. Ristriel shied into the trees, and I followed him, wondering if there might be a wagon among the party. I wouldn't mind a ride.

The horses came at a canter, a party of about four men. No women, no wagons. I shied a little farther from the road. As they neared, my stomach dropped into my hips.

I recognized them. These were men from Endwever.

I slipped behind a gnarled tree, and they almost missed me completely, but a young rider in the back slowed as he passed, calling out to the others. A soft but foul word slipped over my tongue, drawing Ristriel's attention to me.

"You there!" the man called, dismounting. I could remember his family name—Grotes—but not his first name. He was about my age. The age I should have been, that was. "Have you seen—" He paused midstride, eyes wide, and called out to the others again. "I've *found her*!"

I gripped the strap of one of my bags tightly in my hand. Ristriel, still a hart, glanced up at me. "Family?"

"No." My pulse thudded in my neck.

Two of the three men dismounted and ran over; the fourth stayed in his saddle, perhaps ready to give chase should I decide to run. The broadest of them was Callor May, descendant of Farmer May, the one whose scarecrow I had set out before my world turned upside down. I didn't recognize the other man approaching, and wondered if he'd been recruited from another town.

Callor's relief was quickly replaced by a heavy brow and narrowed eyes. "We've been searching half of Helchanar for you, Ceris!

Half-convinced you'd been eaten by wolves or murdered by bandits!" His eyes slid to Ristriel, questioning. "Never seen a hart like that."

"She's the Sun's chosen." The unfamiliar man sounded far more awed. "Of course nothing would lay a hand on her." He bowed to me.

Callor reached to seize my elbow. I twisted away. "Come," he demanded. "Let's take you home."

"If I wanted to 'go home,' I wouldn't have left," I protested. I felt starlight pricking the underside of my skin and urged it down. It would not help me here.

"Surely you jest!" Grotes's hand flew to his heart.

Callor reached forward, and this time my back thumped into the tree behind me, its rough bark catching strands of my hair.

I blinked, and as quickly as two fingers snapped together, there was a body between Callor and me, solid from the shade of the trees, skin pale, hair black as a pupil. Gooseflesh soared up my limbs.

"What the—" Callor and his companions stepped back. On the road, the mounted horseman calmed his startled gelding.

Ristriel tilted his head toward me, though his eyes remained on the Endwever riders. "Do you want to go with them?"

Such a simple question, but relief surged through my chest. "No."

He refocused on the men. "You are not welcome here."

"Who are you?" Grotes asked.

Callor's hand wrapped around the hilt of a short sword at his waist. "Stand down, man. Whatever you are. This woman is of Endwever and has been returned by the Sun Himself to bless our people for our sacrifice." My jaw set at the word *our*. "You have no jurisdiction here."

"No jurisdiction," Ristriel repeated, his voice low and quiet. He took a step forward, and the three men retreated the same distance. "You walk the face of my mother and dare tell me that?"

The shade deepened, as though a second forest had sprouted around us, canopy blocking out the morning light. My lips parted as I watched it creep over the ground like oil, even lift to swallow Grotes's shoe. He noticed and backstepped farther. The unnamed companion followed.

White gleamed all around Callor's irises. He started to unsheathe his sword, but Ristriel's hand flew out to stop him. I thought I saw ice crystals forming on Callor's glove. Tendrils of darkness unfurled into the road. Callor's horse reared and took off while the others wrestled with their own mounts.

"Go," Ristriel whispered.

Stumbling over himself, Callor sped for the road, taking off in the direction he had come, even though his horse had run off the other way. His companions were quick to follow, though Grotes hesitated a heartbeat to look back at me.

Once they vanished around the bend, the shadows receded as though they had never been, and a few spots of Sunlight glimmered through the branches, one falling on Ristriel's hand and turning him translucent.

Ristriel sighed before walking the way we'd been headed before.

I gaped at him and hurried to follow. "I—Thank you."

He nodded.

I marveled. Glanced over my shoulder, but the riders were truly gone. "Ristriel, wait."

He paused, glancing curiously at me.

So many questions pushed through my mind. "I . . . How did you . . ." The darkness had been so intense, yet casting it had seemed effortless for him. I didn't understand the powers of godlings—few mortals could, since our scriptures didn't focus on them.

One question dominated the others. "Why do you need me?" I asked, my bags heavy on my shoulders. "The godlings chasing you, Yar and Shu . . . have you never defended yourself against them?"

"No." In a flash he was a hart again; I couldn't tell if the transformation was purposeful, or what it meant. "No, I have not."

I shook my head. "Why?"

"I do not want to hurt them." He took a few light steps. Stopped. Studied me. "It would do no good, fighting them. I do not *want* to break laws. I don't want to give them a reason to . . ." He paused, monitoring himself, and I dared not press for more, vulnerable as he was. "I only want to be free."

His gaze shifted away. "I was created by war. Born into it. Perhaps that is why I've always hated it. Killing my hunters would not make me free. It would only make me hated. More would come. More will always come."

My throat tightened. I approached him as if he were a real hart, apt to startle if I moved too brashly. "So when the godlings asked if you fight for the day or the night—"

"I have never chosen a side." He dragged his hoof, and in my mind's eye I saw him running his palm over the soil beneath us. "Like the Earth Mother."

That must have been what he meant when he said, *"Walk the face of my mother."* In a way, the Earth was mother to us all. Thus her name. Still, something else nagged at me. "Ristriel, how powerful *are* you?"

He dipped his head. "Not powerful enough. Not where it matters."

I swallowed, trying to find a place for this new piece of Ristriel's puzzle. "Thank you," I said again, surprised at the emotion limning my voice. I cleared my throat. "I . . . did not want to go back."

"You were afraid."

I supposed I was.

"You do not need to be afraid, Ceris. Not with me." His ear twitched.

I nodded, and we started up the road, walking in silence for several minutes. My chest squeezed, and my fingers seemed too full of energy, so I brought up our previous conversation, needing some sort of release.

"You know," I tried, "it is not just dedicating oneself to a godling, demigod, or god that gives mortals hope." We veered a little more from the road, giving us a line of trees for privacy, or protection. Half-decayed leaves from last autumn cushioned my footfalls. "To have hope, to be happy, you must love what's around you. The trees, the air, the flowers, the people, the mountains and hills. All of it. The more love you have for your surroundings, the happier you will be. I think mortals appreciate the beauty of those simple things more than gods do." I could not imagine Sun stopping to smell a peony or listen to a bluebird.

Pausing, I noticed Ristriel was no longer walking beside me. He lingered a few paces back, standing on his legs like they belonged to a newborn fawn. His ghostly form quivered.

"Ris?" I turned back for him. He didn't look at me, so I knelt to be more level with his lowered head. "What's wrong? What did I say?"

But Ristriel was somewhere else, his dark eyes faraway. I reached a hand to him, wishing I could touch him. My fingers passed through his strong, fur-coated shoulder, and it roused him enough for his eyes to meet mine.

A weight sank from the base of my throat to my navel, dragging my insides down.

You were afraid. Yet the fear I saw in *his* eyes . . .

"What hurt you?" I whispered, searching his animal features for answers. "*Who* hurt you?"

We stayed like that for a moment, Ristriel slow to recover. Had my talk of love triggered a sour memory for him?

"Did you lose someone you loved?" I tried.

Ristriel's trembling ceased, and he looked at me with clear eyes. "No," he whispered, like a man struggling for breath. "No, there was no one."

I traced the ghostly edges of his face as though they were tangible. He tried to nuzzle my palm, and when his nose passed through it, he shifted again, this time into an indigo butterfly the size of my hand. He flew ahead, and when I followed him, he said, "We are closer than I thought."

It was then that I decided Ristriel could not be some awful felon, as I had feared him to be at my worst moments. He simply did not have it in him. And even if he *had* done something terrible, he was obviously repentant. Who was I to hold him accountable for something I myself did not understand, when it was blatantly obvious all he wanted was to break away from it?

Sure enough, a few hours later, the forest opened onto a town just a little larger than Endwever, which also nested in the heart of the forest. Many of the houses were similar, and its cathedral to the Sun was nearly identical as well, its torch unlit. People milled about, cutting wood or hanging laundry, bathing children by their porches.

Against my hair, Ristriel whispered, "I will search the forests. I'll be close." A shiver wound its way down my spine, and the butterfly flitted away, every beat of its wings silent as falling snow.

The first people who saw me were a mother and her two boys. Spying a stranger clearly worried her, because she guided them away with her hands. I didn't take offense—strangers hadn't been a common occurrence in Endwever, either, though we were close to the trade route.

An older woman planting in her garden noticed me and came over, wiping her hands on her apron. "And who might you be, miss? Not traveling alone, I hope?"

"Oh, no. My husband is in the forest." I'd last referred to Ristriel as my brother, but this woman was hardly going to trade stories with someone from our last stop. "I think he might be skinning something."

She laughed. "Leave it to a man to let a woman wander somewhere by herself. You have a place to stay? You're here for family?"

The mention of family sent a sharp chill through my stomach. "Nediah, for family."

She nodded. "You've got about five days to go, then. I'm Marda." She extended her hand to me, and I clasped it.

"I'm Ceris." I was always glad to meet friendly folk, but her countenance grew stern the moment I shared my name.

"That's an old name." She hesitated, as though trying to remember something. "What's your surname?"

I considered giving a false name, but I didn't want to lie to her. I didn't want to mask who I was. If I did, it would be like letting the zealots keep my identity for themselves.

"Wenden," I answered.

"From Endwever."

Rumors about me had clearly traveled faster than I had, but it was too late to redirect the conversation. "Yes."

Her hand grew slack, and I released it. "You're the star mother," she whispered, eyes round.

Smiling, I touched her shoulder. "I am, but please don't speak of it."

She nodded as though someone had tied a string to her forehead and forced her to. "I-I won't. Married already?"

I blanched. But surely she didn't know how long I'd been back. "Recently."

She took up both my hands in her own. "It is a blessing to have you here, Ceris. I won't speak of it if you don't wish me to, but do visit Father Meely. He was so excited when word came that a star mother had returned, alive."

Thoughts of Father Aedan made me hesitate, and yet these priests had dedicated most of their lives to the gods. It felt almost cruel to take away what could be a mark of faith for them. That, and I had Ristriel; no one would ever lock me away, so long as he was nearby.

"Of course." I glanced to the cathedral. "Marda, when *did* word come?"

"Only yesterday. Some pilgrims traveling to, oh, I think it was Nediah." She smiled warmly at me. "Mentioned the miracle of a living star mother. They were on horseback, maybe four of them, and a guard."

I wondered if these pilgrims were from Endwever, or if others had taken up a charge in my name. "Thank you."

She released me, and I made my way to the cathedral. I hadn't intended to make myself known, but at least it would guarantee we had a place to sleep tonight. People tended to be gracious when they feared the gods might be watching.

The cathedral's interior was similar to the one back home, although its sculptures and decorations were more ornate and abstract than those I'd grown up with. A gold-leaf Sun greeted me in the narthex, its face jolly and spokes wavy. I smiled to myself, wondering what Sun would think of such an interpretation. Wondering if He ever saw these visages of Himself, and if He appreciated them. Maybe they made Him feel strange the way my statue had made me feel.

I heard a man humming to himself and followed the sound, moving slowly so I could take in the décor. The windows here were not colored, but a fascinating mobile hung in the north aisle, depicting the heavens with geometric renditions of Sun, moon, Earth, and stars. One wall boasted a remarkable old tapestry that spanned a good twenty feet, detailing some obscure battle I'd never heard of. I walked around the atrium, finding a man who had to be Father Meely sitting at a small desk in the apse, copying text from one book into another, his handwriting tight and neat, the side of his hand stained with black ink.

I did not want to startle him and have him miss a stroke, so I let my shoes fall a little heavier as I approached. He glanced up and saw me, then adjusted the crooked spectacles on his nose. "Is that you, Alna?"

"My name is Ceris Wenden."

"Oh, I see." He set down his pen and stood. "My eyes aren't what they used to be unless something is right in front of . . . Did you say Ceris Wenden?"

I nodded, but not sure if he could see it, I added, "Yes."

He froze. "Of Endwever?"

"I am the star mother the pilgrims spoke of."

His lip quivered as he came around the desk, squinting at me. "My goodness, is it really you?" He bowed, winced, and straightened. He looked to be in his late sixties.

I grasped his shoulders to help him balance. "Please, there is no need to do so on my behalf. I've merely come for the night on my journey. I do not wish to be known. Marda asked me to see you."

"Yes, yes! But you must stay so we might capture your likeness—"

"I must leave in the morning to go to Nediah." Perhaps I shouldn't have mentioned my destination, but the kind father bobbed his head in understanding, and I didn't think it would be a problem. If he tried to capture me the way Father Aedan had, I was certain I could steal away again, especially with Ristriel's help.

"But of course. If you would . . . If you would write of your journey, or bless the water, or leave a print of your hand . . . I would be ever grateful."

I frowned. I didn't think I could bless anything. "I would be happy to."

This thrilled him, and he returned to his desk to sort through his limited supplies. I followed him, glimpsing the book he'd been working on, grateful my father had been literate and taught me to read. It took a few lines for me to understand what was written, and I ogled the page. "This is the gods' language."

"Oh yes, yes. Tarnos is entrusted with much of it." Tarnos must be the name of the village—Ristriel hadn't mentioned it. "It is an incomplete guide, of course, but it is our charge to remember what we can and pass it down. That is the third copy I've made, and I'm nearly finished."

I marveled at it, tracing my hand along the edges. "May I?"

"Oh! Of course." He turned the finished copy toward me and again adjusted his spectacles. "You might know a few words yourself."

I didn't, though I had occasionally heard the language spoken in Sun's palace. The book was open to the *T*s, and I carefully flipped back through the pages, watching the words fly by. *Sarn. Pon. Niana. Li. Lamen. Garalus.*

I paused, catching sight of *El* at the top of a page. It was a common sound in godly names. Beside it was written, *Of the; one who is.*

Curious, I flipped back to the *R*s, scanning down the page. Sure enough, near the middle was the word *Ristri.* My breath stuck when I read its entry.

Chains, chained. To be bound.

I pulled my hand away from the book as though it had grown claws. Ristriel . . . one who is chained?

That was the meaning of his name?

I escaped.

What kind of place had Ristriel left, if he was *named after his own captivity?*

"My dear woman, what is wrong?"

Father Meely had tilted his face very close to mine so he could better see me. Rubbing a chill from my arms, I said, "I'm sorry. It's been a long journey, and I find I am very tired. Might there be somewhere I can rest?"

"Of course!" He took me by the hand and led me toward the ambulatory. "I have a room here in this cathedral you may stay in. And do not fret over me; my son is in the village and will take me in for the night."

I swallowed. "Will he wonder why you're not here?"

"I'll promise to tell him tomorrow." He winked at me, and it wrinkled his face in such a way I laughed. "Make yourself at home. I'll see something warm brought to you."

"Thank you." I patted his hand, hoping I did a good job of masking my unease. "May the Sun bless you for your kindness."

Ristriel hovered outside my window just before the last of the Sun disappeared into the horizon.

I sat up on Father Meely's narrow bed, having tried to sleep earlier and finding I could not. I ran my thumb over Sun's ring. "How do you find me?"

He didn't quite touch the windowsill. "I looked for your starlight. Tarnos is not a large place."

So he did know the town's name. I paused for a moment, working through my thoughts. "One of the godlings, from before"—I treaded carefully—"he said he saw 'her darkness' in you. What did he mean?"

His dark gaze regarded me for a beat. "Starlight and shadow are not good and evil, as many mortals depict them. They are simply light and dark. My purpose has always been good, even if I was born of the dark."

Scooting to the edge of the bed, I asked, "What do you mean, 'born of the dark'?"

He studied my face in such an earnest way my cheeks warmed. Did he ever flush, or was he always cool as a summer stream? "I was created in war. The feud between the Sun and the moon is everlasting, nearly as old as they are. I am one of the moon's scars." He considered for a moment, almost touching the cathedral, but refrained, and I wondered at his hesitation. "A portion of her dark side fell to the Earth Mother," he explained, hands clasped together, thumbs fidgeting. "The Earth Mother gives life to all things, and thus I was born."

My lips parted as I tried to comprehend life created in such a manner. "The moon is your mother."

"The Earth is also my mother," he clarified, "but the ways of the gods are not the ways of mortals. It is not . . . the same."

I thought of the pleading look he had given the sky when the moon was out. Did he yearn to have a mother, as a mortal would?

Did he want to be loved by her?

I slunk off the bed and crossed to the window, pressing both hands to its marble base. "Ristriel, who named you?"

His eyes widened, vulnerable and round.

And then an un-Earthly howl sounded beyond the village. A sound I would not have heard if I didn't have starlight within me.

I knew immediately that we had not evaded Ristriel's would-be captors as well as we had hoped. His eyes dropped to my ring.

I twisted the line to black. "We should hurry."

He nodded and vanished. I collected my things and rushed toward the exit, but stopped at Father Meely's desk. The supplies were all there, and I would feel ungrateful leaving him with nothing. So I quickly painted my hand with ink and pressed it into a delicate piece of parchment. He would find it in the morning.

Ristriel met me outside the cathedral's only door, and together we dashed into the forest.

They came for us like wolves.

The un-Earthly howling seemed to reverberate between the trees, not waking a single creature, yet piercing me as though I were canvas and they were the needles, pulling rough thread through my body in misaligned stitches. We passed under moonlight, and Ristriel became a horse. As soon as we stepped back into shadow, he forcefully pushed at me with his head, lifting me onto his back. I barely had time to grab fistfuls of mane before he darted into the forest. He tried to keep to the shadows as before, but the moon was too bright, the trees too squat, and the moment we passed through a glimmer of moonlight, I fell through Ristriel's body as though it weren't even there, barely managing to avoid injury. He became a man once more, grabbed my hand and my bags, and pulled me through the night, occasionally losing his grip due to the magic of the moon.

Branches cracked and the ground quaked as the rhythm of our pursuers grew louder. Ristriel dashed behind a thick, misshapen tree, breathing hard as though he were mortal. "Stay here," he said. "Hide. They've no qualm with you."

I shook my head and grabbed his arm. "I'm not going to leav—"

A whistle through the air was the only warning before Ristriel's eyes widened, and suddenly he jerked away from me as though caught on a line. And he was. In the weak light between the shadows of trees, I could see some sort of ivory harpoon embedded in his leg, silvery light and indigo blood pooling around it.

"No!" I screamed, my skin burning silver. I chased after him, catching sight of Shu, the godling with the silver horns, at the end of the magicked rope secured to the harpoon. The gremlin godling growled at his feet, and Yar wheeled around toward us as though he were his own great mount.

Ristriel groped at his leg, gasping. The shadows began to shift around him, but Shu mercilessly pulled on the rope, dragging Ristriel forward another foot. "None of that."

"Unhand him!" I cried, rushing to his side. I burned brighter than ever before, casting new light in the grove. Ristriel's face was pale and wan, and he shook his head and pushed at me, trying to get me to escape.

But I would not leave him.

Yar came around behind me, stirring old foliage beneath him. If he recognized me, if he knew I had lied to him before, he made no mention. "You know not what you protect." He drew an ivory net from his belt. "Get back, or you will answer for his crimes."

I looked back at the great brute with the blue-striped horns, my hands shaking, my skin burning with starlight I couldn't control. I was angry, I was afraid, and I was hurting Ristriel. I had to be, for he was of shadow, and this power was not.

I was staring at the heartless Yar when I saw a bit of debris pass by him, as though caught on a strong wind. But there was no wind tonight.

I remembered Surril and the halo surrounding her.

Their power attracts the unmade things of the universe.

Yar neared, and I pushed into the starlight instead of restraining it, stoking its heat like I would a fire. I poured myself into my anger, my fear, my *need*, and it brightened more than my eyes should have been able to bear. It lit the grove as if it were noonday. Foliage, debris, and dirt flew around me in a perfect circle, gaining in speed. Pieces of bark tore from the trees to join the fray. Plants uprooted themselves as the tumult gained strength.

Shu lost a spear to the spinning. Yar had to grip his net with both hands. The gremlin flew until his body hit a tree.

"Stop this at once!" Yar bellowed.

But one cannot simply command the stars to stop shining.

I stood in the midst of my tornado and screamed, *"You will not have him!"*

And then my starlight grew so bright I could see nothing else.

CHAPTER 15

I started awake, splayed across the forest floor like a fallen doll, and jerked upright into a sitting position. My breathing was heavy; a few leaves drifted to the Earth. I had not been out long. A smattering of metallic dust covered half of one of the trees hit by the gremlin, and I wasn't sure if it was some sort of godly blood or if the small godling had perished. I saw no signs of Yar or Shu. Even Shu's harpoon was gone. That hungry sensation, not quite fatigue, buzzed through my body.

Ristriel lay in the shadows, still as a corpse. The tree closest to him appeared to be rotting, its branches drooping downward as if to point to the place he had fallen.

"Ris!" I cried, crawling to him. I blinked, trying to see better. My starlight had winked out, and only the light of the sleeping heavens guided me. I took Ristriel's head into my lap. He was cool to the touch, but he always was. His chest still rose and fell beneath the semblance of his clothing.

Panicked, I grabbed one of my fallen bags, looking through it for medicine, bandages, my needles and thread—anything that would help him. In doing so, I noticed a sliver of moonlight across the back of my hand.

Moonlight. I had always thought it weakened him, but did it not also ignite his ability to change? And if he could reorder his body, perhaps he could close the wound in his leg.

I had to try.

Abandoning my things, I rushed to Ristriel and grabbed him under the shoulders. For a being seemingly made of shade and pixie dust, he was heavy as any mortal. I searched our grove, finding moonlight just at the edge of it, where the trees thinned. Above us, a narrow cloud loomed close to the waning moon. I glared at it, daring it to pass over the light.

It took several ungraceful jerks, my feet occasionally slipping on the recently remade forest floor, before I managed to drag Ristriel into the moonlight. The moment the light fell over his shoulders, my hands passed through him, and I had to *push* him in instead. I managed it, and he turned shades of purple and blue, glimmering like an early night sky.

He gasped and sat up, and I dropped against the roots of the tree, fatigue finally smothering me. I looked at his leg, but it was the same ethereal substance as the rest of him, as though the injury had never been.

His dark eyes found mine. "Ceris."

I breathed hard, letting my body relax. "They're gone."

Shaking his head, he came to my side. "You have made enemies of them."

"I hardly care." My ring was still black. Sun would not know unless Yar and Shu told Him, and they did not seem the kind to readily admit their mistakes.

Ristriel paused, staring at me like I'd spoken another language. He lifted a hand, but it was spirit, and it passed through my cheek.

Sitting back, he shook his head a second time. "You mustn't do that again."

"I wanted to help you."

"You mustn't," he repeated, firm. His tone was a mix of anger and fear, just as mine had been moments ago. "You only have so much starlight within you. You must use it wisely."

I paused. *That* was the emptiness I felt, then. The siphoning of my starlight, each time I used it. Sitting up straighter, I found some energy in indignation. "And that wasn't wise? They were going to *take* you, Ris. You might not fight back, but I will."

He pressed his lips together. Looked away. "I should not have bargained with you."

"Too late." I wiped my hand across my forehead. "It's my starlight. I'll use it as I see fit."

"You will become mortal."

"And what's wrong with being mortal?" I pushed myself up, then found I lacked the strength to stand. "I've been mortal my whole life."

He didn't answer for a beat. "It would be a great loss to see you die young."

Exhaustion swept over my anger, uncovering honesty. "Oh, Ris. I don't know if I want a life that doesn't have you in it."

It was more of a confession than I'd intended to make, and a sudden one, for I'd known the godling only a week—two if I counted the time skip—but he was so much a part of my morning, noon, evening, and night I honestly couldn't imagine returning to a life that did not include him, even if I were successful in finding my sister's descendants in Nediah.

He didn't look at me, but knelt, thoughtful, quiet.

Minutes passed. "Perhaps we should go somewhere safer," I suggested.

He glanced up, taking in the metallic spattering on the tree in the wood. "We have time. You need to rest. Your body isn't resilient enough to move on yet."

Resilient enough to birth a star, just not wield the power of one. But I was too exhausted to point out the irony. And so, under Ristriel's silent watch, I fell asleep cradled in the roots of a tree, moonlight on my face.

The dawn was so bold and bright that it penetrated my eyelids, banishing my dreams in a plume of smoke. I opened my eyes and blinked at the brightness, lifting a hand to block it, noting sore muscles as I did so.

It took me a moment to realize it was not the dawn that had woken me, but Sun Himself.

I startled into alertness and sat up, noting the forest around me was bathed in shades of night. And Ristriel—Ristriel was gone.

"What did you do to him?" I launched to my feet, heart in my throat.

Sun raised a golden eyebrow. "To whom?"

My wits rushed to make sense of the situation. The Sun was here. Ristriel must have sensed Him coming, like before, and vanished. Yar and Shu had not yet reported to Him. I did not know Sun as well as I should, but like Ristriel, He was honest, and not one to play games. He did not know.

My eyes adjusted, I lowered my hand. "I-I'm sorry, nothing. Just a bad dream."

Sun hummed deep in His throat. "One of the many gifts of mortals."

I had been searching the woods, wondering if that metallic glitter was still there, or if Ristriel might pop up his head, but Sun's comment jerked my attention back to Him. "Dreams?"

He held out a hand as though offering me something. "Immortals do not need sleep, and so We do not dream. I have always found the idea of a theater of the mind fascinating, and yet it is one thing I cannot, and will not, understand."

"I didn't know." Though it made sense. "They can be very . . . peculiar. Sometimes they are pleasant, sometimes they are scary, other times they are simply . . . there. And they are not always remembered."

He nodded. "Why have you deactivated your ring?"

Flushing, I glanced down at my hand. I twisted the golden loop so the amber band shone across its center. How Sun found me, I wasn't sure, but we had not ventured far from Tarnos, where the ring had last been active. My burst of starlight had likely played a role as well. "I-I tinker with it sometimes. I must not have realized." The lie felt thick on my tongue.

The Sun gazed up at the sky. "I have little time, Ceris. Please, will you come with Me?"

And Sun was so earnest, I nodded. He offered me His elbow. I hesitated, fighting the impulse to turn around, to look for Ristriel. I took His elbow. He was hot to the touch, like a raging fever, but like before, His heat did not harm me. It was quite pleasant, after a chilly night in the wood.

The Sun lifted His foot as if He were climbing a staircase, and the world shifted around us. I did not *feel* it, like I had when Ristriel brought me to my daughter. There was no dizzying sensation, no falling, no wind in my hair. I simply was one place and then I was another, a tunnel of light like a tilting hallway, never ending.

"Tell me of your dream," Sun asked.

I flushed, my lie spinning webs around me. I could not remember my dreams from the night before, so I grasped the first segments of one I *could* remember. "I was a cat, but then I was not."

He glanced down at me, confusion wrinkling the golden skin between His eyebrows.

"That is, I started the dream as a cat, but then I was someone else, watching the cat," I explained. "And there was a ball of string I could not unwind, and it was increasingly frustrating, until I realized it was cheese carved to look like a ball of string." I laughed; it seemed so much stranger said out loud. Remembering my earlier excuse, however, I made up the rest. "And then there was a great wolf chasing me, and my owner was trying to fight him off, and . . . I woke up."

The Sun seemed content with my explanation. "Strange, indeed. I would love to hear more of your dreams."

"I do not think we have the time to cover them all. Besides, the longer you live away from a dream, the harder it becomes to remember."

He waited a breath before speaking. "If you were to be with Me, Ceris, you could tell Me of your dreams every morning."

I shrunk into myself, feeling guilt of all things. Like I was being dishonest with Him—technically I had been—even though I had promised Him nothing.

"Sun, I don't know if—"

"Saiyon," He urged gently. "You may call Me Saiyon."

My earlier thought dropped into the tunnel of light, forgotten. "Not 'Satto'?" That was what many in His palace had called Him.

"I have many names." He lifted His other hand and placed it atop mine, where I held the crook of His arm. "Saiyon was my first."

A mix of cold and heat swirled in my belly. I felt like I had been entrusted with something sacred, and that made me feel loved, special. There were very, very few who knew this name, as I would later learn. I was . . . touched.

"Would you like to see the heavens?" He spoke more quietly now, His voice reverent. "I will show them to you, if you wish."

I gaped at Him, His broad and powerful features. "I-I thought it was too dangerous."

"The danger is held off, for now, but it won't be long before it resurfaces. I would show you the kingdom. And our daughter, if you wish."

Surril! Her name sang in my very bones, but the glee of reuniting with her flashed to fear. Would she tell her father that I had already been to see her? Would I have to falsify my reaction and make it seem like my first?

Would Saiyon accept that I had found another celestial creature to take me, and leave it at that? Would He be angry, thinking I'd endangered myself?

If He truly cared about me, would any of it matter?

Squeezing Saiyon's arm, I nodded my consent.

The light tunnel brightened and spiraled away, and I saw the stars—
so many stars. It awed me no less than when Ristriel had taken me into
the night sky. I wanted to see Surril first—she was my greatest trea-
sure—but fear for Ristriel kept my mouth still. Instead, I let Saiyon
take me where He willed.

I was not disappointed.

He took me deeper into the stars, to wild clouds of every color
and shade imaginable, so vivid and bizarre I could never re-create them
in stitchwork or watercolor or anything else. They were beautiful and
beastly, and we passed through them, clouds of green and crimson and
turquoise passing under my hand. I saw planets. *Enormous* planets made
of swirling smoke, with demigod moons spinning around them, gold,
silver, copper, topaz. I saw *rings* as Ristriel had described, great circles
of worlds light and stone. We passed over charcoal-encrusted ruins,
covered in rolling rocks with jagged edges lined with ice. When I asked
about it, Saiyon told me it was an ancient battlefield from long ago, and
by the distant look in His eyes, I knew it was a battle He had fought in.

I saw enormous moving necklaces of stars, which Saiyon called
galaxies, twirling and beaming, so grand that even Saiyon seemed small
in comparison.

And then He took me to Surril, and I was so glad to see her I
laughed and wept and hugged her. She greeted me with eager arms and
her father with a reverent bow. Again, I could not stay long, and I hated
it, but I took in what I could. Her lovely face, her tinkling laugh, her
stories of the siblings around her and the great storm she had seen on
the Earth Mother, on the other side of the world from where I traveled.

When it came time to depart, she drew me close, our starlight
mixing and brightening, and whispered, "They search north for you."

I knew she meant Yar and Shu. I didn't want to give us away, so I
said nothing but my farewell, tied with a promise that I would see her
again as soon as I was able.

Saiyon took my hand, and we flew through the heavens for minutes that seemed like years. The wonders around us mesmerized me, swallowing me with their vastness, until the tunnel of light rose around me again, and though I did not have the sensation of falling, I did feel a sort of descension guiding me back to Earth.

"Saiyon," I said, after my mortal mind found a way to reorient itself after beholding the kingdoms of gods, "would You not have cared for me had I died like all the others?"

His heat cooled, then flared. "Do not hold Me accountable for the laws of the universe. Would you have no stars?"

"I am not blaming You. I am only asking."

Another low hum emanated from within Him, somewhere inside His chest. "What I know is that I care for you, Ceris Wenden. Star Mother. What I do not know is if I would have loved the others as well."

That word, *loved*, made me shiver despite Saiyon's fiery presence, and I found I could not speak again until my feet touched the Earth Mother's back, returned to the forest where I had slept.

"Thank You, Saiyon." His name rolled from my tongue like a prayer.

He cupped the side of my face, His touch so brilliantly hot, so painfully genuine. "Consider Me, Ceris."

And then He vanished, the dawn rose, and the world seemed dark in His absence.

I oriented myself toward Nediah as best I could before I searched the trees. "Ris?" I whispered, ducking under boughs and startling when a fawn darted behind me. I half expected Saiyon to return in fury, or Ristriel's hunters to come upon me, but the forest was quiet and pleasant, the day's temperature comfortable, the sky blue and clear with a smattering of puffy white clouds.

It had taken him a few hours to find me last time, so I hoped for the best and ate breakfast while I walked, careful with my steps, for those stumpy trees liked to pop their roots aboveground. When noon came and Ristriel still hadn't reappeared, I found a place to rest and pulled out my tapestry to work on his likeness. While I worked, I sang the songs I'd sung to him, quietly at first, then a little louder, getting a peculiar look from a nearby cardinal. I sang verse after verse, and when I finished I started again, pausing my needlework on occasion to pop a piece of cheese or dried fish into my mouth.

When I finished the song for the seventh time, Ristriel's voice said, "Won't you sing it again?"

I turned toward the sound to find him sitting on a thick branch overhead, or rather floating very close to it to give the illusion of sitting. I smiled. "I was worried I'd go hoarse, calling for you."

"For me?"

I nodded, and he floated down, landing without sound on the Earth. He looked ashamed. "I had to leave—"

"I know." I rolled up my tapestry and slipped it into my bag. "I'm glad you did. I don't want anything to happen to you."

He looked at my tapestry, curious, but didn't ask about it. "Where did He take you?"

"To the heavens, and to Surril," I answered, wondering again at the marvels I had seen, but I only said, "I didn't tell Him you took me first."

His lip quirked, and he pointed me more eastward than I had been traveling, waiting for me to start walking before he fell into step beside me. "Ceris."

"Hm?"

He watched his feet instead of me, dark hair falling into his eyes. He looked so human, so alive, but the mirage faltered every time he walked through a beam of Sunlight. "It is a new moon tonight."

Was it already? I was still recuperating from losing time after that battle, when a false new moon had darkened the sky.

"I will be whole the night through," he explained. "If you want, I can carry you to Nediah. We would be there by morning." He paused, and a twig snapped under my foot. "Otherwise, it is a three-day journey by foot."

One night to Nediah. I hadn't realized it was so close. One night, because Ristriel could move so swiftly, even when burdened with me. One night with a godling's magic, or three days on my own mortal feet.

One more night with Ristriel, or three more days.

"I . . . enjoy walking." I tucked a few stray hairs behind my ear. "Three days isn't long." Remembering Surril's warning, I added, "But I suppose it would be better for you, to put distance between the hunters and us."

To be free of me and start a new path, but my throat was too tight to say as much.

Ristriel glanced over his shoulder. "They will not catch me." His gaze returned to me like an early spring wind, and it raised goose bumps on my flesh. "But Nediah is what you want, isn't it?"

I rolled my lips together, thinking, my pulse quickening ever so slightly. "It is one of the things I want."

Daring to meet his gaze, I noticed that he'd stopped walking, and so I halted as well. He lifted a hand, then dropped it, unable to touch anything in the light of day.

Unable to touch me.

Looking away, he began walking again, but we only went a few paces before he stopped once more and faced me.

"When you said . . ." He hesitated, stood straighter. "When you said I was the one who took care of you. Ceris . . ."

I wrapped a hand around my braid and squeezed it, unsure what he was trying to say.

He swallowed, a very human gesture. "You are the only one who has *ever* cared for me."

Those words settled in my bones like a midwinter night. I closed the distance between us, made the semblance of touching his arm. I wanted to cradle his face and bring it close to mine, lean my forehead against his, but such a thing was impossible. It infuriated me and gave my voice an edge when I next spoke. "Those who haven't are fools. You are kind and true, Ristriel, and noble and loyal and everything good. You are worthy of all the universe has to offer you. All *I* can offer you."

I would have kissed him then, had he been tangible. I had only ever kissed Caen, and only then on the day I had left. I hadn't even kissed Saiyon, though I had given Him everything else. But I would have kissed Ristriel there in the forest to seal my promise, to clear my confusion, to speak what words were too weak to relate. For indeed I did care about him. I didn't want to admit it then, but I was falling in love with him.

He looked at me as though he might cry, which made me want to cry, and he bowed his head to me, whispering, "Thank you," in the most sincere, featherlight manner I had ever heard.

"We should take the southern route," I whispered, smiling to reassure him. "I have good word from a certain star that we'll be the safest that way."

We continued walking, stretching one day's travel into three, if only to maximize our time together.

Near dusk, when I was preparing our small camp, Ristriel tensed. I knew immediately that our pursuers from the night before were close, so when he gestured for me to hurry in a different direction, I did so without word, sprinting as best I could without sound. The ground declined, and we reached a swift-moving but shallow stream and crossed it quickly. Ristriel darted back the way we'd come, breathtakingly fast, and dipped into the trees. A moment later, a flock of starlings rose from the trees a good distance from us. He was trying to throw our pursuers off our tracks.

He returned just as swiftly. Night swarmed us, and without the moon, I couldn't see where I was going. Ristriel, physical once again, took my hand and guided me. I remembered him saying Saiyon could not find him in his ethereal state. Could Yar and Shu better hunt him when he was physical?

Tonight was the new moon . . .

I heard our pursuers in the distance, just as I had at the cathedral.

"Don't breathe," he whispered, and pushed me against the nearest tree, the bark clinging to my dress like nails. He pressed himself against me, toe to toe, hips to hips, shoulders to shoulders, and not breathing became increasingly hard. He was a godling, a shapeshifter, but he felt every bit a man. Even his clothing felt real, for I clung to it with my fingers. I focused on staying dark, on keeping my starlight buried.

Like on the battlefield, blackness began to seep out from Ristriel, soft as incense, swirling and clinging. It made it look like the tree itself was growing up around us, making us part of it, concealing us from the rest of the world. It reminded me of what he'd done to the riders from Endwever, but this darkness seemed more encompassing. More absolute.

On another night, it might not have been enough, but without the moon to illuminate us, it was a powerful ruse. My breath burned within my lungs as the sounds of pursuit grew louder, *louder*, and then softer as they passed by us, growing distant.

I gasped for air, breast heaving against Ristriel's chest. We stayed like that for minutes after the forest quieted, pressed together like lovers. I touched his hip, and he settled his chin atop my head, breath in my hair.

His darkness receded like paint washed away in the rain. The starlit forest seemed bright in comparison. For a moment we looked at each other, noses nearly touching, our faces little more than shade and shadow.

I allowed myself to wonder, briefly, if giving myself to him would hurt as it had with Saiyon, or if I would hurt him, because of my starlight.

But then Ristriel stepped back from me, his hands running down my arms until they grasped my fingers. "The war continues," he murmured, soft as a moth's wings. He looked back at the tree, sorrow limning his features. I couldn't see what he saw in the darkness, but as we departed, opposite the way Yar and Shu had gone, I thought I smelled the faintest wisp of rot.

After that day, Ristriel changed. He was lighter, happier. He asked me to share stories of my life, my family, my pranks, and I gladly did, finding joy in remembering the life I had left behind. He, in turn, talked about the places he'd seen, using names I couldn't pronounce and architecture that sounded impossible until he shifted into a semblance of it, allowing me to glimpse the mysteries on the other side of the Earth Mother. It started a game with us, where I would name a creature and he'd shift into it, making me laugh, especially when he exaggerated size or color. He truly had seen all the world, for there was not a single beast, even mythical, that he did not know, but he showed me many I had never heard of. Saiyon had opened the heavens for me, but Ristriel showed me the magic of my own world.

Near the end of the day, I asked him, "Ris, what is your true form? Your original shape?"

He paused, his shape stuck on a funny creature called a "giraffe." "I don't know. I don't remember. But . . . I like this one."

He shifted again into a man. The man I had come to identify him as. It felt like a true form to me, for though mankind comes in every shape, size, and color, Ristriel was always consistent in his interpretation. Always the same face, the same hair, the same build. Always beautiful, and never a stranger.

"I like it, too." I wanted to take his hand, but the Sun still shone upon us, so I settled on wishing for it instead.

CHAPTER 16

Ristriel was right.

In our three days of walking, the wood thinned and opened, and the fourth morning we topped a hill and looked out over a wide expanse. A large lake shimmered in the distance, and beyond that the spikes of a faraway mountain range, but before all of it, nestled in grassy hills, was the first true city I'd ever seen.

Nediah.

A thick stone wall surrounded it, but from our vantage point, I could see its houses and shops, clustered close together like sleeping mice. The city arched up, encapsulating one of the hills, and a great cathedral sat at its highest point, its golden spire shining in the morning light. I squinted—there was something else on that spire, but I was too far away to see what.

"That is it," Ristriel murmured. "Your new home."

"It might be. If the Parroses live there, and if they accept me." I kneaded a knuckle into my stomach. It was tight and uneasy, which made the thought of breakfast unappealing.

"They would be fools not to."

I smiled at him, warmed by the words. "Come with me, Ristriel. Walk with me."

He nodded, and we descended the hill together. When we reached the next, I noticed the cemetery.

It was outside the city, marked off by a four-foot fence studded with spikes to keep out wild animals. It was large and green, and the smell of honeysuckle wafted from it.

Changing direction, I moved toward the fence. There were a few people within. I came to the fence and followed it around until I found the gate. As soon as I entered, a man who looked to be in his late forties approached me. I had expected Ristriel to flit away, to hide in my hair or my pocket, but he stayed by my side. The day was warm, the sky spotted with clouds, and his colors made him appear ordinary.

"I'm the keeper here," the older man said. "What are you seeking?"

"Parros family."

He nodded as though the request were perfectly normal, which gave me hope. Gesturing for us to follow, he walked toward a small building I'd thought was a sepulcher, but turned out to be a utility shed and office all in one. He flipped through the pages of a tome on a crooked table.

"G-14." He pointed south. "Look for the pegs in the ground."

I glanced to Ristriel, hope rising in my throat. I walked south, noticing metal pegs in the ground stamped with letters and numbers. I found row G easily, and lot fourteen was near the other end of the fence. Some of the graves were like the ones in Endwever, weathered and illegible. Some were only months old.

"Parros," I said, running my hand over the closest one. *Yosef Parros,* passed two years ago at the age of fifty-one. "The surname is here, all right. I just need to find them."

I'd run through the meeting in my mind so many times, sifting through different scenarios accounting for all sorts of reactions. Mistrust, disbelief, happiness, tears . . . I'd tried to prepare myself for every possible outcome. The worst-case scenario was either not finding my family at all or finding them and being outright rejected, in which case I'd have to make my home somewhere else, or take Saiyon up on His offer.

I glanced at Ristriel, wondering if he could ever make a home among mortals, or if he'd be forever running, leaving me behind to grow old without aging. Would he stay by my side, if I chose to stop moving? Would he be able to?

"Come with me to the city?" I'd never been an anxious person, but facing that large place on my own became suddenly daunting. I'd never been to a city before. Part of me wanted to turn back into the forest and simply get lost in it, never to face another human being again.

But Ristriel nodded, and I breathed out my relief. Once we left the cemetery, he said, "I will have to be careful if there are crowds, but I will do my best."

Crowds, because anyone might simply walk through Ristriel instead of bumping into him, and that could cause anything from confusion to a riot. As Ristriel had said, humans were superstitious creatures. "Thank you." I let my fingers pass through his, and a cool chill ran up my arm. Ristriel stepped closer to me, enough so that, were he solid, our shoulders would brush. I wished that I could feel his hand in mine as I approached this enormous place where I knew no one. So I could have something steady to hold on to. So that he could whisk me away if something went wrong.

I glanced up at the Sun, willing more clouds to bar the light.

Then I turned my ring off.

There were guards at the gate, but they stood there casually, welcoming the coming and going of visitors. The wall was old, perhaps built long ago as a fortification in battle, and the city was densely packed within it. The crowded streets, crammed with shops, homes, and people, were not good for Ristriel, but I marveled. The throngs were thickest down the large streets, especially toward the centers, where people of all sizes and shapes pushed past one another, or shouted so their haggling could be heard over their neighbors'. We avoided the worst of it by following the narrower routes close to the wall, hugging the stone as we passed tradesmen and sweetshops, skinny houses sharing walls, a horse market. I found two men sitting outside a closed tavern, playing a game of stones, and asked them if they knew where the Parroses lived. They did not, so we moved on. I asked a woman leading a child by the hand, but she did not, either.

I had some hope when we stumbled across the blacksmith, smoke rising from his bellows. I had been told the Parroses had left Endwever to pursue metalworking.

But the blacksmith was not a Parros, and the name was unfamiliar to him. He wasn't even sure how many blacksmiths the city had. Was Nediah so large?

We wandered a little farther, and I found a woman selling warm sweet buns from a basket and used a bit of my precious coin to purchase one. Ristriel melded with the shadows until I returned, and then he walked by me once more, occasionally flashing solid when we passed under stone bridges that shut out the Sunlight. Beneath an especially large one, I finally did grab his hand, squeezing much too hard, but he didn't so much as wince. He clasped my fingers tightly, until we passed the bridge and he became a spirit again.

The city spiraled upward like a conch, and the more we walked, the higher we climbed, the ground slowly elevating a bit at a time until I could see over the main wall. I stopped here and there, asking if anyone knew of the Parros family. Most willingly answered, all said no. Even Ristriel took to asking around, approaching those who looked less savory, who might take advantage of a lost woman. He gathered nothing of use, either, though he did get directions to a second blacksmith. The man's forge was closed when we arrived, but a neighbor confirmed he was not a Parros, either.

The cobblestones were rougher than the natural Earth, and by the time evening settled over the city, my feet ached. I knew I had much of the city left to explore, that I should not give up yet, but my heart was heavy, and my ears buzzed with the noise of so many bodies. At least no one looked at me strangely, for in a place this large, strangers were common. At first, it was a relief not to be noticed. But after several hours, I began wishing someone would shout out, *Star Mother!* and cause a stir, and a crowd would form, and *one* of them would know about the Parroses who'd moved here so long ago, and who had graves in the local cemetery.

Instead of continuing to wind around the city, we cut through it by taking a stairway between high stone walls, wide enough for only one person to pass at a time. Ristriel walked behind me, encouraging me when I had to stop for a breath, pressing a hand into the small of my back, for like beneath the bridges, the stonework blotted out the Sun. I leaned into his touch, and not only because I was tired.

We emerged at the top of the hill-like city, the setting Sun bright, its golden rays washing over Nediah, and Ristriel's touch evaporated. We had come out near the cathedral. I paused simply to gape at it, for it was the largest church I'd ever beheld, easily seven times the size of the one in Endwever. Its gray stone turned white the farther up it went, where the Sun had bleached it, and its golden spire was enormous—at *least* two stories, but it was hard to judge from the ground. I wondered how anyone had managed to get it up there. Fastened to the spire was a golden Sun, rays like waving daggers, without a face. It had to be the size of a house.

If there was anywhere that would help me, this was it.

I crossed the road toward the heavy double doors at the front. I was approaching the steps leading up to them when Ristriel spoke. "Ceris."

His hand was out, like he wanted to touch me. The Sun's rays were so bright here I could see through him, despite his best efforts. I quickly surveyed our surroundings. A few people milled about, but thus far, none had noticed him.

I gestured for him to come up the stairs, into the shade, but he shook his head. "I will wait for you out here. I dare not step into His house."

"He isn't here." I pointed to the sky.

But the godling's resolve didn't waver. "I dare not risk it. Neither for myself, nor for you."

Pressing my lips together, I forced myself to nod. I had never been timid, even as a child, but in this massive place, I desperately wanted Ristriel by my side. "I'll be swift."

Ristriel managed a weak smile, then stepped away. Somewhere in the bright bands of evening Sun, he shifted, and a midnight butterfly swept around the cathedral's far corner.

Steeling myself, I entered the cathedral, pulling back on the right door with all my weight to open it. The hinges were well oiled; no creaking announced my presence.

The cathedral was enormous, but otherwise quite similar to the others I'd visited. The aisles were wide, the floors made of granite, or perhaps marble, with long yellow carpets trailing their center. The nave was lined with enormous arches, the crest of each carved with a Sun. These Suns were simple, without faces, and had only six spokes. Suns and stars were carved into the columns as well, and at the columns' bases, the image of a dark circle pierced with a sword. I wondered if that represented the moon.

A hymn rang through the halls. As I walked, I noticed a large children's choir rehearsing. Perhaps one of them was a Parros, but I dared not interrupt their song. I saw no caretaker or priest, so I let myself wander, circling around the aisles, taking my time gazing at portraits and sculptures in the transept.

It was there I saw something that made my breath catch. A copper bust, turned turquoise, in a crystal case atop a podium, barred off by both a wooden railing and a velvet cord. It was a depiction of a woman, and a star was carved upon her brow.

I knew her immediately, before even reading her dedication.

Star mother.

I quickly read the engraved plate beneath her likeness. Her name was Agradaise, chosen by the Sun nearly five hundred years before I was. Chosen from Nediah.

And she was buried here as well.

Shivers coursed up my arms and down my legs. I whirled around, looking at the cathedral through new eyes, its aisles and arches suddenly like a maze I was trapped in. I retraced my steps as the choir started another song. Near the apse, I found a cleverly hidden passageway that led down into the cathedral's basement.

Into the crypt.

I descended the stairs, the air growing significantly colder. Below, everything was solid, common stone. Large shelves had been carved into the wall, some holding coffins, others bearing exposed bones.

Agradaise was not hard to find. Her tomb was above the floor, in a fine coffin made from magnificent marble limned with gold. How far the people had gone to mine it, I couldn't guess. It was raised on a stone dais, surrounded by the same golden cords protecting her likeness upstairs, though these were braided together to make them thicker. Like my statue in Endwever, the edges of the coffin were worn and smooth from the passing of thousands, if not millions, of hands. She had lain down here for twelve hundred years, after all.

"Agradaise," I whispered, hoping I pronounced her name right. I would not think of lifting the lid—I would find a skeleton there, perhaps laid with a crown and glass roses. But I did lift my hand to the smooth marble edge of her casket. If I said her name to Saiyon, would He remember anything about her? How many star mothers had passed between her time and mine?

Running my fingers across the cool stone, I whispered, "Agradaise, I wish I had known you."

And then my vision burned white.

CHAPTER 17

I was still in the cathedral. The stone remained firm under my feet. The musty smell lingered in my nose, and the chill slid beneath my clothes.

But my mind was elsewhere.

Everything around me was white and pearlescent, not unlike starlight. Not unlike Saiyon's palace, for there was nothing, and yet at the same time *everything*. I could sense forms around me too bright to behold. I heard distant peals of laughter and something like birdsong but distinctly *other*. The presence of deities and spirits enfolded my skin like warm breaths.

It was so overwhelming, so utterly beautiful, I began to cry.

A figure broke away from the others and moved toward me, her visage just as bright as everything else, yet her form had more definition. Like she was allowing me to see past her glory, similar to what Saiyon did. Her face was comparable to the bust, but here it looked ageless, beautiful, without flaw or blemish. Without any of the cares of the world.

"I have heard of you, Ceris." Her voice was music no mortal could hope to compose. "I would have liked to meet you."

I blinked, but the tears continued to stream down my face, like I stared at Saiyon in His full power. "Are we not meeting now?"

She reached forward and touched my chin, though her fingers were insubstantial. "You are lovely and strong. You will look after our stars until we meet them again, won't you?"

I realized at that moment, clear as dawn, that I was peeking into the great hereafter promised to star mothers, though I had not the power to fully behold it.

Reaching up, I wiped my sleeve across my eyes. But when I opened them again, the crypt surrounded me. The stone seemed so plain, so lifeless, compared to my vision. The marble I had just found exquisite seemed made of dust. Everything was too dark, too shadowed, too cold.

Even Saiyon's palace could not compare to what I had seen, and now that it had been taken from me, I felt empty.

I pressed one palm, then another, against the coffin. "Agradaise?" I whispered, willing her to return. Grasping for another peek into that beautiful paradise surrounding her. Were my parents there, my sisters? Caen?

Nothing happened.

"Agradaise?" My voice echoed between the stone walls. Stepping over the yellow cords, I threw my body onto the coffin. Pressed my forehead to it. "Agradaise, come back! Please, I beg you. Answer my questions!"

The crypt remained cold, still, and quiet. But I did not weep more. I didn't feel anything.

It was dark when I emerged from the cathedral. The choir was gone. There was a woman, perhaps a steward, polishing the pipes of an organ, but I didn't ask if she knew anyone by the name of Parros. I didn't want to speak or be spoken to. I felt so displaced, so out of my element, my mind couldn't make sense of it. Even more so than when I had reappeared in Endwever only to discover it was not the same little town I had left.

I had seen what my fate should have been, and it scarred my mind the way Saiyon had scarred my spirit. And I didn't understand. I couldn't comprehend why I had survived when every other star mother before me had passed on. I didn't know where my family was, or where they would end up. Where I would end up.

The Earth Mother seemed too solid, too dreary, too cold. I didn't want to be there anymore. Ristriel had promised I wouldn't be alone, but he couldn't stay with me, not if I stayed in Nediah. And even if I managed to find the closest thing I had to kin, our blood would be so different, they'd be strangers, just like everyone else. They wouldn't look like me, or my sister, or remember me or her. Even my own daughter was forever away, unreachable by my own means.

I didn't belong here. I had glimpsed the place I was meant to be, and I ached for it like I had always been there until this moment, when I was cruelly ripped away. I didn't understand how the afterlives worked. What if I found myself as alone after death as I was now? What if I was cursed to always be alone?

"Ceris?"

I looked up, only then taking in my surroundings. Cobblestones under my feet, dimly lit by a single window of what looked like a cobbler's shop. My feet were dragging in the gutter. The road was mostly empty, save for two gentlemen laughing about something down the way. There was the distant sound of music, perhaps from a local pub, but I couldn't tell where it might be.

And it was cold. So very cold.

Hugging myself, I turned toward Ristriel. The moon hung in the east, shining on his head and shoulders. The rest of him was solid. A passerby likely wouldn't notice the difference.

I took a deep breath to steel myself, but it came with a shudder. A look of pain washed over Ristriel's face. He moved toward me and took my hand, pulling me closer to the cobbler shop until he was out of the moonlight.

Then he held me, and my heart broke, fresh tears coming to my eyes. I leaned into him, smelling snow and autumn skies, my own heat reflecting back to me. His shirt was soft. Had it always been that way, or had he made it soft for me?

"What happened?" he asked. "What did they say?"

I shook my head against his shoulder. "No one spoke to me. No one living."

Pulling back just enough to see my face, Ristriel asked, "What?"

"Agradaise's tomb is in there," I whispered. "Star mother. And I saw her. She spoke to me somehow. I saw the hereafter where she lived, and I knew I was meant to be there. My family was meant to be there. But I don't know if they went there, or if I will, or if I'll ever see them again." Sniffing, I wiped my eyes with the pad of my thumb. "I'm lost, Ris. I'm lost, and I don't know where to go."

He didn't answer immediately. His chest rose and fell, and I rose and fell with it. "We will find them."

"But are they even mine to find?" I gripped his shirt tightly in my fist. "Only so I can watch them die, over and over . . . and over."

Another shuddering breath shook me. I turned my head into Ristriel's neck, but he stepped away, leaving me even colder than I was before. I looked at him, confused, but he didn't return my gaze. He looked at the cobblestones, beyond them.

"I'm so sorry, Ceris."

Again I wiped my eyes. "You are the only constant I have."

But he shook his head. "I am not." He stepped away from the wall, his hands in tight fists at his sides, and looked upward, every inch the picture of a man supplicating heaven. "Do you know how time works, Ceris?"

I blinked, uncertain I had heard him correctly. Clearing my throat, I answered, "Of course I do. Sixty seconds in a minute, sixty minutes in an hour, twenty-four hours in a day. Three months to a season, four seasons to a year—"

He shook his head, and my voice cut off.

"Mortals have depicted time in many ways." He looked just beyond me, his dark eyes boring into another plane. "Circle, loops, falling sand . . . but time isn't like that at all. Time is like music. Imagine the keys of a harpsichord, or the strings of a harp, only they play ever higher and ever lower, never ceasing. Eternal music. Time is like that.

"Time is a realm beyond our own. It is not a god or a being, but a piece of the universe itself. It is older than all else and yet has no age. It is an endless orchestra, for every living creature and spirit has a song.

"When I escaped—" He paused, throat working, choosing his words with care. "When I broke my chains and fled, I fled into the chords of time. Time is more eternal than those who would capture me. Time makes others forget. I thought . . . if I could lose myself in time, or *take* enough of it, they would forget about me, and I would be free."

My heart cracked at the story, and I moved toward him, but he lifted a stiff hand, stopping me.

"I found a weak spot. A soft note, and it allowed me to pass through. To enter time itself. And I strung its music around me. As much as I could get. But Sun and His soldiers realized what was happening and came for me, forcing me to flee. I stole enough for mortals to forget me, but not for gods to."

He met my eyes, shadowy hair falling across his forehead. "Ceris." He swallowed. "I took seven hundred years."

The number made my heart jump.

"I knew it was yours after . . . after I used time to pull us from that field." He hugged himself, shrinking. "The song was the same. Your song. It was your time I took. I didn't know. I didn't know *you*."

I opened my mouth, closed it. Tried to wet my dry tongue and found it nearly impossible. My pulse hammered in my neck and wrists. "Seven hundred years," I repeated.

He nodded.

I needed to sit, but there were no chairs, so I leaned against the shop wall. Its cool, smooth surface sucked heat from my skin.

And I thought of the long grasses, the rotting trees, the autumn leaves in the midst of spring. I thought of my spoiled meat and rusted coins, of long hair and long nails. I knew he had broken the law in the field, but I hadn't realized the extent. Time was leaking from him, altering the things around us any time we stayed in one place too long. Perhaps even making a trail for Yar and Shu to follow.

Numbness spread through my fingers, my cheeks, my lips.

"Ceris . . ." He struggled to continue. "The soft note I entered . . . I was able to come into the music because that note was so weak. It was . . . dying."

Dying.

I closed my eyes, and I was on that not-bed in the heavens again, my body blazing, my abdomen crunching, my star ripping from my womb.

"I took all of it." He whispered now, bent over like he was in physical pain. "I took your time of death, Ceris. I took the years from your chord. I shifted your fate seven hundred years."

My chest had become so heavy it was hard to breathe. I had lived not because of my own strength, but because of the meddling of a runaway godling. I had been barred from the paradise of star mothers, severed from all those I knew, because of him.

My voice was no stronger than a frog's when I asked, "Can you not give it back?"

The moon rose higher, casting her light onto him, and he seemed to shrivel in response. "I have lost so much of it already, Ceris. Even if I could give it to you, I wouldn't be able to send you back."

Memories of Agradaise flooded me, untold beauty lined with despair.

Emptiness.

I could never go back. I was well and truly lost, separated from my loved ones, cast out of the paradise that was supposed to be mine.

Trickster.

I turned my back on him, one hand against the shop for support. "Ceris—"

"Please go." My voice was a whisper yet sharp as a knife.

He drifted after me. "I didn't think—"

"Go!" I shouted, loud enough that the laughing men at the end of the road paused in their conversation. I did not turn. I did not look at him. I dragged one heavy foot in front of the other. "I would rather be alone."

Such was the fate he had given me. I walked away, and Ristriel did not follow.

CHAPTER 18

I had been robbed of time. Or rather, time had been robbed through me.

That was it. I wasn't resilient, I wasn't special. It was a coincidence with unintended side effects. A star had died—the very star that powered Ristriel's chains—and Ristriel escaped. Then I had given birth to Surril at the same instant Ristriel fled to time to shake his pursuers . . . and my dying body had allowed him to steal time for himself. He had literally cut my death out of the strings of fate. Out of the chords of time.

He had preserved my life in the process. One might think I would be grateful to be alive. And perhaps I would have been, had Agradaise not come to me.

I had my daughter to live for, of course. But how could I live for a being I could not even inhabit the same space as? Who was independent and well all on her own, without the care of a mother?

The universe had literally continued spinning without me. For seven hundred years. Was I even still a part of it?

My hand drifted to my ring, still lined black.

Did Saiyon know? But how could He not?

And how dare He not *tell me* if He did? He might not know I traveled with the godling who had stolen time, but I had told Him about the time discrepancy. *Seven hundred years.* He had paused. Considered. And *said nothing.*

Were mortals so unimportant that gods and godlings alike didn't think twice about our welfare? About what *we* wanted?

I was glad for the night, for I would not have been able to bear the presence of people as my mind sorted through this revelation. I did not wander too far; I did not know the city, and there were certainly dangerous men within its walls, lurking about. I absently followed the music until I found the tavern, then looped around and climbed back to the peak of Nediah, to the cathedral. Ristriel was nowhere to be seen, not that I looked for him. But the woman from before was locking the doors. I approached her, trying to straighten my back and look friendly, but the weight of time itself seemed to press me down, as though I were just as old as all the years I had lost.

"Pardon me." My voice had aged as well. "I'm so sorry. I'm a traveler, here to find family. And I haven't yet. I . . . I need a place to stay."

The woman pulled the key from the lock. She didn't appear unfriendly, only uncertain. "There's an inn just down this way that will take you in. It always has a room to spare."

I considered this. I should have enough coin for a room at the inn.

But Ristriel was less likely to return if I stayed in the cathedral.

It wasn't hard to summon the starlight to my skin; it tended to respond to my emotions, and while they were a mess, they were strong. The woman gasped and dropped her keys.

I guiltily pulled the light back in, losing only a minute fraction. "I'm sorry, I didn't mean to startle you."

"Are you she?" the woman asked, leaving her keys on the steps. "We heard rumor that a star mother lived. Are you—"

I simply nodded, and tried not to cry. For some reason, being reminded of my fate by a stranger made it more palpable. But to my relief, the woman fetched her keys and shoved the largest into the lock on the rightmost door. "I have somewhere for you to rest, my dear. Please, you must be weary."

And I was. For I truly hadn't rested for seven hundred years.

I slept fitfully in the small room where the kind woman had made a pallet, so when dawn neared, I rose early, folded my blankets, and snuck away out a side door. I did not have the energy to explain my story again. I did not want to be worshiped. I did not want to speak of Agradaise. I had taken what I needed, and that would be all. I was lost, but I had to find my way somehow. And the only direction I had was to continue searching for the Parroses.

Or.

As I walked away from the cathedral, my bags weighing down my shoulders, my eyes dropped to my ring. I ran my thumb over its smooth surface. Twisted it on, to the amber band. Off to the black. On, off. On, off, before dropping my hand, the band still set to black.

Or I could tell Saiyon I would come with Him and be, as He'd promised, a queen over all the beauty He'd shown me.

I did not think Saiyon had ever lied to me, but like Ristriel, He had certainly held back truths very pertinent to my existence. I did not love Him, but perhaps I could grow to. He was a noble being, bound by duty, and that was admirable. He had never been unkind to me. In fact, He seemed remarkably humble, for a god, like He, too, was weighed down by something unseen.

Just as Ristriel was.

I pushed thoughts of the godling from my mind.

Were those my only options, then? To find my sister's descendants and make a place among them or to return to the arms of my child's father? And yet if my kin did *not* accept me, that left only one choice.

No, it didn't. I could travel the world. Sell my embroidery, live off charity, discover the places Ristriel had told me about, where giraffes lived and towers touched the clouds. I could return to Endwever, set my own rules, and live happily there, a beacon of hope for my people. I could, perhaps, not find myself in Saiyon's *bed*, but in His employ, and in return see my daughter as often as possible. Find purpose, or at least peace, in her. For despite everything falling apart around me, one truth was immutable. I loved my daughter. I missed her terribly, and her absence was a dull ache in the back of my heart that could not be satiated by mere stargazing.

I mulled over these thoughts as Nediah awoke around me. Any smiling faces I encountered, any merchants I visited for food, I asked about the Parroses. Like yesterday, none were able to point me in a clear direction, though one woman walking a goat on a leash advised me to ask the local cartographer. It took me two hours to find his shop. It was locked, the windows dark. I banged my head against his door twice before breaking away and finding a place to sit on the curb. Someone limping by with a crutch asked me for money. I had little, but I always had the option of selling my spirituality to the cathedral, so I gave him a few coppers. The rest I would need to keep for the inn tonight. After that, I'd have to find something to sell. I'd since trimmed my nails, but my hair was still especially long from the effects of Ristriel's misuse of time. It was streaked with silver, but one could always dye it, if I needed something to sell.

My heart twisted, thinking of him. Thinking of his arms around me, before he confessed what he had done.

I wished I had never visited Agradaise's coffin. I would rather have ignorance in peace than this confusion. This ache.

Sighing, I pulled myself onto sore feet and continued my search. I had made my way to the northwest side of the city, no closer to finding who I needed. I chose to forego dinner. If I was lucky, some bread or soup might be included with my room at the inn. If I could make it to the cathedral before dark, I might be able to remember where the stewardess had pointed.

Shopkeepers had begun to pack up their wares with the setting Sun when I found another long set of stairs to climb. I was about halfway up them when a jay flew over my head and landed on a rooftop ahead of me. It glimmered like the midnight sky.

My chest pulsed painfully, like my heart was the end of a flail. "I'm not ready to speak with you."

But the jay said, "I found them, Ceris."

I paused, though the immature and petulant part of me wanted to give him a crude gesture and continue onward, uncaring. "The Parroses?"

The jay nodded. "They live about a mile from here."

Old hope surged in my chest. However I wore my despair, I could not leave this stone unturned. Grasping the handles of my bags, I said, "Show me."

Ristriel gave me a somber nod and flew ahead, as slowly as a bird could without losing the air beneath its wings. My sore feet forgotten, I hurried after him. It wasn't until I'd covered a full mile that my thoughts whispered, *Trickster.* But despite his confession, I could not believe Ristriel would purposefully hurt me, so I followed him besides.

The throngs thinned, and the street I followed slimmed into an easy road, turning into a residential area of the city. Narrow houses packed each side of it, some sharing walls, some with spaces only as wide as a man's shoulders in between. There had to be fifty in all. Ristriel flew around the corner and landed atop the fourth house in the row. A wreath made from torn cloth knotted together hung from its door. I slowed as I neared it, out of breath, night descending around me.

I approached the door and stared at that wreath, wondering which of my practiced scenarios would present itself. I was under the eave, so I couldn't tell if Ristriel was still there, or if he had flown away to leave me in peace. I wasn't sure which scenario I preferred. But surely he'd stayed nearby, in case this was the wrong home? In case they didn't want me?

I glanced behind me, half expecting to see him there. The street remained empty.

Holding my breath, I rapped hard on the door. I wanted to make sure I was heard. Then I waited. The urge to weep overcame me, but I stuffed it down. I could not have their first impression be of me crying in the street, so I stood tall, adjusted my bags, tidied my hair. Shuffling sounded from within, and a woman about ten years my senior opened the door.

She bore no family resemblance to me, not that I'd expected she would. Her pale eyes studied my face. "Can I help you?"

Behind her, a child scurried to the door to get a better look.

"I . . ." My throat closed, and I gently cleared it. "This is going to sound very strange, but my name is Ceris Wenden. I've come here from a village called Endwever. My family . . . married into your family a long time ago—"

The woman gasped, a hand rushing to her mouth. I'd forgotten what I was going to say next; she'd startled the words from my mouth.

Her hand slowly lowered. "I know *exactly* who you are."

For a moment, my heart didn't beat.

She opened the door a little wider, and the child, a blonde girl of about eight, poked her head under the woman's arm. "Ceris Wenden," the mother said. "You have . . . You have a statue in the Endwever Cathedral."

Hope lifted my shoulders. "Yes."

"Your nose . . ." When I touched it self-consciously, she let out a nervous laugh. "I'd heard rumors, but I thought they were just that."

Knitting my fingers together, I prompted, "You know me?"

She nodded. "The story of our family's star mother has been passed down for generations. I . . ." Her eyes watered. "I-I married into it, but . . ."

She pulled her daughter in front of her, settling a hand on either of her shoulders. "My name is Quelline. And this, this is Ceris."

The child smiled and waved.

My jaw slackened. "Ceris?"

"It's a family name. The first girl in every generation is named after the star mother. And you . . . you look just like the drawings." She stepped back, revealing a set dining table and a fire blazing in a cozy hearth, and waved me forward. "Come in, come in! Please . . . I heard a star mother had returned. I never thought it would be you . . . That was six hundred years ago!"

Seven hundred, but I didn't correct her. I was too enthralled by her smile, by the warmth of the room, by the adoring eyes of the child who shared my name.

"Come in!" Quelline took my elbow. "And tell me everything. *Everything.*" She hurried inside and called up the stairs. "Ruthgar! Come down, come down! Our star mother is *here!*"

CHAPTER 19

I had been wrong. I had not run through *every* possible scenario in my mind. When the women who volunteered to sacrifice themselves for new stars were told their names would be honored and remembered for eternity, it was true. In my case, literally true.

After the introductions—Quelline and Ruthgar, who had one daughter, Ceris, and lived with Ruthgar's mother, Yanla, and his father, Argon, who came home an hour after I first knocked on the door—Quelline opened a polished wooden box kept on a high shelf in the front room and set it on the dining table. From it, she unrolled two tapestries stitched in a delicate hand, both comprised of lines and writing in varying colors—one full, the other nearly so. They were old and weathered and hemmed multiple times to combat wear; I recognized it as a record of my family line. My genealogy, preserved.

And there were so, so many more of them than just the Parroses, for names had changed over and over again in marriage. In truth, it was lucky the name Parros had brought me here at all. As though I had wished upon a star, and it had come true.

"Here." Quelline pointed at, but did not touch, the delicate blue thread listing my name. In the light of a dozen candles, it looked green. A white star was stitched above it. My parents' names were not there, but my sisters' names appeared next to mine. The tree descended from Idlysi, not Pasha, and branched off again and again, some of the branches ending abruptly, others shifting off the tapestry, making me wonder if there was another cloth containing their family, or if they'd simply been forgotten to favor other families.

There were *so many names*, but one recurred throughout every generation: Ceris. Ruthgar even had a sister in a nearby village whose middle name was Ceris. Idlysi's first daughter was Ceris, and *her* daughter was Ceris, and another of Idlysi's granddaughters was Anna Ceris. There were boys named Cerist to make it masculine, and middle names strewn in throughout the tree, occasionally abbreviated to C. where space grew thin.

I read every single one of them until the end. Tapping my nail delicately near the bottom, I asked, "And these people are all still alive?"

"I think so." Ruthgar rubbed his chin. "My cousins"—he pointed out three names—"are in Nediah. They . . . They would be incredulous to know of you."

"I might not believe it," Argon grunted, "if the rumor of a star mother returning hadn't already come by. Only a week ago."

Quelline shook her head. "But her *face*, Papa." She returned to the book and pulled out an old sketchbook, its pages yellowed, and sheepishly set it before me. "They're not the originals. We don't have those, but they're very good copies. Our ancestor Erick Trent made them, but I don't know which one." She pointed out the name in two different places on the genealogy, one naming Idlysi's great-great-grandson, the other naming a man too far removed for me to guess an accurate relation. Carefully she opened the book, and sketches of my statue from the cathedral looked back at me. Every angle had been sketched: below and to the right, to the left, even just pictures of my feet. Quelline turned another page and blushed at the faded watercolor there. It depicted my face accurately, but I had golden-ginger hair and deep-brown eyes. My eyes were gray, my hair a simple mousy brown, streaked silver like an old woman's.

"I certainly look more regal, here," I joked.

Quelline smiled. "Not at all." She stared at me until she caught herself, and flushed. "I'm sorry, I just . . . It's strange, seeing your face move. Stories of you are told every spring solstice. You're . . . You're a fairy tale."

"The one that lived," Argon chimed in, sticking a lit pipe into his mouth. "How did you do it?"

I spied movement from the corner of my eye, but when I turned toward the window, all I could see was darkness on the other side of its pane. I wondered if Ristriel was watching, or if he had left for the night.

Or forever.

My chest grew so tight at the prospect I missed a breath. My stomach soured. My fingers chilled.

Ristriel had kept his end of the bargain. He had brought me to Nediah, and to my distant family, safely. He had done his duty, perhaps alleviated his guilty conscience. He had no reason to stay.

I will be your companion as long as you wish.

Suddenly a cup of water was being pressed into my hand. Quelline smiled warmly at me. "I'm sorry, you must have had a long journey. We should eat."

"Oh, no, it's fine." I took a sip, cool water struggling to flow down my tangled insides. "As for surviving"—I glanced out the window again—"I'm not sure."

They accepted my lie easily. "It's because she's strong," Yanla croaked, then coughed. Her health was less than pristine. "Because she's a Parros!"

Quelline laughed. "She's a Wenden, Mama." She glanced at the genealogy. "That name was lost a while ago."

I nodded, solemn. "That's what happens when you have a family of all daughters."

Argon said, "Let's summon the others!" The cousins, he meant.

"Tomorrow." Ruthgar stretched his back. "We're all pressing against her and breathing on her. Give her a second to settle down. She still needs to eat. We all do."

Quelline passed her husband a wry smile. "You just want to keep the glory to yourself."

"Can she sit by me?" little Ceris asked, jumping beside Quelline. "Please?"

Quelline grinned. "Of course, my dear. It would only be proper, to sit by your namesake."

The genealogy was put away, the chairs filled, and stories shared late into the night. I was happy, but my gaze kept wandering to the window, looking for a midnight jay.

We talked a long time. Ruthgar worked in construction, half of his wages coming from a landowner in the city who hired him to do repairs on various houses and shops. He and Quelline had met at church as adolescents. Quelline's family lived on the north side of the city; her parents were deceased, so she'd lived with her aunt, uncle, and cousins in her youth.

Ruthgar, Argon, and Yanla did their best to describe grandparents and great-grandparents from memory while Quelline put on dinner. I tried to help her, but everyone insisted I rest and talk, and so I did, telling them about becoming a star mother. The story had been passed down over the centuries, but the details had warped and changed.

"No, I was *not* married, but I was betrothed," I said, correcting Argon's telling. "The two strongest contenders were Anya and Gretcha . . ."

Nostalgia filled me, making me feel top light and bottom heavy. For me, the events I related had happened only a year ago. For them, it was, as Quelline put it, a fairy story.

The whole tale spilled out of me, including the part Ristriel had played, all the while trying to ignore the sinking feeling in my gut as I relayed his part in my coming here, leaving out a few incriminating details.

"I'll show you my daughter before we go to bed," I promised once I'd finished. "She is lovely."

"And the horse man?" little Ceris asked, a smudge of creamed corn on her chin. "Where is he?"

I opened my mouth to answer, but I wasn't sure what to say. *Just outside,* though that may not have been true. *He went home,* but Ristriel didn't have a home to go to.

I set down my spoon, my appetite suddenly gone.

What was it that I wanted? My time back? A promise of paradise?

A fugitive godling who smelled of winter and shrunk in Sunlight?

Reaching over the table, Quelline set her hand upon mine. "I'm sure Surril is lovely."

To Yanla, Argon asked, "Where's that spyglass?"

And then the room went dark, and thunder rolled through the sky.

My heart launched into my throat. Little Ceris shrieked. Quelline and Ruthgar both scrambled for candles. I stood, my appetite suddenly gone. I knew that sound. I'd heard it once before, in a field near Tarnos, when the moon had vanished from the sky.

"Gods help us," Yanla whispered.

Ruthgar snapped, "Gods are the problem."

I turned to Quelline, who said, "It's the war. The gods are feuding." So it had reached even Nediah, then.

Argon murmured, "Maybe it's real thunder this time."

"Third time it's happened," Quelline whispered, even as I heard running feet in the street outside. Not simply fleeing citizens, but heavy steps, clinking with armor. I thought of the guards I'd seen earlier and rushed to the window, though the view was poor from the house.

"Before," Quelline continued, "it was far off. We just saw lights in the sky. The next time it was closer. We saw the lightning, the fire. The Sun and moon, warring for the sky."

Ruthgar shook his head. "Storms. Just storms." He sounded as though he were trying to believe his own words.

I wrenched the door open and stepped outside, both startled and relieved to see Ristriel there, standing as a man, staring up at the sky. "Ris!"

"They are celestials." Ristriel responded as though he had heard the others' conversation, and perhaps he had. His tone was matter-of-fact. "They were created in opposition to one another, and Moon has never been happy with less. The workings of mortals are beneath them." He glanced from me to the Parroses crowding behind me. "They will tear this city apart."

Yanla fainted. Argon didn't move fast enough to catch her, but he grabbed her arm, slowing her descent to the floor.

"You're still here," I whispered, my insides twisting in a different pattern.

Quelline was frozen as a game piece. She said something, but I couldn't hear it over the *boom* overhead, so loud I had to cover my ears. My teeth clanked against each other. The noise rattled from my skull to my toes.

I ran out into the street, Quelline shouting after me, and stared up at the dark sky overhead, seeing the residue of a silvery explosion; perhaps the collision of celestial godlings far beyond what my mortal eyes could see.

A colorful blast that reminded me of the space clouds Saiyon had shown me burst to the west, just beyond the city wall. Distant screams followed.

"Saiyon!" I screamed into the sky, hands forming fists at my sides. "Saiyon, stop it!"

But of course He couldn't hear me.

Thunder rolled. A red streak like angry lightning rent the sky. I searched for Surril, but the smoke and clouds and lights hid her from my eyes.

At least the stars were too far away to be affected by this. We, unfortunately, were not.

Another *boom!* hit. I didn't see color or light, but the ground beneath my feet shook, and I toppled sideways, nearly hitting the cobblestones. A hand grabbed my elbow, righting me.

Ristriel.

He watched the sky, the lights of war reflecting off his dark irises. Quelline remained in the doorway, Ruthgar just behind her.

Ristriel's earlier words rang in my memory. *They will tear this city apart.*

"Why here?" I whispered. "Have they followed us again?"

Ristriel shook his head. "The gods war throughout the heavens. It is happenstance that we see this one." He pressed his lips together. After a beat, he added, "They are not concerned with the Earth Mother."

"We have to lead them away," I whispered. "Somehow. Away from the city."

"They do not care about either of us." Ristriel turned from the light show. "They will not notice."

He took a step down the road, and then another, until I caught his forearm.

"Where are you going?" Fear strained my words.

He looked past me to my family, standing in the doorway. To other faces pressed to the windows surrounding us, watching the celestial war with open terror. The city rumbled, and another far-off spark lit the sky.

"To protect the city," he whispered.

I shook my head. "No. We'll run. We can make it out—"

He broke from my grasp, taking my hand and interlacing our fingers. "If I am to pass as a mortal"—he looked into my eyes, and I fell into his—"I must heed the lessons you've given me."

"Ris—"

"Protect those weaker than myself." He smiled softly. Raised his free hand and drew a knuckle down the side of my cheek. "Everyone here is weaker. I will keep you safe. I promised."

Tears clouding my vision, I shook my head. "No. You kept your bargain. You brought me to Nediah. You don't have to keep me safe anymore." My chest heaved as though I had run a mile. Fear clawed at me, anxiety that if he left, I would never see him again.

I realized in that moment that what I wanted more than anything was to have him by my side. To run with him through meadows and listen to his stories, as he listened to mine. To banter about needlepoint and discover the creations of the Earth Mother.

I had seen the paradise that awaited star mothers, but I was not dead yet. And now that Ristriel was leaving me, I wanted nothing more than to live beside him.

That smile remained on his lips. "But I am the one who takes care of you."

He kissed my forehead before stepping back, just past the reach of the shadow cast by the eaves. When the next spark of light cut the sky, he shifted into a ghost and whisked away on the wind, so fast I could not discern him from the night.

"Ris!" I shouted, chasing after him. I made it halfway down the road before I stopped.

But I would not be helpless.

I stalked back to the house, tripping once as the ground shook. An explosion overhead lit the road, but I didn't look up. Quelline and Ruthgar were outside now, watching the heavens with awe and horror.

"He's gone to fight for us." My tone was hard so it would not bend to unshed tears.

Quelline blanched. "Will it hurt him?"

I thought of the harpoon embedded into his leg and swallowed. There were certainly things in this universe that could tear him apart, ethereal or otherwise. "I don't know. But if he survives, it won't go well for him. He is wanted by them, and when they see him, they will know he is here. I need somewhere to hide him." If he survives. If he survives. If he survives.

I couldn't dwell on that now.

Quelline pursed her lips together in thought, barely noticing the next burst of warfare overhead. Then she snapped her fingers. "I know where we can hide him. In fact, it's perfect."

And when she told me, I had to agree.

I thought to watch the battle from the wall, until a churning orb of power collided into it.

It spat from the heavens, too bright to look at, silver and dust and rabid energy. It struck the fields beyond the city, then skidded across the Earth until it burst against Nediah itself, breaking apart stone that had stood since before I was born.

It was a wonder the Earth Mother didn't wake, with a god and demigod battling so close to Her. Then again, perhaps they were the reason She slept.

Many, like me, stood outside their shops and home, staring in awe, fear, or both, watching lights streak across the sky. Others shut themselves up in their homes without even a candle lit, their shutters drawn closed, as though their scant protections might succeed where the city's stone fortifications had failed.

I made my way toward the enormous cathedral, for it was the highest part of the city, but changed direction when I saw a full pile of firewood outside what looked like a bakery. Leaving all sense of modesty behind, I scaled it and scrambled onto the roof. If anyone was inside and heard me, they showed no sign.

Standing there, I hugged myself against the chill of night and watched as a deep shadow grew between bolts of lightning, heavy and dense as tar. I knew it was him, somehow, and when the next silvery volley crashed down, Ristriel bent around it and lobbed it back. Not hard enough for it to reach the heavens, but it sailed off into the distance, crashing elsewhere where there was no town. For Ristriel knew every town and city that stood, and he would not destroy one to protect another.

I remembered Argon asking about a spyglass, and I wished I'd lingered long enough to grab it, for I sensed more was happening that I couldn't see. Starlight rose in my veins, and I quashed it with relative ease.

With the speed of a shooting star, Ristriel streaked across the sky, a snaking cloud of shadow and violet light. A new explosion burst into being as he stopped beside it, but this one wasn't like the others. It was a blue bonfire stemming from a single log. Like a mighty axe, Ristriel cut the log in two, breaking the volley from its course.

Something thundered behind me, and Nediah shook, nearly toppling me from the roof. I fell, skinning my knee through my dress, bruising my hands. I slid down the shingles of the bakery but regained traction before falling off. Getting my feet under me, I darted back up the gable, this time clinging to the wide chimney at its crest.

And I saw them. An army of godlings, too far away for detail, and Ristriel a massive eel winding around them, snatching them up and spitting them out, flinging them both heavenward and Earthward, stopping only when thunder struck, and then he zipped across the sky once more, spread out as shadow, and stopped a ball of Sun fire from crashing into the city.

I breathed hard through my mouth, clutching the chimney, as the fight went on and on, shifting west as Earth turned, slowly, so slowly, moving away from Nediah. I watched, I feared, and I prayed. And as the quaking slowed, the thunder grew distant, and the lights danced away, I knew two things for certain.

First, Nediah was safe.

Second, I had been wrong in my earlier assumption. There was something else Ristriel had hidden from me.

He was no godling.

CHAPTER 20

Ruthgar found me as I ran back toward the house, the battle nearly over but not yet.

Breathless, he said, "Quelline is—"

"Help me," I pleaded.

He nodded, and together we ran through the city, the downhill streets speeding our steps. Wherever I could I checked the sky, watching as a dark shadow fell, fell, fell. Nothing chased it, nothing stopped it.

I ran as hard as I could, not even feeling pain when I tripped and smashed my hip into the cobbles. Ruthgar was there beside me, my blood kin many times removed, pulling me up and showing me the fastest way past the wall.

My lungs burned, my calves ached, my heart hurt. I let my emotions soar, and my starlight lit up the fields beyond the city. If Ruthgar had harbored any doubts of the veracity of my story, they vanished in that moment.

We found him collapsed in the wild grass, his breath strained, his eyes closed. But the moon was distracting the heavens with her selfish war, and so we were able to help him. Ruthgar threw him over his shoulders, and I tossed a cloak atop him, snuffing out my starlight so it wouldn't exacerbate his condition.

The journey back took longer. Exhaustion pulled at us even while need and uncertainty pumped energy through our limbs. The roads were uphill, some steeply so, and Ruthgar looked ready to collapse by the time we reached the cathedral a couple of hours before dawn. Quelline had waited for us that entire time, lurking by a small back door with a rounded top, something a child's playhouse might have had. It led to the basement, away from the eyes of priests, not far from the crypt that bore Agradaise's body.

What better place to hide a creature of the moon than at the Sun's own house?

The cellar was chilly, partitioned by stone walls, and small. There were some food stores—wines and jams, mostly—and a pallet of blankets thrown together by Quelline. A basket of food and water sat beside them, as well as a lit oil lamp.

"Bless you," I whispered as I helped lower Ristriel onto the pallet. He had been nothing but man-shaped ink before, but now his color was coming back, making him look a little more human.

"Is he . . . ?" Quelline asked.

I touched Ristriel's face. He wasn't responsive, but he breathed, and at that point, that was all that mattered. He'd worried Saiyon would sense him here, but his energy was so dwindled, I wasn't concerned. Besides that, we weren't *in* the dedicated cathedral, only beneath it.

"I'll make sure we weren't followed." Ruthgar hunched over like an old man. Quelline, her lips pinched together, rested a hand on his shoulder.

Looking from one to the other, I said, "I am indebted to both of you."

Quelline smiled. "I'll check on you soon."

The two departed, making sure to secure the door behind them.

I let out a long breath, reaching for the water to calm my burning throat. Ristriel did not need food and water, but I lifted the bottle to his lips anyway, and to my surprise and relief, he drank some. I tried to make him comfortable the best way I knew how. I smoothed hair from his face. Listened to his breathing, slow and even, its rasp gradually lifting.

Safe beneath the cathedral, tucked away from the war, sleep weighed me down like lead. I turned down the oil lamp, afraid a passerby might notice its light around the door, and laid my head down on Ristriel's shoulder, watching his chest rise and fall.

I noticed, as I drifted into slumber, that he had a heartbeat, too.

Worry clawed within me at dawn, when Sunlight seeped into the cellar. Whatever had happened during the night, Saiyon's kingdom still rose, eventually. I wasn't sure without a timepiece, but the night had felt too long. As if Saiyon had lost a little time as well.

It was not the hours of the day that worried me, but Ristriel. He was a being I had never before seen sleep, yet he remained unconscious on the cellar floor, even when I tried to rouse him. I whispered his name, shook his shoulder. Ran my fingers through his hair. He looked peaceful, at least. I did not know enough about celestial beings to determine his wellness. Part of the problem was that I didn't truly know *what* Ristriel was. When the moon and the Earth Mother came together by chance, what did they create?

But he still breathed, so I merely had to hope for the best. Perhaps Sunlight or moonlight would help him, as it had after Yar and Shu caught up to us in the forest. But unless he took a turn for the worse, I didn't want to risk bringing him outside. Not where the people of Nediah and the gods of the heavens could see him.

The food Quelline had left for us had spoiled overnight, reminding me of Ristriel's confession. Of the time he had stolen, which leaked out of him like butter in an overworked pastry. Pushing the food aside, I tried once more to rouse him, even singing Surril's lullaby to him. I ran my palm over his chest, my thumb over his lips.

"I forgive you," I whispered, hoping the words might incite some sort of reaction. They didn't. "I forgive you, so wake up. Please? You did it. I'm safe. We all are. Just don't leave."

I had so many more questions for him. So many things I still needed to say.

After ensuring Ristriel was comfortable, I braided my hair and moved toward the door. I needed to update Quelline and the others, ask their advice, find something new to eat. The light outside was so bright my eyes watered and I sneezed. I pressed the door closed tightly behind me, grateful the cathedral was surrounded by cobblestones that wouldn't show any tracks. Not that the people of Nediah would be looking for their savior—if they even knew he existed—but I would not let Ristriel be caught because of a small mistake on my part.

I barely knew the city, but I managed to find my way back to Quelline's home. Knocking softly on the door before opening it, I found Argon alone in the front room, sitting by the embers of an old fire, a bowl of porridge in his hands. When he saw me, he went back to the table and ladled me a bowl of the cold oatmeal, which I accepted gratefully. I sat near him, leaning toward the embers.

"He's fine, for now." I stirred the oatmeal.

"They're all asleep upstairs. Told them I'd keep watch," Argon explained between bites. Gesturing to the bowl, he said, "Yesterday's breakfast, but better than nothing."

I smiled at him. "I certainly won't complain." I needed more rest as well, though my mind was painfully awake.

I planned to finish my breakfast, gather my things, and leave a message with Argon before returning to the cathedral. Then Ristriel and I could sort out where to go from there. I very much wanted to stay in Nediah, but I also wanted to stay with my wayward "godling," and it was evident that Nediah couldn't house him forever.

Godling. Yet I didn't know what else to call him.

I set the bowl aside and grabbed my bags, fixing each crosswise over my shoulders. "Tell Quelline we're fine and to come only when—"

Distant shrieks sounded outside the house. Argon and I exchanged a tense look before hurrying to the door. Had the battle resumed? It was foolish to think celestial beings would go to war with one another only under the cover of night. Ristriel was still asleep. He would not be able to defend us again.

My heart sickened as I opened the door.

But the commotion wasn't one of fear. There were no un-Earthly weapons sailing toward the city wall or sparks or explosions in the sky. Argon and I turned toward the cathedral, where a massive pillar of flame burned.

A gasp like a man's dying breath pulled from Argon's throat. "Gods above . . . another star mother is to be chosen from Nediah."

But as I shielded daylight from my eyes and peered toward the massive cathedral, blood surging through my veins, mouth dry, I saw what Argon did not. "No, it's not the torch. It's the spire."

The golden spire, something not made to burn, gleamed wildly against blue morning sky. A breeze passed, carrying its heat. The shrieks died down to silent awe. Neighbors stepped from their houses to gape. I heard footsteps, and Ruthgar came out behind us, followed by Quelline, who rubbed at the dark circles beneath her eyes.

"What does it mean?" Argon asked.

I let out a long, trembling breath. "It means the Sun wants to speak with me."

CHAPTER 21

Saiyon knew I was there. The ring allowed Him to track me, and I had switched it on a couple of times, nervously fiddling with it, only a day ago. I doubted Saiyon would promenade into the city itself, though He didn't seem to have any qualms about showcasing His power right inside its walls. I feared returning to Ristriel, in case I was being watched, though I kept my ring black. I was sure Saiyon had lit up the cathedral because it was a temple to Him, not because He knew Ristriel recuperated there. I was also sure this was a meeting I could not put off.

So I started for the city wall.

Quelline grabbed my sleeve. "W-Wait. The *Sun*?"

I nodded. "It isn't the first time." I tried not to let my own nerves hinder my voice. Placing a hand over Quelline's, I added, "Don't worry. He won't hurt me."

To my relief, I believed those words.

I insisted on going alone, and it was an easy, unimpeded walk, for everyone was going to the cathedral to talk about the star mother or whatever it was they thought the flames meant. I moved away from them, past the shops and markets, beyond the stone wall collapsed from the battle. I passed a farm, into pastures dotted far off with sheep, where I twisted my ring again, its center gleaming amber. I walked, and walked, and walked, until finally I'd put enough distance between

Nediah and myself that the sky flashed and Saiyon appeared, blazing and golden, clothes billowing in a celestial wind. The sky darkened slightly, a portion of its light siphoning down to create this image. He was not as bright as He'd been in His palace, and His eyes took on a more golden sheen than diamond, but they burned with restrained fury.

I switched off my ring.

"You are harboring a criminal." It was not a question, but an accusation. His voice was deep and hard, His face stern and flat.

"You and Your war threaten the lives of thousands of mortals," I spat back, hands on my hips. "Which problem would you prefer to discuss first?"

Saiyon scowled. "Celestial affairs are not your concern."

"I believe a threat to my life and the lives of my family are very much my concern."

He inhaled, bristling, then exhaled, defeated. "I was not aware you were here until recently. Very recently."

I shook my head and folded my arms. "Did your soldiers tell you, or your bounty hunters?"

A growl sounded deep in His throat, reminding me of my first "lion" impression of Him. "He is a criminal and must pay for his crimes, Ceris."

"And what did he do?" I asked, stepping closer to Him. I was angry, *He* was angry, and yet His heat didn't flare. His hands didn't move to strike. He had no desire to harm me. "Escape an unjust prison?"

I could tell by the opening of Saiyon's face that He had not expected me to know that much. But His features immediately hardened. "He has broken eternal law. He tampered with time."

"*My* time, but you failed to tell me such."

He simmered.

"Have You not done the same?" I countered, trying to keep my voice even. If Saiyon was willing to temper Himself for my sake, I could do the same. "You held him against his will."

The Sun God shook His head. "It is not against universal law to keep him."

I flung my arms out. "No. *You* said—"

"I said *mortals* cannot be forced to do a god's bidding."

I ground my teeth together. "*Mortal* law does not permit you to hold someone against their will if they have done nothing wrong." Saiyon opened His mouth to retaliate, but I forced in, "*Before* his dealings with time, had he done anything wrong?"

Saiyon's flames darkened. He was just as angry as I was. "He is not mortal."

"And yet he lives among mortals."

Saiyon scowled. "Mortality has no claim on him."

"*I* have claim on him!" I snapped, and I might as well have taken Shu's ivory spear and run Saiyon through with it. His expression melted into something painful. Only for a moment, for He was a god and had had tens of thousands of years to learn to school Himself into the semblance of omnipotence. But though I had seen the hurt, and I did not want to cause it, I did not regret my words.

"I have claim on him," I repeated, softer.

He studied me longer than was comfortable, and His fiery brow lifted. "Of course . . . it makes sense."

I hugged myself, feeling vulnerable. "What does?"

His mouth turned down. "You will deliver him to Me, Ceris."

"Or what?" I stepped closer again, but Saiyon was hardly cowed by me. "If celestial and mortal law is so separate, can You even order me to do that? Can You punish me? Will You hurt me, Saiyon, kill me? Or will You imprison me the way You did him?"

He flared, heat so powerful I had to step back. He reined it back in.

"It is my charge," He ground out. "I must secure balance in the universe, regardless of who tries to destroy it. Regardless of My feelings for you. He must repay the time he took. He must restore the chords. I will burn down every mortal city you hide him in if I must."

I gaped at Him. "You would never be so cruel."

His light flared again, so bright that I could not bear to look . . . until I realized it was not Saiyon who glowed so brilliantly, but the sky. Or one small point of the sky. I knew its light instantly, its warmth, the voice I could feel but not hear.

Surril. My star.

Saiyon turned His head skyward. "You *dare* oppose Me in this?"

But she did. I could not see whatever trouble she was causing, but it was something Saiyon could not ignore.

He blazed red and turned back to me. "You blame Me for the damage done here, but you are misled. Ask him, Ceris. Ask him why this war started. Ask him how it is *his* doing." His voice was low, tinged with rage . . . but something sad weighed down His words, and at that moment, I could not determine what.

Saiyon flashed away, Surril retreated, and I stood alone among the trees stippling the wide spreads of pastureland, more confused than ever.

I walked back slowly, my energy drained, my mind heavy. I didn't understand where mortal laws ended and celestial laws began. I trusted Saiyon, and yet I wanted to trust Ristriel with everything I was. It gave me peace to know Surril watched over me, even when I could not see her, and yet her intrusion only raised more questions. Did *she* trust Ristriel? Could she watch him from the heavens as she did me? Or did she oppose her father only to support me?

Why did Saiyon want me to ask Ristriel about the war?

I rubbed gooseflesh from my arms when I neared the city. A baker had a cart of hot buns near the wall. Grateful to have my things with me, I eagerly paid him for two and ate every last crumb as I climbed the rising streets of Nediah, licking candy gloss from my hands. It was about noon, if the sky was to be believed. I thought of the times

I'd gotten bored enough in Endwever to pull one of my pranks, and laughed at my younger self. How simple life had been then, to have such a small world to bask in, a husband already chosen for me, and a future mapped out by someone else!

There was still a crowd when I reached the cathedral, though the spire had ceased burning and showed no damage from the heat. It reminded me of myself, burning alive in Saiyon's bed and walking away without any physical scars. I stopped and closed my eyes, pushing the memories away. But something struck me: Saiyon could see my soul's scars just as well as Ristriel and the godlings did. Past looks He'd given me, things He'd said to me, made sense—He felt guilty for giving them to me. Then, like now, He had followed the laws of the universe. And He still wanted me, despite the disfiguration of my spirit.

I was not so naïve to think He loved me more than the law, however. I didn't think He was able to.

Guards had gathered around the cathedral, trying to calm the crowds as people shouted questions about the gods and star mothers and blessings and curses. My attention pushed past them, to the towering monstrosity of worship looming over me. I thought of the priest in Tarnos, and his book of the gods' language. Could this cathedral, being so large, so old, and so prestigious, have something like that? A book of celestial law, perhaps? Something that could help me sort out this problem and save Ristriel from his fate? I had not noticed one before, but then again, I had not been looking.

The least I could do was try.

I slipped through the crowd, finding gaps in it where others had grown tired and gone home. I was nearly to the steps when a guard put his hand out in front of me. "None may enter."

Without stopping, I unleashed my starlight, burning like a new wick before him. He quickly cowed away, eyes round. "Let me pass," I demanded, and he did. My light died before I reached the front door, but it had started a commotion behind me. Good; let the onlookers keep the guards busy. I had work to do.

The breathtaking stained glass and oil paintings, sculptures and busts, mosaics and columns, were practically invisible to me at that moment. I sought something pragmatic, not ornate. I did stop once at Agradaise's bust, studying her face in copper, remembering it bathed in brilliant light. Wondering when I would get the chance to ask Saiyon her story, if He even remembered it.

But she was dead and could not help me now, so I bowed my head in a plea for forgiveness and continued my search, checking alcoves, shelves, and tablets along the walls. I walked through the ambulatory and looked in each chevet, then came around the cathedral again, checking drawers and slinking behind roped-off sections. I found books, but most of them were familiar hymnals or scriptures—the same pages I could have read back home.

Footsteps alerted me to another's presence, and I saw a priest approaching me. I straightened, keeping my chin held high. If the guards could not keep me out, he certainly wasn't going to, either.

"I'm looking for records," I explained.

He readily ignored my question. "You are she."

He must have spoken to the stewardess, but I couldn't be sure. "I beg your pardon?"

He came within three paces of me, clasped his hands together, and bowed his head. "Star Mother, it is an honor."

"My name is Ceris."

"I know who you are." He lifted his gaze to take me in, and something about it made me feel as cold and metallic as Agradaise's bust around the corner. "I have communed with the Sun. You must return to Him."

I blinked at him. Had Saiyon really spoken to this man, or did he fancy himself a revelator? It did not take an extensive education to interpret the relationship between star mother and Sun.

I took a breath to steady myself and fuel my patience. "I am looking for records of celestial law. The workings of the universe. What may have been passed down and shared between the walls of this church."

Tilting his head to the side, the priest gave me a patronizing smile. "The only laws that need concern you are that we are to worship the gods and read their scripture. Within their words is all you need to know."

I did not hide the scowl infecting my face. I set the hymnal down and stepped from the alcove, brushing by him. "You know nothing."

I turned and started for the front doors, but the priest followed me, talking over my footsteps, his voice growing a hair louder with every syllable passing his lips. "Are you mad? You of all women have *lived*, and the Sun touches this very cathedral, and you walk away from it?"

When I did not turn, he sped up and slipped in front of me, blocking my path. "The sire of your star may be a god," he panted, "but you are still a virtueless woman. Why not return to He who has claimed you?"

The blood drained out of my face even as my hot pulse pushed it back into my cheeks. I glowed, not because I meant to, but because my temper flared dangerously close to the line of my control. "How *dare* you."

To my amazement, the priest looked over my skin, dazzled by my starlight, seemingly unaware that he had just insulted my worthiness as a woman. "Sun be praised."

I almost spat at him that the *Sun* hadn't given me this light, Surril had, but I thought better of it at the last moment. I wouldn't waste any more of it here. Reining in as much of my anger as I could, I feigned astonishment. "He is here. He awaits us in the street."

The priest blanched and whirled toward the doors so quickly he tripped on his robes. And in his eagerness to meet his god, I fled in the other direction, picking my way through a side hall behind the ambulatory. The décor fell away within a few steps, the walls turning into uneven stone, cold and unadorned. This was a better route, besides. It would do no good to reveal Ristriel's hiding place to the crowd outside.

When I stepped into the crypt and saw Agradaise's casket, a chill overcame me, eyes watering in remembrance of the beauty of my vision. Beauty I'm sure could only be described in the gods' own tongue. To say I did not still yearn for it, that I did not ache to see it again, would be a lie. I would ache for it all my mortal years. But my fate had changed inextricably, and I could not yet confirm it hadn't been for the better. There was beauty to be found outside the hereafter. Beauty I knew completely, beauty I had touched, beauty as complex as the depths of the night sky.

Thoughts of the self-righteous priest winked away, as insubstantial as a summer snowflake.

I shoved open the narrow door to the cellar with my shoulder and took another six steps downward. The lamp was lit, flickering with what little oil was left. Cool relief drowned me when I saw Ristriel sitting up, elbows resting on his knees, head down. His blacker-than-black hair covered half his face, but he glanced through the locks when I approached.

Dropping to my knees beside him, I asked, "Are you all right?"

The corner of his mouth ticked. "It will pass."

I took his hand in mine and looked it over, running my thumb across his palm, tracing his fingers with my own. He watched like it was some sort of dance he was beholding for the first time.

I saw no injury—no cuts, no bruises, no scrapes, on his hand or elsewhere—but that didn't mean they weren't there. Ristriel wasn't mortal, after all.

Which made me remember.

I lowered his hand softly. "You have never lied to me."

He stiffened and winced, affected by injuries I couldn't perceive. "Never."

"But you have never corrected me, either."

His eyes met mine, knowing.

I let out a long breath. "You are not a godling."

He hesitated for several heartbeats. For a moment I thought we were back to our old game, me dying to know the truth and him evading it. But instead he answered, "No, I am not."

I'd known as much, yet hearing his confirmation spiked alertness in me. "Then what are you?" Surely he wasn't a demon. He was much too kind for that.

Ristriel considered for a moment. "By the classifications you would understand, I am a demigod."

My heart thudded a little harder. A demigod. The second-most-powerful celestial being. So many questions filled my mind, but the loudest was the one Saiyon had told me to ask. *Ask him why this war started. Ask him how it is his doing.*

"The war," I began, but Ristriel took up my hand, staying me.

"I will tell you everything you want to know." His eyes were so deep, so endless, so sad. "Even if it angers you."

My throat tightened. I forced it to swallow. "I'm not angry. Not anymore."

His lips twitched again. "Did He tell you already?"

Shaking my head, I said, "He only told me to ask." But it seemed Ristriel would have revealed the truth either way.

"It is my doing, this war." His voice was husky, just above a whisper. "I am the one who prevented it. And because I escaped, they war with one another again."

I shook my head, confused. "Ristriel, *who are you?*"

"You asked me, before, who gave me my name."

One who is chained. That was what Father Meely's book had read. We'd been interrupted before he could tell me.

"The Sun God named me," he went on. "But mortals gave me a name as well. They called me 'Twilight.'"

A shiver coursed its way from my crown to the backs of my knees and up again. Twilight. *Twilight.*

Gods in heavens, it all made sense. The night came on so suddenly now; I had thought it strange, in the back of my mind, but never examined it. But I remembered. Before the torch lit in the church in Endwever, before I ever met Saiyon . . . I remember the dim indigo light that covered the sky after the Sun had set, and before the moon rose. I remember having more warning before darkness fell. I remembered *him.*

And I had the distinct impression that I was the only mortal left who did.

"It's as I told you . . ." Ristriel pressed into the cool stone at his back. "I was created by a shard of the dark side of the moon and the Earth Mother. But neither of them claimed me. I was reckless in my youth, unguided and unsure of myself. The Sun won His war and captured me, chaining me in the veil between His kingdom and hers, so the moon could never again assail Him at times of strife, when He is split and weakened."

I gaped at him, but I couldn't close my mouth. He had told me how the moon had stolen her light. I felt like I was outside of my body, a third party listening to a story I could never have fathomed on my own. A demigod created by accident, forced to guard the space between kingdoms . . . it was beyond any fairy tale.

It was no wonder he knew the geography of Earth so well. He'd watched it from the sky for . . . how long? Millennia, surely. I could not think of a single tale or fable in which there was no twilight.

"The power of the stars held me in my prison." He was whispering now, watching his hands again. "And I . . . I couldn't . . . be there anymore. I was alone, save for just after Sunset and before Sunrise. Then I could see the Earth Mother and Her mortals for a short while. Learn their habits, their names . . . but they never noticed me. But Moon's and Sun's powers would press against me and send me back into the darkness."

He pushed the heels of his hands into his eyes and curled around himself.

Pushing myself onto my knees, I put my arms around him, comforting him as he had comforted me in the dark streets. My mind reeled, trying to imagine . . .

Darkness. He'd lived in darkness, alone and lonely, as stronger gods and demigods rose in the heavens.

I thought of Saiyon, and the considerate things He'd done for me, the way He'd tucked my hand in the crook of His arm. Could He really be so cruel?

"And then a star died." He kept his hands where they were. "A star died, and my chains loosened, and I ran. I stole time and hid on the Earth Mother. I don't think She even knows who I am, She's slept so long . . ."

"Ris."

He was somewhere far away, somewhere dark and lonely, somewhere I couldn't reach him.

I waited, squeezed tighter, then spoke his name again. "Ris."

He didn't respond.

I let a glimmer of starlight seep through my skin, and an indigo sheen rippled across his skin and clothes. "Ristriel."

He lifted his head, his expression so vulnerable, so childlike, so *mortal*.

"The war is not your fault," I admonished, pulling back to better see his face. "They have struck against each other since before your creation. Their war is what created you in the first place."

I tried to find more words. *You didn't deserve that.* But they all seemed so weak, so small. Not enough.

I ran my palms down his arms, resting them at his elbows. "Thank you, for telling me."

He didn't answer.

We sat in silence a long moment, our breaths the only sound between us. The oil lamp flickered. I wondered how long it would burn. I could not let it go out. I could not leave Ristriel in darkness.

"A star died before I became star mother," I whispered. "Was that the star that freed you?"

He rested his chin on his knees. "I believe so. My chains must have drawn their powers from it."

I nodded, piecing together our timelines. He's been running for nearly a year, then.

"Will Saiyon—the Sun—Will my presence make it easier for Him to find you?"

He glanced at my ring.

I wrenched the priceless band from my finger and tossed it across the cellar. He watched it roll and bounce across the stones, spin, and settle.

"We're in the Nediah Cathedral," I said.

"I know."

"Is it safe for you to leave?"

He glanced up at the stone ceiling as though he could see to the sky. "No. Not yet. It's ill advised for Him or His servants to trespass a city, but they will not hesitate long."

"I need to see Quelline so she knows I'm all right." She'd last seen me marching off to meet with the Sun Himself.

He studied my face. Swept a few strands of loose hair from my cheek. "Go."

"But you'll be alone—"

"Ceris." His expression turned sweet, loving, and in it I saw endless years. The face of a demigod. "I have spent my entire existence waiting. A few hours is nothing."

I stared at him, heart surging, breaking, pounding.

And I knew what I had to do.

CHAPTER 22

I wound my way to Quelline's home, the streets of Nediah seeming steeper than they had been. The house was quiet when I slipped inside. I wasn't sure where everyone had gone; the abnormal activity had disturbed people's normal routines, and Nediah was not yet functioning as it should. Some might have been resting upstairs, but I didn't search for them. Instead, I went to that polished box and pulled out the fragile tapestries of Idlysi's genealogy.

Unfurling the cloths, I ran my hand over the names, printed in stitches, some faded, some bright. It was everything I had missed . . . It was everything I could never have, regardless. If I had passed on to the hereafter, perhaps my family would have followed me. For all I knew, they had gone without me. I knew only this—I would never meet the rest of them here on Earth. No string of fate or chord of time would allow it. Still, I took a fine yellow thread from my bag, and beside my name at the top of the tapestry, I stitched a simple six-pointed star, and beneath it the letters S-U-R-R-I-L, because my daughter was the reason we were remembered.

I rested my head and closed my eyes, succumbing in part to exhaustion. In a dazed half dream, I relived my time in the heavens, with Saiyon and Fosii and Elta. I reappeared in Endwever. Saw my statue for the first time. Ran my hands over my family's tombstones. Traveled alone until I met a midnight—a *twilight*—horse in the forest. I played every hour, every day, of my journey with him. The mysteries in the moonlight, the late-night chatter, every song sung and joke told. I relived my fears, my worries, the chase. The harpoon embedded in Ristriel's leg, his body pressed against mine as shadows concealed us in the forest.

Returning to myself, I raised my head, wiping away a single tear with the pad of my thumb.

The door opened, revealing Quelline, a cloth sack of groceries hanging from her shoulder. "Oh, Ceris! I was worried about you." She set the bag down and hurried to my side, taking my hands in hers. "Are you well?"

I nodded. "He merely wanted to talk."

Quelline searched my eyes. "Talk with a god . . . I'd never have believed it before yesterday." She paused. "What's wrong?"

I smiled and blinked away another tear. "I have to leave."

Her face slackened. "Leave? B-But you just got here!"

"I know." I wiped my eyes again. "I know. And I may come back. I want to. I want to know you, and little Ceris, and Ruthgar and Argon and Yanla. But I have to leave. I have to protect him."

Quelline studied me. Let out a long breath that deflated her shoulders. "But of course you do." Her eyes shimmered, but she smiled at me. "He brought you here to us. He saved us. I want you to help him, too."

A wet chuckle tore from my throat, and I threw my arms around Quelline's neck, holding her tightly to me. She embraced me back, and we both cried into each other's clothes, leaving marks of family against the fabric.

Quelline pulled back first. Patted my hands. "You'd best go now, or Argon will convince you to stay. Here." She went to her grocery bag, then to her cupboard, to pull together a fine meal for me. She wrapped it in a fraying cloth and handed it to me as if it were a newborn. "Come home when you can."

Home . . . yes, Nediah was home now, wasn't it?

I thanked her, kissed her cheek, and placed the food reverently into my bag. Then I stepped outside into the evening light. The streets were already less crowded. People no longer had the balm of twilight to usher them home; they simply had to be there before the darkness consumed them.

I started for the cathedral, lifting my head toward the sky, to where I knew Surril would be, and whispered, "Thank you."

The Sun was setting when I returned to the cathedral, making the enormous church throw a cold shadow over me and half of Nediah behind me. It was poignant and poetic, as if Saiyon was trying to make a point to me, even though I knew it was just happenstance that I had approached the cathedral from the east.

The crowd had dispersed, and both the cathedral's spire and its great torch remained cool. Crouching, I grasped the cellar door's handle before filling myself with a deep, reassuring breath. I could not change the past, I could not control time, and I could not barter with the gods, but I could follow my heart, and thus my path was clear.

It was dark inside; the oil lamp had burned out. Panic had me stumbling down the short stairs, but Ristriel's voice in the dark reassured me that he had not left. "You came back."

My breath escaped in a sigh. "I promised I would." I left the door cracked so I could have a sliver of light as I searched the things Quelline had left to see if anything was worth taking. The blanket was still good, but the rest was unsalvageable. My ring glinted on the stone, limned black. I was tempted to retrieve it—if nothing else, it would sell for a high price. But I worried that even turned to black, it would allow others to track us.

"We need to leave," I whispered. "He knows you're here. I'm worried the godlings He'll send for you will destroy this place." The battle with the moon nearly had.

Ristriel's brows lowered. "But your family is here."

"My family is there." I pointed up. "And she likes you almost as much as I do. She intervened for you today."

He blinked, speechless, as though he could not fathom *two* people caring about his welfare.

I took his hands. "Do you know where we can go?"

He pressed his lips together, taking a moment to think. I could almost see his thoughts spinning, his knowledge bending and stretching like taffy. "The Losoko Canyons."

I had never heard of them. "Canyons?"

He nodded. "They're one hundred seventy-three miles south of here. They run deep into the Earth, shadowed even at noonday." A spark of hope lit his eyes. "Perhaps there, the Earth Mother's power can conceal both of us."

I bit the inside of my cheek. "That is a long way."

"I will carry you whenever I can."

Steeling myself, I said, "Let's go now."

Ristriel took my bags onto his shoulders. I left a quick note of gratitude beside the lamp before slipping outside and tugging the door gently closed. Behind me, the Sunlight snuffed out, pulling us into the moon's kingdom. She made her slow climb into the sky, but the heavens were pocked with clouds, which would help us.

Her light beamed between a gap in the clouds, silver light spilling a few feet from us.

"Wait." I grasped his elbow, stalling him. "Before we touch the moonlight." I stood before him, my toes and chest an inch from his, my hands by my sides, my face turned defiantly upward.

For a being who had watched the world turn for thousands of years, he had an adorably naïve and reserved expression on his face. "Ceris." My name sounded like a long-kept secret.

I pressed a hand to his chest. He leaned into the touch. I drew even nearer to him before his eyes softened. "Ceris, we can't."

I didn't budge. "Why not?"

His dark eyes dropped to my lips. "Because you are a star mother. You are His."

I waited until he met my eyes again to say, "I am no one's but my own."

The waxing crescent moon slipped behind a cloud, darkening the city. His hands came under my jaw, fingers tunneling into my hair, and his mouth lowered to mine, cool and soft. His touch was like the morning after the first frost, or an early spring breeze. He smelled of winter storms and wide-open plains without a house or human in sight. His kiss ignited something in me, something exciting and deep that neither Caen nor Saiyon had been able to touch. Craving it, I pushed myself onto my toes, fearing for a heartbeat that my forwardness would startle him. But he pulled me closer, tilted and claimed me, and I surrendered to him, falling against him, parting my lips, exploring him as he explored me. Time and heaven ceased to exist. In that moment, the universe was only us, shadow and starlight, lovers dancing in wild grass under the violet haze of twilight.

And yet time waited for no one.

I drew away from him slowly, reluctantly, and peered into his lidded eyes. "I choose you, Ris."

His expression was so sad, yet so joyous, it made me hurt. He kissed me again, fervent but brief, before breaking free to whisper, "We must run while we can."

So we did, down the spiraling streets of Nediah, over arching bridges, around shops and pubs. Ristriel had to return my bags before we reached the broken city wall, when the moon again stole away his body. But once we passed the guards at the gate, a thick cloud favored us. Ristriel took me into his arms immediately, and we flew across the low hills and pastures surrounding Nediah.

I clung tightly to him, looking over his shoulder to keep the wind from my eyes, taking in the world as we swept by it: trees, gardens, valleys, creeks. We wove through brambles and thickets, passed over an ancient stone bridge crossing a fast-moving river bloated with spring runoff. Ristriel watched the moon carefully, and set me down just before the cloud moved so I would not fall.

He became a horse, identical to the one he'd been when we first met. I followed him at a steady jog, my body exhausted but alert. The shallow shapes of faraway mountains had risen up in the distance, and I could tell they would be mighty when we neared.

Another cloud swallowed the moon's silver light. This time, I rode on Ristriel's back, my fingers tangled in his dark mane. I hunched low over him, trusting my care to him despite my lack of horsemanship. Wind whisked by me, deafening my ears to everything else. A few raindrops struck my cheeks. At this speed, they pummeled me more like thrown pebbles than beads of water. I smelled the sharp tang of a nearby saltwater lake.

The stars not hidden by clouds watched us, twinkling in wonder.

The mountains, which reminded me of a fabled dragon's back, grew larger and larger as we neared. The ground hardened, the wild grass and weeds in it becoming lean and sparse. The way became rocky, which would have been a problem for an ordinary horse, but Ristriel trod on, gracefully picking his way through. His neck sweated beneath my hands; were he a ghost, he would not have suffered for the effort. I pressed a kiss to it and whispered words of encouragement, though I'm not sure if he heard me. I had yet to hear any sounds of pursuit; in truth, our escape had seemed too easy.

The mountains grew exponentially, until they stood as massive giants fallen from some ancient war, their bodies turned to stone.

Ristriel slowed as the ground inclined toward them. Beneath the stone behemoths, there was not a sliver of moonlight to be seen. I could barely make out the path ahead of us, and I dared not use my abilities to light the way for fear of hurting Ristriel.

An uneven bar of black stood in the mountains ahead of us, not unlike the pupil of a snake. A pass through the cliffs. We moved far faster than any mortal could, but there were limits even to Ristriel's speed. We could be only halfway to our destination at best. These weren't the canyons, merely a barrier between us and our hope.

Ristriel saw her before I did; he dug his hooves into the ground, throwing his neck back to keep me from flying over his head. I startled, my skin glowing as the moon for a second before I snuffed it out.

Then I heard thunder.

No, not thunder—the shuffling of boulders as they tumbled down the cliffs. Squinting, I made out their uneven shapes as they came together against the pull of the Earth Mother, forming a body with a small head and massive limbs. The being glowed a pale green where the rocks held together, creating an asymmetrical net of light. The godling herself was at least thirty feet high, and she pushed out her stony arms, blocking our path.

She had no eyes, yet I could feel her watching me.

"Ceris of the Stars and Ristriel of the Skies." Her voice was gravelly and low. "The Sun searches for you. You may not pass."

My stomach sank. I tightened my hold on Ristriel's mane and asked, "You fight for the day?"

"My fight is not with the skies; I only heed the call of other gods while mine slumbers." She didn't budge even a hair. "The Sun has called for you, and for he who has stolen time. You will not pass."

I looked over my shoulder, expecting godlings with nets and harpoons to come running at us any moment. For now, the rocky slopes remained empty.

"Let us pass, please," I pled to the godling. "I am my own ruler, and he is in my charge." I indicated Ristriel.

The godling's green lines brightened. She did not move. I was not sure if Ristriel could overpower her without the light of the moon, and I was afraid to see him try. The mountains were wide and great; we could not simply go around them. Perhaps Ristriel could fly over if we waited for daylight, or follow them to where the moon touched, but I could not go with him if he did.

He stepped back, his coat darkening, as though getting ready to charge.

I slid from his back. He hesitated when I did so. Shifting away from him and closer to the godling, I allowed my skin to glow.

"You will not let me pass?" I repeated, my voice growing hard. "Am I not a mother, like the sleeping god you serve? My daughter and the other stars in the heavens bless all on the Earth Mother, even you. I, who stand for the deaths of thousands of women who relinquished their lives to protect the soil on which you stand. Who have kept stewardship over the Earth Mother since the dawning of Her time." Bits of dust and rock began to swirl around me—I had not intended to do that, but my words carried emotion, and my powers were still new and unpracticed. "Will you truly stand here and forbid me passage, on the word of a god whose true name you do not know?"

Ristriel stood silent behind me. I watched the godling, and she watched me, for several heartbeats until she lowered her arms.

"You speak well, Star Mother," she said. "I will let you pass, for your womb and your scars. Your fight is not mine."

The green light vanished, and the boulders that made her crumbled away, rolling back to where they had come from, across the Earth and up the cliffs, laying the way bare before us, unguarded. My body slackened, sore, as though I had run the distance from Nediah myself.

"I have lived far longer than you," Ristriel whispered beside me, "but I could not string together such powerful words."

I lifted my hand and ran my thumb over his muzzle. I had not tried to be clever or poetic, or even brave. I had simply let my heart speak for me.

I climbed atop Ristriel's back, and we soared through the gorge, desperate to make it to the Losoko Canyons before dawn.

CHAPTER 23

The pass was long and narrow, not unlike galloping through the body of a serpent. Its walls were steep and tall, and above them I could see the moon when clouds did not float past Her, but the mountains were so dark and cavernous, the moonlight never touched us. Ristriel surged onward, far steadier and quicker than any horse, fed by the shadows. My body grew sore and tired from the ride, and I worried my hands would remain permanently clenched for how tightly they held on to his mane.

In about two hours' time, the pass began to open up, and again a few patters of rain kissed my face and hair. The mountains broke into a deep, wide, and dry-looking valley, as though spring had yet to come to this part of the world, if it ever did. Instead of grass, there were patches of dry shrubbery half made of needles, half of bones, and the Earth underfoot became dusty, slashed with red. I knew Ristriel could tell me why, but I dared not interrupt his ride or slow our progress. We had perhaps four hours left before dawn, and the spotty cloud cover would not last forever.

Taking in the landscape, I painted a picture of it in my mind so I could later re-create it in thread. This long escape alone would make a beautiful tapestry, though surely it would take me years to create.

The Earth flowed beneath us like the ocean. The mountain range behind us opened like the maw of a great wolf, stretching farther and farther away. The ground continued at a steady incline. Soon more boulders and strange rocky structures pebbled our way, bizarre and still as statues, perhaps the bodies of godlings long since claimed by time.

Ristriel slowed, his lungs heaving, and when he stopped I slid off him, stumbling on aching legs. I pulled the waterskin from my bag.

"I need to rest only a moment," he said, his voice sounding from somewhere other than his mouth.

"You are so strong." I ran my hand down his muscled neck. "We must have come a hundred miles already."

"One hundred forty-seven and a third," he panted, and I smiled at him. He lifted each of his legs, one at a time, stretching them out. The clouds, which grew steadily thicker the farther south we traveled, broke again, momentarily flooding the land with moonlight. I gazed up at the moon, wondering if she watched us, until the breeze pushed the clouds over her once again.

But the wind carried something else, an ethereal sound I was becoming increasingly familiar with, and it sent chills over every inch of my body.

The sound of pursuit.

I whirled around, facing the pass I could no longer see amidst the distant mountains. "Ris."

"Get on. Quickly."

He bent his knees and I scrambled onto his back, barely able to situate myself and my bags before he took off again, a shadow against shadows. He never even suggested we hide as we did in the forest, and it took me a moment to realize why.

The sounds of the chase were louder than they'd been before. More complex. Wings, hooves, and feet thundered toward us. We had more pursuers, and they were not *searching* for us. They knew exactly where we were.

A soft cry climbed up my throat. We were so close. *So close!* The Losoko Canyons, at Ristriel's speed, were only an hour away. But Ristriel was tired, and these godlings were not. Their pursuit grew louder, louder, *louder*.

"Ceris!"

I hadn't realized my skin was glowing. Ristriel shrunk beneath me, his steps wavering. Gritting my teeth, I willed it back into me. It was slow to obey, for panic was blooming in my heart. But I managed it, and Ristriel gained speed, for what little good that would do. His second mother slumbered beneath us, unaware Her child ran for his life. And his first mother spat upon us, for the clouds broke, and Ristriel gave way beneath me.

I flew forward, weightless, the world spinning around me, items spilling from my bags. Just before I hit, shadows surged up around me. It felt like falling into cold foam, and they slowed my descent enough that I didn't break anything when I hit shoulder first, then hip. Part of my skirt tore as I slid across the dusty Earth, red particles flying around my head as I coughed.

"Ceris!" Ristriel was behind me, trying to help me up but unable to do so. "I'm sorry. I'm so sorry—"

"I'm fine. I'm all right." I pushed myself up, trying to bite down on a wince. I looked skyward. Any moment now the moon would hide again, and Ristriel would be whole. We were so close—

An ivory arrow pierced the ground inches from my hand. I stared at it, my mind slow to comprehend what it was.

I heard the whistle of a harpoon next. A cry stuck in my throat as it neared.

Ristriel spun around and caught it by the shaft, its tip inches from his hip. It was of celestial make, so he could touch it even in his ghostly form.

I realized then that Yar and Shu had managed to hurt him before only because they'd had the element of surprise.

As though summoned by my thoughts, I saw the horned godlings closing in, their bodies like centaurs', moonlight glimmering off their blue- and silver-striped horns. Beside them was a creature as ghostly as Ristriel, her upper body humanlike, her lower half like a comet trailing behind her. Another of our pursuers was three times as wide as a man and dark as loam, eyes glowing gold in the darkness. Some resembled dogs, others resembled Yar and Shu. Eleven in total. They surrounded us in an uneven circle, every last one armed with shining ivory weapons.

My starlight shimmered. I held my breath until it faded.

A demigod could easily overpower a godling, but not eleven of them. Especially not when his companion continually deprived his strength with her own.

But even the Sun struggled against the moon, so perhaps there was hope. Or so I thought, until a bonfire exploded behind me. Spinning around, I looked into the fiery, gemstone eyes of Saiyon.

The Sun God Himself, come to capture His quarry. He held in His hand a great pearlescent sword so sharp it hurt my eyes to look at it. It was too broad and heavy for any mortal man to wield, and its point hovered close to the ground.

Ristriel stepped in front of me. He flashed solid for a moment, but in Saiyon's presence, he couldn't hold his form, even with Saiyon dimming His power. At first I thought the Sun God was so radiant because the cloak of night emphasized His light, but then I wondered if this was Saiyon in full, not a division of Him. Which meant capturing Ristriel was critical enough that those on the other side of the Earth Mother were still waiting for dawn.

Even as the thought entered my mind, I heard an explosion overhead, though I dared not take my eyes from Saiyon to look. I knew the sound. Recognized the sparks in my peripheral vision. While we stood here on the Earth Mother, the war between day and night continued above us—or perhaps Saiyon's soldiers were simply distracting the moon so He could finish His business with Twilight. After all, He was encroaching on her kingdom—I wasn't sure if the Earth Mother claimed Her own, with Her face turned away in sleep.

"Let's end this, Ristriel." Saiyon's voice was like a great low trumpet, too strong and loud for this quiet place. "You cannot wield time forever. If you try now, I will kill you where you stand."

My breath stuck in my throat. My skin flashed silver. Demigods were immortal, but perhaps the death Saiyon intended was not the same as the death I knew.

Ristriel stood tall. "You cannot deal Your justice upon the Earth Mother."

Saiyon frowned. "And She cannot offer you sanctuary in Her slumber."

I tried to put a hand on Ristriel's arm, startling him. He glanced at me, his dark eyes determined in their set but fearful in their depths. Focusing on Saiyon, I said, "What must be done? For You to let him go?"

A thin breath passed from Saiyon's nose. "He cannot be *let go*. He is the only barrier between day and night."

I held His gaze and stood tall. "You are a god of law, Saiyon. Explain to me how eternal chains are a just punishment for the recklessness of a newborn being."

Saiyon's light blazed a little brighter; there was strain in His features as He reined it in again. Ristriel stepped over to shield me, but I knew Saiyon would never hurt me.

When the god did not answer, I asked, "Can You?"

His diamond gaze flickered to His subjects surrounding us. His jaw set stiffly, but He managed, "I cannot."

I breathed out a sigh of relief. "Then I ask again. What must be done, for him to earn his freedom?"

Saiyon did not respond for nearly a minute. The tension flowing between us, and between Ristriel and the godlings, made drawing breath a laborious effort. And yet His eyes never left mine. Just like when we first met, I sensed He was peering beyond my mortal façade, deep into me, to something even I did not know. My understanding was so limited then, and yet I had spoken simple facts that even the Sun God could not deny. In truth, looking back, I am surprised He cared for me enough, at that time, to barter with me. Then again, a god of justice could not be entirely deprived of mercy.

When He spoke, it seemed to shake the Earth Mother Herself. He spoke to Ristriel. "The war will continue."

Ristriel looked away.

Sighing a great, summery breath, Saiyon said, "He must repay all the time he stole."

Indigo light flickered across Ristriel's incorporeal form.

"How?" I pressed.

"In Oblivion," Ristriel whispered. Eyes on Saiyon, he murmured, "It is the space beyond stars, an otherworld unclaimed. It has been my home since shortly after I was born."

His prison, he meant.

"That is cruel," I said.

Saiyon flared brighter; even the godling beside Him had to step away. "I am bound by the laws of the universe. The loss cannot be acquitted, even for you." Fiery gaze back to Ristriel, He asked, "How much of the time you stole is still in your possession?"

Ristriel tensed, and I knew it was very little. He must have spent a great deal of it before meeting me, trying to displace himself from the heavens. The rest had been leaking out of him in the fortnight since.

Old anger bubbled in my stomach, pushing my starlight outward. Ristriel did not shrink from it, but he became even more transparent in its light.

But Saiyon—in the moment my starlight filtered through my skin, I saw, for an instant, golden threads around Him, connecting Him every which way to the heavens overhead. Bright chords, leading into forever. I blinked, and they were gone.

I understood then how true His statement was. Saiyon was truly and literally bound by celestial law. Ristriel wasn't the only one who bore chains.

Even the gods were not truly free.

"It still isn't right." My voice was barely a whisper. "Had You not chained him—"

Ristriel lifted a hand to stop my argument.

"Perhaps you are right," Saiyon said, "but I am not the one on trial. You are young, Ceris Wenden, even for a mortal. You have not truly experienced war. The turning of the universe does not hinge on your decisions. What I did was done to spare My people, and yours. You feared for the mortal city, did you not? Would you tell Me with an oath of truth that you would not sacrifice one to save the rest?"

Pain tinged my jaw, I clenched it so tightly. I could not answer Him.

My silence answered for me.

"In My kingdom," Saiyon went on, "there are many more lives at stake than there are people in Nediah."

Tearing my eyes from Saiyon, I looked over the godlings around us, armed and ready, cold gazes set on Ristriel. They could capture him, hurt him, given the command. But if the moon came out, Ristriel might be able to fly away. Leave me behind and save himself—

"Spare her, and I will come."

Ristriel's voice was hot iron pressed to my heart. "Ris, no."

He turned to me, reaching for my hands, but in Saiyon's aura, he could not take them. A sad, heavy smile tugged on his lips. "I knew the laws when I broke them."

I searched his eyes, blinking back tears. "You were hardly given the chance to follow them."

He lifted his thumb and wiped it under my eye; I felt only the cool touch of autumn there. Leaning close to me, his cheek hovered at my temple. So quiet no one else could hear, he whispered, "You have taught me what it is to love, Ceris. So long have I watched it from the skies, but I never understood it until now. It is truth, it is promise, and it is sacrifice. I don't regret any of it, even if my chains become eternal. I will be happy in that dark place, so long as I can watch you thrive.

"I love you, Ceris."

My heart shattered as he pulled away. My limbs grew so cold I could not move them. Even my starlight had burrowed too deep inside me to surface.

Ristriel turned toward Saiyon. Moonlight peeked and rippled across his back, turning him from a demigod into a ghost, a specter, something unreal and unreachable. My heart bled with his every footstep. Every inch he moved away from me felt like a thousand miles, and my spirit opened up and cracked like the canyons we had almost reached.

Would this be our goodbye? I hadn't even been able to touch him.

He would repay seven hundred years, alone in the dark. Even with my starlight, I might not live to see the end of his sentence. He would have no one to fight for him, to free him. He would be chained forever. Both of us would be alone.

"Let us be done with it," Saiyon said.

It is truth.

Ristriel bowed his head, subservient.

It is promise.

Saiyon lifted His sword.

It is sacrifice.

Sacrifice.

"Stop!" I cried, flinging my arm out as though it could stay the Sun God's blade. "Stop! I will serve the time myself. I will take it. I will serve his seven hundred years!"

Ristriel whirled around, obsidian eyes bright and disbelieving. The godlings were so still they appeared no different from the rock formations around us. Saiyon's eyes brightened, and His brow lowered.

"You cannot. He must pay his price."

Ristriel looked at me the way he had the first time I'd thanked him. Like he could not believe I would make such an offer. Like he might weep.

Like he could not believe I loved him, too.

"Is it law?" I begged, voice shaking.

Saiyon nodded, once.

"Then he will serve beside me." I stepped forward, until Saiyon's heat flared across my body. "I will serve half his time. If it appeases the *universe*, let him start before I do and finish first, too. But I claim three hundred and fifty years of my own. Surely this is just enough for a creature wrongfully imprisoned!"

Saiyon's mouth set in a hard line. I remembered our argument outside of Nediah. *I have claim on him!*

Saiyon hadn't denied me then, and I knew from the anger lining His face that He would not deny me now.

Perhaps I understood more of the laws than I had believed.

"Ceris, no." Ristriel's words were strained with emotion, like it physically hurt him to speak.

I did not look at him. I held Saiyon's gaze defiantly. My starlight uncovered itself, burning brightly, a soft, cool light against His vivid, scalding blaze.

Even now, I could not tell you how long we battled each other in silence, unblinking, powers pulsing. It might have been only seconds;

to me it was years. And years to gods were as inconsequential as seconds to mortals.

"I will accept your offer—" Saiyon growled.

"No," Ristriel begged.

"—on one condition," Saiyon finished.

I squared my shoulders. "Name it."

Saiyon sheathed His sword. "You will spend your years in My kingdom, with Me."

My starlight dimmed, leaving me with that powerless hunger. Despite my previous dealings with the Sun God, I had not expected this.

I would not be beside Ristriel in Oblivion. I would not be able to reach out to him, comfort him, console him.

But nothing in all space and time could stop me from loving him.

"Agreed." My voice remained steady.

Saiyon's relief was almost hidden. Almost, for I noticed the breath that loosened His shoulders. "So it is done."

"Wait."

Saiyon flared, His patience thin as eggshells.

"I swear an oath of truth that I will give him to You." Now I did look at Ristriel, and the pain in his stance, in his countenance, made my spirit weep. "But give us until dawn. You stand on the Earth Mother and judge during the moon's reign. Take out our sentences when Your sovereignty is in full."

I could not separate from Ristriel without saying goodbye. Without touching him one last time.

Saiyon's lip curled. He did not like this.

Ristriel murmured, "I, too, take an oath of truth. I will not run or flee. I will return to my chains at dawn."

An explosion popped overhead, drawing Saiyon's gaze to the ongoing war above. "Very well." His tone was low and sour, but resigned. He said nothing more, only waved His hand to the godlings surrounding us.

They dispersed in flashes of Sunlight. Saiyon lingered only a moment, watching me, before He, too, returned to His war.

I exhaled, and my strength fled with the breath. I fell to my knees in the dark, the clouds coming together once more, the ensuing thunder sounding more like an oncoming storm than a fit of godly rage. Perhaps in Her dreaming state, the Earth Mother cared enough to shield us from celestial carnage. In Saiyon's absence, beneath the growing cloud cover, Ristriel was again whole.

He knelt beside me and took me into his arms, pressing his forehead into my hair. "No, Ceris," he whispered, his tears against my scalp. He spoke as though he could still convince me to withdraw my claim. "No, please."

Pulling back, I cradled his face and kissed his lips, tasting his sadness and mingling it with my own. "I will not leave you to the darkness." It was a truth, a promise, and a sacrifice. "I will always come back to you, Ris."

I held him, and he held me, and we mourned together, though in truth, in the deepest parts of our hearts, we had both known this would be our fate. We were both beings trapped outside of time and punished because of it. And we would pay it back together.

We had only hours before dawn, and we did not waste a single minute. We made our promises and whispered our prayers. Lay against the Earth Mother and discovered each other slowly and thoroughly. It took only a glimpse of moonlight for Ristriel's clothes to become skin, and I knew him as I could know any man. We came together, learning, moving, shuddering, and I understood then what lovemaking should be, and I held it in my heart, protecting it with every ounce of power my star had bequeathed me.

When the sky threatened dawn, we held each other and repeated our promises, mingled with apologies. I sang to him and he kissed my forehead, tracing his fingers down the silver streaks in my hair.

When the Sun rose, two fiery godlings appeared on either side of us, armed with ivory spears, heads mounted with tall, flaming helmets. They held out their hands, and bound by oath, Ristriel stepped into them.

My heart had already broken for him, but when Ristriel flashed away in the possession of those godlings, my spirit broke, too, and I fell to the dust and wept for him, until every tear I had to give spilled to the Earth Mother.

Saiyon's projection, standing behind me, waited for me to finish before taking me back to His palace.

CHAPTER 24

My time with Ristriel did not result in a child.

Part of me despaired that it hadn't, for I so desperately wanted a piece of him with me, something I could hold and cherish, since Ristriel was locked away in a place I could never hope to find, and three and a half centuries is a very long time to someone who was not quite mortal.

Another part of me was glad that I hadn't conceived, for I dwelt in the Palace of the Sun, and I did not know whether a child of Twilight would have survived within its walls.

I was confined to the palace, but I was not chained, nor was I kept locked up in my room. Even so, for a month I would not leave my bedchamber, with its not-walls and not-furniture. When I wasn't abed, weeping for my loss, I lay on the floor, staring into the star-clustered sky, whispering to Surril. Often, she whispered back. Fosii and Elta, again appointed to my care, tried everything in their power to make me smile, but Surril was the only balm to my ache, and I blessed her with every scar she had given me, seen and unseen unlike.

After the first month, I grew defiant. I pushed the boundaries of my prison, for I saw it only as a prison then. I walked to the edges of the palace and dared to jump into the sky. I went where I was not welcome—the armory, other godlings' quarters, even Saiyon's. I would not call Saiyon by the name He had entrusted to me. I would not call on

Him at all, and I starkly ignored Him when He came to me, no matter how kind, angry, or sorry He appeared.

Time moved on as it always does. I was allowed my stitching, and Elta retrieved for me the longest piece of canvas I had ever seen. I started from its topmost corner, stitching into it greens and browns and grays, depicting Endwever as I remembered it, the cathedral and the forest, telling my story from the beginning. When I got to the second scene, where the torch lit, my stitches came uneven and loose so often I unpicked it more times than I could count. Anger and sorrow do not make for a steady hand.

I took my stitching of Ristriel and soaked it with tears night after night for six months before finally attaching it to my tapestry. I ran my hands over it gently, afraid of wearing down the fibers, and did not hide it from Saiyon when He visited me. He kept coming back to speak to me, to apologize, even, for the laws He was bound to uphold, despite my harshness toward Him. And harsh I was.

I discovered what I had not during my pregnancy—that my world *could* be viewed from Saiyon's home. I needed only to climb to the highest point of the palace, and from there I could look over not-spires to the Earth Mother. She looked very small from that place, like I could hold Her in my hand. I watched the Sun's light draw across Her face and waited for a shadow lit by stars to descend in its wake, dividing Saiyon's kingdom from the moon's. Twilight's presence forced their war to a stalling point, for the moon could not cross His power and Saiyon did not wish to. Twilight touched the world for barely half an hour at a time before withdrawing into Oblivion. Twice per turn of the Earth Mother. Each time his colors shone, I sang to him the songs we'd shared on Earth. I sang from the moment he appeared to the moment he vanished, no matter how depressed or weepy or hoarse I was. I sang to him, day after day, month after month, year after year, never sure whether or not he could hear me.

Two years passed before I resigned myself to my fate. Two years before I could conquer my misery and take care of myself, as I knew Ristriel, Surril, and even Saiyon wanted me to. I finally opened up to Fosii and Elta, telling them stories of my childhood in Endwever and my journey to Nediah. As I stitched picture after picture in my tapestry, I told the godlings about the workings of humans. Of wars and storms and happy times below. I know they reported what I said to Saiyon, for He later presented me with a sort of spyglass that, when I stood on that high spire of the palace, I could use to see Nediah. I watched Quelline and Ruthgar live and grow. I saw little Ceris turn into a woman and marry and have a Ceris of her own. I watched Yanla, and then Argon, pass away, and mourned apart from my family, who would never see my tears. I watched Quelline and Ruthgar pass as well, and Ceris's family expand and grow.

My tapestry grew rapidly, then much more slowly as I ran out of stories to chronicle. I had Fosii and Elta beside me, my spyglass, and Surril, but I grew painfully lonely. Saiyon continued to visit me, sometimes briefly, sometimes longer when I allowed conversation. Time played on, scarring over my injuries, stitching together my heart where it could. My anger slowly subsided, and I even found myself smiling again, laughing at times. Saiyon was constant and noble and truthful, and as years and years passed, I found myself growing fond of Him. Never once did He mock me or rage against me, even when I left His side to go to my spire and sing to the Twilight. Never once did He question or cajole me. He simply let me be, and let me heal, and let me suffer in my loneliness while He suffered in His, until I cracked for need of wanting and love. For fifty years He waited for me, whether I wanted Him to or not. In the fifty-first year, I finally came to Him.

During my time in the palace, I spared five star mothers, for Saiyon's seed took only when there was a gap to fill in the night sky. Through our love I bore Him five more stars, each as brilliant and playful as Surril. She loved her two sisters and three brothers and danced with them

249

in the heavens, forming shapes and patterns beautiful to behold. Like Surril, each star blessed me with light, making me a little less mortal with each new life. And though I was meant to serve out my sentence within the confines of the palace, Saiyon took me heavenward often so I could be with my children, because with them I was at my happiest, and He so dearly wanted me to be happy.

And so time went on, and on, filled with old promises and nightly songs, until 350 years from me, and the same from Ristriel, had fallen into the coffers of time, mending the music that had been stolen from it.

I was not there when Saiyon journeyed into Oblivion at the end of Ristriel's sentence. But I have heard enough from Him, and from Ristriel, to piece together what happened there.

Ristriel lifted his head, wincing at the bright light filling the space where he knelt, held up by bright chains made of starlight, waiting for the Earth Mother to turn so he could watch her for the sliver of time he was given. So he could hear the distant song that soothed him, for never once had it failed to come in 350 years. It sparked the hope that dwindled each time the darkness returned, and kept him sane against the pull of his captivity.

"It is done." Saiyon, red and smoldering, held back His powers as best He could. "You've only minutes left."

Relief washed over Ristriel. He sagged against his chains, grateful.

"Ristriel."

He lifted his head once more.

"You must pay back what you have kept," Saiyon said. "You must return the last of it."

Ristriel met Saiyon's eyes, incredulous. He tried to stand, but the chains forced him to hunch. "I will not."

Saiyon dimmed further. "You must. It is the law."

His chains pulled tight. "Do you not know what those minutes are? They are the first that I took."

Saiyon nodded. "I know."

"They are the time for which fate meant to claim her." His voice weakened, disbelieving.

Saiyon nodded again.

Furious, Ristriel tried to stand again and nearly managed it. "You would have her die? After all the time You've had with her, after all the new stars I've seen? You would let her die?"

"She may not." Saiyon's voice was tired and strained. "The time of her death is past. It may merely be replaced, and she will go on as she has before, upheld by the starlight within her."

"But it might not. It might snap back into her song and end it entirely."

Saiyon bowed His head, His body heavy with sorrow. "It is the law" was all He could offer.

Ristriel's chains pulled on him harder than ever before.

Below, the Earth Mother turned, and his power descended upon Her, showing him the oceans and seas, the land and mountains, hills and valleys, and all the people upon her face. And he heard my song so faintly, so far away. A truth, a promise, and a sacrifice.

And so Ristriel reached deep within himself, grasped on to the last of my time, and swallowed.

Saiyon heard it and stiffened. "What have you done?"

Smiling sadly, Ristriel answered, "I've taken it into myself. You and the universe will never have it."

Saiyon blazed. "You fool! Do you not know what will happen, if you make a mortal's death part of yourself?"

But of course Ristriel knew.

It would make him mortal.

Mortality spread over him like a rampant disease. His violet glow diminished, his starlight chains snapped, and his lungs struggled to work, for a mortal could not exist within Oblivion.

Cursing, Saiyon grabbed him and pushed him onto the Earth Mother, into the midst of a night-fallen forest, and Ristriel lived.

When Saiyon returned to me, He already knew what choice I would make. He'd always known.

It broke my heart anew when He asked me anyway.

"Saiyon." His name was a cleaver rending me in two. All in all, I had spent 351 years in His palace. For three hundred of them, I had held Him, loved Him, and cherished Him. But my path had been set before I ever left the Earth Mother, and no amount of time could heal the scars Ristriel had carved into my heart.

My true love was waiting for me.

I touched Saiyon's face. With so much starlight in my veins, He felt as warm as another human, even through the flames that licked His golden skin. Blinking back tears, I kissed His lips, His nose, His forehead. He embraced me, flames living and dying in endless cycles. Saiyon was not capable of weeping, which was for the better. Had he wept, I might not have had the strength to leave Him.

"Remember the star mothers," I chided Him. "Remember their names and their stories. Tell them of the hereafter and leave them their choice. Tell them of me.

"You will find her," I promised. "You will find the one who will endure Your strength, who will climb the heavens and break Oblivion on Your behalf. And she will stay here, and guard Your stars and Your heart, and You will never be alone. But I cannot be that person for You."

He held me tighter, almost to the point of pain.

"I will sing for You." I stroked His fiery hair. "I will sing for You as I did for him, every dawn and set, so that You will remember I love You, too. I will sing for You as long as I have a voice, for we both know I am not eternal."

I sang my first song for Him then, and note by note He let me go, His goodbyes unspoken.

I descended back to the fields and forests of my birth, wearing the new ring He had made me.

This one, I did not take off.

In the light of the third-quarter moon, I found my feet again on solid Earth, surrounded by real trees, beneath a sky full of stars that couldn't show their true colors. My clothes, once spun of light and not-fabric, were simple and homespun, mortal. It took me a moment to recognize them as the ones I'd been wearing when I last touched the Earth Mother. How out of fashion they would be now, nearly four centuries later. My hair, entirely silver with starlight, hung over my shoulders. I swept it away, searching my surroundings. The forest was dense and thick, heavy with shadows. Once, it would have terrified me. Not so much time had passed that I had forgotten hiding from wolves or running from bandits. But there was no fear in me now, only sorrow, and anticipation, and a need that had not been quenched since I was far more mortal than I was now.

I had forgotten what a deep spring forest smelled like, and I breathed it in, admiring the way my skin pebbled in the cool air. But I was not here to admire the Earth Mother's gardens, nor to reflect on the existence I had once known. I was here for him.

It took mere thought to ignite my starlight, which lit the grove to nearly white, startling a roosting bird and silencing the first crickets of the season. Tree leaves, new and green, took on a gemlike quality. A curious breeze rustled through tender branches.

I was home.

"Ris?" I called, starlight dimming to a faint glow, just bright enough to guide me. "Ris?" I wandered between trees, careful where the forest floor dipped and roots rose. A twig snagged my hair; dogwood brushed my skirt. With every step, my trepidation grew. I did not suspect Saiyon of foul play, but He had returned me to the Earth Mother seven hundred years late before, without realizing it. What if Ristriel was on the other side of the world? What if I never found him?

I moved quicker, leaping through the brush, calling out his name. No. We would not be alone. We had both given up too much to never find each other again.

A song broke through the trees, faint, hushed. I paused, listening to its familiar, haunting tune. I knew that song. I had sung it to the skies twice a day for 350 years. My breath caught at its beauty. So long . . . it had been so long since I heard his voice.

Surril twinkled above me, lending her encouragement.

I moved as swiftly as the dense forest would allow, following that song. My skin prickled into tight gooseflesh; my heart beat hard and fast. My eyes searched every shadow, yearning to find his face.

The melody grew louder. I was close, so close—

I found him alone at the bank of a brook, in a narrow grove open to the stars. Moonlight drifted over him, but he remained whole, his demigod luster gone. That was the first moment I knew he was mortal, though he did not tell me the story of how until later.

He stopped singing mid verse and spun toward me, wide-eyed as a new fawn. As though this time *I* was the ghost.

We stayed like that, staring, incredulous, remembering the sight of one another. It was tense and reverent, shattered only when Ristriel mouthed, "Ceris."

Starlight beaming, I ran to him and threw my arms around his neck. He held me tightly, lifting me off the ground, burying his face in my hair. He still smelled of winter nights and midnight, but his skin had lost its coolness. I clung to him, disbelieving, sobbing.

"I heard you." His tears traced my neck. "I heard you sing."

"I promised." I took his beautiful face in my hands and kissed him, remembered him. "I promised I would always come back for you."

Our tears swept together and fell to the Earth, and beneath them echoed a faraway groan, as though the Earth Mother Herself stirred at our reunion and shifted to cradle us together, Her forgotten son and a mother of stars.

EPILOGUE

The tapestry ended shortly after that, but the story of Twilight and the star mother was passed down to their children, and their children, and their children, and all could see the tapestry in the great shrine built to them and remember the story as Ceris had sewn it.

The silhouettes in the forest, connected by spinning stars, represented the sharing of starlight. That Ceris had given it, and Ristriel, no longer weakened by it in his mortal form, took half of it into himself. It is said Ceris told him, *Let us live long lives at each other's sides, and die together when it is time,* but no one really knows for sure.

The persons stitched next, seventeen in all, mortals with bright, shining faces, were their children. Their names have been passed down over centuries, though some argue that Renellis was older than Quelline, and others argue that Quelline was actually the firstborn. The pattern their likenesses are stitched into leave the answer up for debate.

But all agree on the ending of the tale, not because it's stitched into the seven-hundred-foot tapestry, but because it's sewn into the sky itself. The six stars of Ceris and Saiyon, with Surril at the top and the north star at the bottom, burning brighter than all the rest. Those who know the story understand the north star isn't simply a single light, for Ceris and Ristriel, after living long enough to meet their grandchildren and great-grandchildren, and their great-great-grandchildren, and theirs as well, made a hereafter of their very own, combining their remaining starlight and using it to propel themselves into the sky to be among Ceris's stars, and with the strength of their love and the power of the Sun God, they stayed there together, two beings burning brilliantly together as one.

ACKNOWLEDGMENTS

It's ironic that this book revolves so much around light, because it helped pull me out of a dark place. I had gotten into the habit of running before walking, of stretching too thin, and it broke me for a bit in 2019. This novel was my recovery. So while it might be weird to thank a book, I want to thank *Star Mother* first and foremost.

I want to thank my wonderful husband, Jordan, who makes my writing possible, who forgives my silence in the car because he knows I'm in "book land," and who nurtures our family so that creativity and accomplishment can bloom. I would wait 350 years, and more, for him.

Thank you to Joanna Ruth Meyer, whose stellar talent planted the seed for this story and whom I roped in as a beta reader for it. Now she'll never be rid of me!

Many, many thanks to Tricia Levenseller, who has proved to be one of my best critique partners and who always delivers no matter how many pages I slam her with.

My utmost appreciation goes to Rachel, Rebecca, Kim, Leah, and Whit, who helped polish this sucker in its early stages. I keep putting those last two on tighter and tighter deadlines, and they always manage to make it work!

I owe so much to my agent, Marlene Stringer, aka the broker of my word babies, and to my editor, Adrienne, who sees the potential in everything I plop on her desk. Thank you to Angela, who has been with me through fourteen books now and who tastefully points out my errors, and triumphs my strengths. And of course, my utmost gratitude to the 47North team, to those that proof and kern and layout and all that other super fun stuff that makes a book nice.

If you are someone who bothers with reading acknowledgments, then you'll know I'm going to finish off with my thanks to God, who guides my paths and directs my inspiration . . . and may very well have been the One who carved the way out of darkness and pointed me toward *Star Mother* in the first place. ;)

ABOUT THE AUTHOR

Charlie N. Holmberg is the author of the *Wall Street Journal* bestselling Paper Magician series and the Amazon Charts bestselling Spellbreaker series. She is also the author of the Star Mother series and the Numina series, as well as five stand-alone novels, including *Followed by Frost*, a 2016 RITA Award finalist for Young Adult Romance, and *The Fifth Doll*, winner of the 2017 Whitney Award for Speculative Fiction. Born in Salt Lake City, Charlie was raised a Trekkie alongside three sisters who also have boy names. She is a proud BYU alumna, plays the ukulele, and owns too many pairs of glasses. She currently lives with her family in Utah. Visit her at www.charlienholmberg.com.